Winner of the 2017 Pacific Northwest Book Award

PRAISE FOR

MARROW ISLAND

"Smith's excellent command of language gives life to arresting characters and their creepy surroundings, keeping the suspense in this dark environmental thriller running high." —*Elle*

"*Marrow Island* is transporting." —*Vanity Fair*

"This alluring novel explores the darkness of love, how it can cajole you into danger or tip your actions toward cruelty. Clean but intoxicating writing . . . Ambitious."
  —*New York Times Book Review*

"Beautifully wrought." —*O, The Oprah Magazine*

"An elegant writer to watch. [Smith's] *Marrow Island* is an ambitious literary novel with an intensely personal core."
  —*Minneapolis Star Tribune*

"Smith's book captivates in the first few pages and delivers a gripping, compelling story throughout."
  —*Milwaukee Journal Sentinel*

"Engrossing and atmospheric, a thorny meditation on environmental responsibility with a big haunted heart."
  —*Miami Herald*

"Smith marries haunting, lyrical prose with the page-turning urgency of a thriller. Warnings of the environmental and geological disasters that threaten us are woven seamlessly into a beautifully crafted story of loss, love, and rebuilding. A gorgeous, compelling novel."
—Cari Luna, author of *The Revolution of Every Day*

"An eerie, haunting mystery."
—*Woman's Day*

"Tucked into this suspenseful plot are stunning and important reflections on nature and the environment, its awe-inspiring power and the many ways humanity both detracts from that power and willfully ignores it—and how that shapes our lives."
—*Shelf Awareness*

"Ambitious and provocative. This eloquent and soft-spoken novel explodes as it confronts eco-terrorism, natural disasters, and radical Catholicism . . . Spellbinding."
—*Signature Reads*

"Excellent . . . Smith's story carries the same heft, descriptive nuance, and narrative spark that distinguished her debut [*Glaciers*], but this time, she more finely hones her characters' emotional rhythm and atmospheric location to create a thoroughly eerie reading experience capped off with a startling conclusion."
—*Publishers Weekly*, starred and boxed review

"Wrenching and limpidly written . . . Smith is excellent at showing the terrible things people can do for the sake of their ideals . . . A near-perfect read."
—*Library Journal*

"A stunning novel about sacrifice for the sake of survival in the aftermath of natural and man-made disasters . . . In graceful and dolorous prose, [Smith] captures a dense and dramatic landscape, evoking questions of what it means to harm—ourselves, our surroundings—and to heal. Engrossing eco-fiction, eerie and earnest."
— *Kirkus Reviews*

"A compelling, complex meditation on both the power and the vulnerability of the natural world."
— *Booklist*

"[*Marrow Island*] is weird and glorious and I loved it."
— *Book Riot*

"[A] marvelously spun post-disaster story. The author reaches into the depths of our connections to our pasts, our loved ones, [and] our devotions."
— *My Edmonds News*

"[*Marrow Island*] is moody and atmospheric, and [Smith's] descriptions are stunning . . . It's quite an immersive reading experience."
— *Fourth Street Review*

"Atmospheric, intense, and mysterious—Alexis Smith's *Marrow Island* is a smart novel, richly peopled and lyrically written. Smith is a writer genuinely at home in the natural world, and willing to write truth, darkness, and beauty into the island landscape. She understands well how environmental pressure translates into human pressure and loss. An important, gripping book."
— Megan Mayhew Bergman,
author of *Almost Famous Women*

"A foreboding, compelling story of humanity's uneasy relationship with nature and with each other, told in lyrical language that continually propels the reader further in . . . Between the suspense of the story and Smith's poetic prose . . . *Marrow Island* is a gripping read."   — *St. Louis Post-Dispatch*

"I was already happy to count myself among Alexis Smith's admirers, but *Marrow Island* has brought me to a new level of fandom. From the intricately suspenseful plotting, the remote and intoxicating atmosphere, and the haunted, flinty heroine at the center, this novel absorbed me with the force of a seaside storm, leaving me awed and breathless."   — Laura van den Berg,
author of *Find Me*

"Returning to the islands of her youth, Lucie Bowen finds her long-lost soul mate caught up with a mysterious commune called Marrow Colony and finds herself with no choice but to face the painful past. At once a page-turner and a sustained lyrical meditation on a beloved landscape, this novel also shines a spotlight on the anxieties of living in a world with such environmental uncertainties. The depth of what we possess—and what we stand to lose—is achingly drawn."   — Amanda Coplin,
author of *The Orchardist*

"Conjuring a lush and mysterious landscape, *Marrow Island* investigates the impact of the losses of the past—be they loved ones, failed quests, or the environmental calamities brought on by our collective blindness. By turns elegiac, compelling, and timely, it seeks real answers and finds the possibility of miracles. This is a beautiful novel."   — Edan Lepucki,
author of *California*

MARROW ISLAND

MARROW ISLAND

ALEXIS M. SMITH

Mariner Books
Houghton Mifflin Harcourt
BOSTON   NEW YORK

First Mariner Books edition 2017

Copyright © 2016 by Alexis M. Smith

Reading Group Guide copyright © 2017 by Houghton Mifflin Harcourt
Publishing Company

Q&A with Author copyright © 2017 by Alexis M. Smith

For information about permission to reproduce selections from this book, write
to trade.permissions@hmco.com or to Permissions, Houghton Mifflin Harcourt
Publishing Company, 3 Park Avenue, 19th Floor, New York, New York 10016.

www.hmhco.com

Library of Congress Cataloging-in-Publication Data
Names: Smith, Alexis M, author.
Title: Marrow island / Alexis M. Smith.
Description: Boston : Houghton Mifflin Harcourt, 2016.
Identifiers: LCCN 2015037467 | ISBN 9780544373419 (hardback) |
ISBN 9780544373426 (ebook) | ISBN 9781328710345 (pbk.)
Subjects: LCSH: Secret societies—Fiction. | Cults—Fiction. | BISAC: FICTION /
Literary. | FICTION / General.
Classification: LCC PS3619.M538 M37 2016 | DDC 813/.6—dc23
LC record available at http://lccn.loc.gov/2015037467

Book design by Brian Moore

Printed in the United States of America
DOC 10 9 8 7 6 5 4 3 2
4500661956

for Amy K.

PROLOGUE

This was my last glimpse of Marrow Island before the boat pulled away: brown and green uniforms clustered on the beach, tramping up the hill to the chapel and through the trees to the cottages of Marrow Colony. The boat wasn't moving yet, but the uniforms already seemed to be getting smaller, receding from my sight, shrinking into a diorama, a miniature scene of the crime.

Carey had helped me into the boat. I sank to the wheelhouse deck and curled into myself, sitting knees to chest, spine to prow. Joshua Coombs was calling out on the radio, requesting an ambulance to meet us in Anacortes. Katie tried to come aboard, but Carey hollered something to her and she ran back up the dock. He squatted next to me and spoke softly, just by my ear.

"We need to take off your clothes."

They were soaked through; I wouldn't be warm until I was dry. I understood that this was first aid; I understood that he was doing his job as the park ranger. I just didn't have it in me to participate in my own rescue. I was spent, scraped, and bruised. I leaned into him, eyes closing.

"Stay awake, Lucie," he said. "A little longer. Listen to my voice."

He lowered me carefully to my back, his parka under my head, and called to Coombs for scissors.

Carey kept talking, narrating as he undressed me, threading one arm through a sleeve, gently rolling me, tugging the shirt up my torso, lifting my head. I knew his hands were on me, but through my cold flesh they felt like the mitts of a giant, huge and heavy. He took off my socks—my shoes were long gone, in the field? in the ruins? in the woods?—and cradled my heel in his palm as he lowered it to the deck. My thoughts had stopped making sense; I tried to visualize Carey's words as he spoke, *I have to cut these off.* Then he slid the small sharp scissors up the outside of my leg through my jeans. He hesitated around my hip.

"Please try—can you be very still?" he asked.

I was shivering uncontrollably. He rubbed my legs up and down under a blanket, telling me about circulation, about blood, about heat. I drifted.

"Stay awake, Lucie."

Coombs was starting the boat. Katie came back with more blankets. Carey told Katie to get down on the deck and wrap herself around me. She lay down beside me on Carey's parka, pulled me into her body, and rubbed my arms and back. He covered us both with the two blankets.

I breathed into the wool as the boat lurched through the swells, nausea rising up instantly. Katie seemed never to stop panting from her run up the shore. The bass beat of her heart, the thrust of the boat through the waves, and the feeling of fullness at the back of my throat. I wanted to purge everything inside me, but my bearings held.

"Don't let her go," I heard Carey say.

· · ·

At the hospital in Anacortes, they treated me for hypothermia, but they were confused; I was going through more than one kind of shock. Carey told them I'd been lost on Marrow Island overnight—he didn't know the rest of it yet—and they saw his uniform and took his word. When they asked me what and when I had last eaten, I shrugged, though I remembered my last meal well—the mussels, the heady broth, the bread, the wine, and the birch liquor—and the cramps in my stomach that started not long after. The memory of food brought on the first hunger pangs; the craving for energy, for heat, my metabolism waking up. They were so strong they stabbed at my guts, but the nausea lingered. I couldn't imagine putting something in my mouth, tasting, swallowing.

Katie told the intake nurse she was my sister, and I didn't correct her. They let her sit by my bed all night.

"I'm not leaving you alone with her," Carey told me. She was standing right beside him when he said it, but she didn't defend herself. I didn't know what to say; I wanted them both.

Katie held my hand for hours, while my temperature rose and patches of my flesh became livid. I could feel the drunken movement of blood and plasma through my body, my cheeks throbbing, my toes and fingers buzzing. My breasts felt like meat cold from a locker. Eventually Katie slept, head next to mine, nose to my cheek, like when we were girls, like that first night after the quake, clinging to each other under a Mylar sheet in the gymnasium. I listened to her sleep; I felt her moving through her dreams.

Carey sat in a chair by the door, waiting for the sheriff, though he shouldn't have—he should have been back on Marrow at his post, taking the state troopers through the woods, writing official reports. Soon enough everyone would be looking for all of us, with questions. But they would find what they were looking for at the Colony without our help. And by the time they asked me to tell my part, they would have a story of their own and they wouldn't veer from it, no matter the details I offered.

My notes were probably already in the sea or burnt to ashes. I tried to reconstruct the days in my mind, building a timeline, sorting details, drawing up the images of pictures I had taken, of things I had seen. I cataloged the different scents in the layered stench I gave off: conifer needles, stump rot, burnt lichen, fungi spores—all washed with the yeasty brine of bodies. Mostly my body. But other bodies, too.

In the weeks after, back in the city, I woke alone in my third-floor apartment every morning. Outside, buses lumbered down Fremont Street, shopkeepers turned over their Open signs, people drank their coffee, checked their phones, walked their dogs. The city repeated its relentless, noisy cycle just like it had every day before and after that week I spent on Marrow. I listened, I watched. After the May Day Quake, over twenty years before, Seattle had rebuilt itself, from concrete rubble heap back to silver city, lessons learned, so we tell ourselves. Otherwise, what was the point of it all? What unlikely comfort we find in the refrain *build, destroy, repeat.* There are always survivors left to pick up the pieces. There's always someone to tell the tale.

I had my own refrain: I told the story of those days on Marrow hundreds of times in the first few months—to the state police and the FBI, the grand jury, to my fellow journalists, to the editors who wanted me to write a book, even—because of Sister J.—the archbishop of the Seattle Diocese. I answered their questions honestly, and all the details were true, but the telling began to feel like a betrayal. I told them the story and they typed it up and it became tabloid-television lurid. Marrow Colony as cult. Marrow Colony as failed utopia.

Build, destroy, repeat.

From my hospital bed, from my apartment, from the courtroom, I saw Marrow Island and Sister's Colony pillaged, and all the people there who were scraping out a little space for themselves — their only hope to live gratefully, daily, in the service of the planet — they were evicted, displaced, incarcerated.

Now I am five hundred miles away in the dry, pine-scattered forests of eastern Oregon, but every time I dream, I find myself back on the islands. In some dreams, I relive the events as they happened. In others, I realize I'm dreaming, and I try to undo the past, to make different choices. Either way I wake up feeling lost. How did I get here? How did this happen? I might be the only one left who knows.

The newspapers have moved on to other catastrophes. The Colony's history will fade into the archives; the colonists will become ghosts. No one will remember the names of those who performed a miracle on Marrow Island. I have never said so to anyone — not even Carey — but I forgive them. I forgive them for trying to kill me.

One

THE ISLANDS

———

ORWELL ISLAND, WASHINGTON
OCTOBER 8, 2014

THE SUN HAD just set. I turned down the lane to the cottage, arrows of light shooting from clouds on the horizon. The air was warm, with a chill settling at the edges. Tall trees darkened the driveway. I could see the shape of the house but few details. My phone lit the way through the front door and kitchen to the fuse box. I switched the breakers, heard the fridge rattle and an encouraging tick from the water heater, turned on a few lights. Faded notes in my mother's hand were taped to everything— on light switches and cupboard doors and appliances—explaining how and what to do to revive the place. I read each one, not ready to rely on my memories. Mom had been renting the cottage out to friends and acquaintances for years. But this was my first time back since I was twelve.

As I hauled my bags from the back seat of the car, I heard sputtering chirps echoing in and out like synth beats at a club. Then, realizing the incongruity, I remembered the time a bat the size of my palm had become entangled in my hair one summer evening, just a few feet away, in the garden. I looked up to see them sweeping the air overhead, feasting on the moths and other insects attracted by the porch light. I shuffled up the driveway as fast as I could, luggage raking the gravel.

On my way back for the box of groceries, I noticed a glow among the swaying trees — not the moon, which hadn't risen yet. A light in an upstairs window at Rookwood, the big old house across the lane. I wasn't completely alone on the far side of the island.

Weary from the drive and the long ferry ride, I went straight to bed, up the ladder to the loft in the eaves. The ceiling was so low, I crawled to the pallet bed on my knees.

When I was a kid, I could walk upright if I tucked my head. Every night I read until I fell asleep with the lamp on. So Dad started calling it my lighthouse. He could see my windows from down by the shore where he cleaned crab pots or smoked salmon or drank beers with Mom and talked about the things they didn't want me to hear. When they came back to the cottage, he would climb up the ladder to kiss me good night and turn off the light. I remembered the smell he brought in with him: night, alder smoke, an abalone wetness.

I woke early. Woolly fog wrapped around the small windows, and condensation dripped down the wooden sills, the white paint puckering and peeling away. The ceiling was still blue, with faded golden stars painted all over the slats. Once there had also been paper stars hung from the beams with fishing line. I listened to the muffled lap of the waves against the dock below and guessed that the tide was high.

As I climbed down the ladder as gracefully as I could, creaks sounded out from the rungs that I used to flit up and down like a chickadee. In the morning light, I saw everything I had missed the night before: Grandma Lucia's lace curtains still hanging in the east windows, a row of agates along each sill, the wool rag rug in the living room—worn to threads in places. The smell of wood smoke was in everything. It had already seeped into my hair, though I hadn't built a fire. I knew by the note Mom had left on the closet door that there were *extra coats, hats, etc.* inside, but when I opened it, I took a step back. They were Dad's coats, boots, vests. A box full of knitted caps, rain hats, work gloves. Some of them had been Grandpa Whit's first. I closed the door and tore the note down. Then I went around tearing all the notes down.

After the earthquake and Dad's funeral, it took all the money we had to get to Seattle to Mom's parents' place. Mom signed up with a temp agency as soon as we unpacked our things. There were ruins everywhere and plenty of work in reconstruction. She did anything they offered her, directing traffic for utilities crews, sorting salvage at warehouses where people could haul loads of debris. Eventually she worked in the office of a property developer. She supported us with that work, within a few months finding us an apartment, acquiring health insurance, sending me to the parish school, Our Lady of the Lake. And repairing the cottage. Making sure the county didn't condemn it and tear it down, like so many other buildings rattled by the quake. She used what she learned working for the developer to sidestep occupancy requirements, to get waivers and stays, to hold on to Dad's childhood home. It hadn't been ruined, just abandoned. *Not abandoned,* she had told them, *just temporarily vacant.*

Reconstruction all over the region took years, but it wasn't long before people wanted to get away from the city and the glassy, haunted look it could have, when everything new just reminded them of what had been there before. Mom started renting out the cottage to pay for taxes and utilities. Occasionally a friend of mine would report that she had slept in my lighthouse room. I would change the subject. I would avoid that friend for a week.

There was a new mirror above the sink; the old medicine cabinet had come off its rusted hinges and crashed in the quake. I had not been tall enough to see most of myself in it then. I was unrecognizable now, eyes cottony with sleep, hair flared up on the pillow side, ponytail askew. I had fallen asleep in long underwear and a wool cardigan with elbow patches. I looked like the morning after a wild L.L.Bean catalog shoot. I had friends in Seattle who cultivated this look. They showed up to work like this — wherever they worked: hair salons, universities, butcher shops, ad agencies. I preferred to look like I had my shit together, even when I didn't.

Mom sometimes told me I looked like Grandma Lucia, Dad's mom, with her wavy black hair — she wore hers in a bob — and big brown eyes and high cheeks. I understood this to mean that I looked like my father, too, but that she couldn't bring herself to mention him. I combed out my hair with my fingers, washed the sleep from my eyes.

I sat in front of the stove on a cedar stump, staring through the dark opening into the cold iron belly. My mother had insisted (House Rule #2: Replenish Supplies) that the fire box always be full, and it was: dry kindling, extra-long strike-anywhere matches, and a Sunday paper from over two years ago, wrinkled and crisp.

A fire needs three things, I told myself. My dad used to say it all the time.

I rifled through the box and pulled out the paper. Seattle headlines: the new socialist mayor, raising the minimum wage, the lawn wars, the first of what would be several years of summertime droughts, the year of the worst wildfires in Washington's history. It was the year protesters camped out on golf courses and organized the guerrilla gardening of food plants and fruit trees all over the city. I had reported on it for *The Stranger*. I had followed a group of anarchist gardeners as they planted by night, with work gloves and headlamps, hauling old pillowcases full of homemade compost and worm castings to weedy parking medians and abandoned lots all over the south end of Seattle. In the light of day, their gardens were sloppy but darling; touring the city in the morning, you never knew what you would see, what formerly trash-dotted roadside scab of broken concrete and dirt would suddenly be speckled with squash seedlings and hand-painted signs in rainbow colors with slogans like FOOD NOT LAWNS and OCCUPY THE SOIL.

It hadn't been my first feature, but it had been my first to lead the region's media coverage of anything. The paper in my hand had come out a full month after my article. I turned to the inside page and there he was: Matthew Cartwright, the locavore chef and food activist who asked me out over a bucket of homemade fish head fertilizer. His handsome, bearded mug —the same one that led my own story—had sold urban homeowners all over the city on tearing up their lawns and starting worm bins. We had been lovers for over a year after that, and during that time I had stopped reporting on anything related to the movement. I had spent weekends tearing up blacktop, amending soil, digging holes for a public fruit and nut arbor on Beacon Hill, and hours helping him with the onslaught of media that came in the wake of my piece.

After all that work, all that time on his projects, I didn't measure up. When I let go of my own work, my own priorities, I lost the qualities he had been attracted to in the first place. That's how he put it. He loved the woman I was before I was in love with him.

Since the breakup, I had worked for two papers and been laid off by both. Freelancing and adjunct teaching were not paying the bills. I couldn't afford my apartment anymore.

I tore the article into long strips, visualizing my dad's method, twisting handfuls into long bunches with flares at each end. I shoved Matt's smug face to the back of the stove with a stick, piled other sticks around it. For a full minute, the fire scuttled through the paper, licking at the wood. The kindling crackled but didn't catch. Smoke swallowed the log. I could almost hear my dad sucking air through his teeth the way he did whenever I insisted on doing something without his help, even if I didn't really know how.

A fire needs three things: *a dry bed, fuel, and room to breathe.* Maybe I hadn't given it enough room to breathe.

Everything in the cottage seemed closer than it ought to be. I pulled too hard on drawers; I ran into the corner of the cutting board with my hip. I opened a sticky cupboard door straight into my forehead. It felt like it would bruise. I sat in a kitchen chair and laid my head on the table, cheek on the cold Formica. Beside me, my workbag held my computer, notes for articles I had pitched or was thinking of pitching. Since Mom had handed over the deed to the cottage, I only had one story on my mind. It was a more personal story than I was used to writing: this trip back to Orwell and Marrow; how the two islands had changed since the disaster. I had pitched it to an editor at the *Pacific Standard* who wanted more — visuals and an arc.

There was an envelope sticking out of the front pocket of my bag, a letter from my only childhood friend from the islands, Katie. We met at Orwell Village School when we were eight, when my parents moved back into Dad's childhood home and he took a job at the ArPac Refinery on Marrow Island. I was an only child; Katie was, too. They lived a mile away through the woods, and over the years we wore a path through the trees between our yards. She became a kind of sister I would find and lose and find again over the years, after Mom and I moved away, through high school, when we went off to college. I had thought I lost her for good a decade ago. But then this.

I pulled the letter from its pocket. There were other papers behind it, in a manila envelope: the deed to the cottage I was sitting in. I dragged everything out, spread it out on the table.

Mom had given me the deed and Katie's letter at the same time, in a little bundle tied with string. We were sitting in the atrium of Café Flora, drinking mimosas at our monthly brunch. I had opened the envelopes, confused: the deed, with my mother's signature and the stamp of a notary, the address and a description of the cottage on Orwell Island; then the beat-up letter with the return address simply *Kathryn Paley, Marrow Island, WA 98297*. The postmark on the letter was three weeks old.

Orwell and Marrow were two separate islands, but they were often mentioned together because they were so remote from the other islands in the San Juans — right up against Boundary Pass and Canadian waters — and they relied so much on each other. Before the earthquake, the only ferry service to and from

Marrow had been from Orwell. After the quake, there had been no reason to go to Marrow at all, only reasons to avoid it.

Unless you were someone like Katie.

"I guess she's still living out there on the commune?" Mom had nodded at the letter, tipping back the rest of her mimosa. Mom had never trusted Katie and had once told me she reminded her of a feral cat. "I guess she finally settled down."

"You're giving me the cottage," I had answered.

"It was always yours, Lucie."

"We both know that's not true," I'd said.

We had looked at each other for a long time, and the bright expression she was wearing faded. There were so many lines on her face. There had been times over the years when I knew she wanted to be rid of the cottage, when it was a burden to her. And to her new husband, who worked for a developer and saw the "potential" in tearing the place down and building something modern.

"You can always sell it." She had leaned toward me, put her hand on mine. "I know you could use the money."

I had thought about texting her before I left for Orwell, letting her know I was going to check on the cottage. But I didn't. I had written to Katie, though. A postcard, mailed a few days before the trip, telling her I was coming.

I pulled on my boots and one of Dad's old coats from the closet, took my coffee and Katie's letter out to the porch. I sat on the steps and reread the letter, looked over Katie's tight cursive—tall, compressed letters strung together and tilting across the unlined paper so that I tipped my head to the right as I read.

Dear Lucie,

I've tried your old address & the e-mail at the newspaper. No luck. I'm assuming your mom & stepdad haven't sold their house on the lake, so hopefully they'll get this to you. I'll keep this short, just in case. I've written a few long letters that came back to me.

I've read your articles and I'm so proud of you. You always knew what you wanted to do, and you went for it. I always admired that about you. I think I was jealous, even. I never knew what I wanted to do, so I tried everything.

Things changed for me at the Colony. It was supposed to be a three-month externship, but I knew I belonged here. There's too much to explain, but you would be interested in the work we've done here. Your interest in the state of the planet, your sense of justice. You always needed to see things put right. I want you to come see what we've done on Marrow. It hasn't always been easy, but the work we've done here is unprecedented. We've transformed the island, Lucie. The island everyone abandoned. Have you even been back to Orwell in the last twenty years? You should come home, Lu.

I've been here for almost ten years & I've thought of you every day. How could I not? How could I have thought I was putting distance between us? Sometimes I even think I see you, down at the end of the table at meals, like at summer camp, or wandering the shore with your head down, looking for agates. Then I blink, and you're gone. I know how it sounds — but there it is. I'm saying it because you probably won't even read this.

I miss you, Lu.

Katie

Squinting into the fog, I could make out a faint light still shining from the window at Rookwood, but the mist and trees obscured most of the house. It had been the summer home of Maura Swenson, an artist and heiress of a lumber and mining fortune. The Swensons were lumber millionaires, maritime industrialists. Maura built Rookwood in 1918, in the Arts and Crafts style, as a showcase of Pacific Northwest materials. Great fir beams and limestone flagging from her father's mills and quarries, stones from the Skagit and Snohomish riverbeds, hardwood carvings of ravens and pine boughs in the eaves. All handcrafted. Every inch. Grandpa Whit and Grandma Lucia had been the caretakers. Maura willed them the cottage and the land it was on when she passed away.

Maura's daughter Julia had been like a grandmother to me after my own passed away. I could still remember the timbre of her voice and the waft of her eau de toilette. I ran in and out of Rookwood all summer long, chasing Julia's cocker spaniel, Daisy, in the yard. Katie and I had played hide-and-seek in the immense house. For weeks after the earthquake, Mom and I stayed with Julia at Rookwood, not sure if our own cottage was safe. We ate strange meals from the well-stocked but ancient pantry. Julia taught me to wedge clay and crochet lacy coasters, telling me the stories of her favorite saints, the patrons and patronesses of the sea, of boatmen, of laborers, of children. We would pray together for my dad's safe return every night.

The expanse of the Salish Sea and all its islands were invisible from my spot, but I could hear its restless pulse, feel the ebb and flow. Like putting your ear to someone's chest and feeling the course of the blood, the steady thrust of the heart. I closed my eyes and tried to draw the image out of my memory: beyond the shore, at the distance of about twelve nautical miles, lay Marrow Island—where Katie was living now, on a commune; where my father and eight other men were burnt to death after the earthquake.

Two

THE WOODS

—————

CAREY WAKES AT dawn to get to the ranger station by eight. It's a forty-minute drive from where we are, down three Forest Service roads near the Wolf Creek Trailhead. He kisses me behind the ear and slips out of bed, tucking the blankets back around my body. No central heat in the cabin; it's always cold in the morning. He starts the coffee and oatmeal and heads for the shower. I stare out the window at the pine trees, listening to the birds, the air-splitting jeer of a jay, the constant trill and chatter of the flycatchers. I close my eyes again and just listen. There's a pine with one lazy arm draped over the roof that scratches the outside wall in the breeze. I've become so accustomed to the sound, it almost disappears. I try to pick it out under the birdcalls and the river, the shower and the coffeemaker.

The faucet squeals when Carey shuts off the water. His movements are quiet, deliberate. Maybe it's from working in the wilderness. He doesn't stomp around like some men, putting his full weight into everything. It's like the signs at the trailheads: LEAVE NO TRACE. He recognizes the traces left behind by other men and a few women. I see the marks in him, too. As he comes back into the bedroom, the floor creaks. I roll over and watch him pull on a pair of briefs, socks, an undershirt. His khaki shirt and trousers hang from the back of the door.

I slip out of bed and go to the bathroom. The coffeemaker is sputtering its last drops into the pot.

"Pour me a cup?" I call from the toilet.

It's waiting for me on the table.

It's still too hot to drink, so I stand on my toes and kiss the back of his neck. We don't talk much in the morning. He portions the oatmeal and butters toast, and we sit down to eat. There's a pile of mail on the table and Carey glances at it. The letter on the bottom, which I tried to hide below the bills, was for me. I let it sit there a week before Carey opened it for me and I read it by the fire, half thinking about tossing it in.

"Have you answered her yet?" he asks.

I shovel a full spoon of oatmeal into my mouth and shake my head. He doesn't look upset, just confused.

"It's not like you to run away from something," he says, biting off a corner of his toast.

"It's exactly like me to run away," I say through my oatmeal. "What else would I be doing here?"

He locks eyes with me, shrugs.

"Other than you," I say, too late.

He swallows the rest of his coffee and takes his dishes to the sink.

"Deathbed request, Luce. Don't get many of those in a lifetime."

Jesus, Carey. Always taking the high road, I think, but don't say. I can't say anything. My cheeks are hot; I know he's right.

He pours the rest of the coffee into a thermos and puts a can of soup and a sandwich into his lunch pail. He hadn't bargained on me coming out here when he accepted the post in the

Malheur. He asked me to visit and I came. After three weeks he had asked, "So I guess you're staying?" And I had said, "I can't imagine leaving." The *you* was implied, I thought. I can't imagine leaving *you.* I just couldn't say it at the time. Two months later and I'm still not saying anything right.

He doesn't look at me as he's getting ready to go. I meet him at the door, put my hand on the deadbolt but don't turn it.

"I'm sorry," I say.

"I know," he says, leans down to kiss me. I kiss him slower and deeper, and feel his hesitation, feel him trying to swallow the hurt. I let him go and open the door. He gets in his truck and backs down the bed of pine needles we call a driveway, lifts a hand to wave before he pulls onto the blacktop. I watch from the porch, the burnt-sugar taste of his mouth still in mine.

Back in the cabin I pick up the letter. It had been forwarded to Carey's PO box in Prairie City. When I saw the letterhead with the roses and the cross, I had a good idea what it would say.

April 5, 2016

To Miss Lucie Bowen,

    I am writing on behalf of Janet Baldwin, formerly Sister Janet Baldwin, one of our own, the Sisters of the Holy Family. As you may know, before her conviction and incarceration at the Women's Correction Center in Walla Walla, Janet was diagnosed with progressive adenocarcinoma. She refused radiation and chemotherapy offered by the State during her incarceration. After several weeks, hospice workers and the Chaplain successfully petitioned for Janet's compassionate release. The Sisters of the Holy Family were moved to take in our sister Janet, and we are seeing her through her final days here in Spokane at our Provincial House.

Janet has made few requests, but she wished for me to contact you especially, and asks if you are able to visit her here. She believes that you may have something that will help her in her final hours—a keepsake of your time together, perhaps. She cannot be more specific—her mental capacities are failing—but believes that you will know what she needs. Even if you do not have the item, I believe that your presence would be a comfort to her. Janet speaks of you often, with such warmth.

We can accommodate you here at the Provincial House as our guest. You are welcome to share in our meals and Communion as you wish. I have provided my mobile phone number. You may call anytime to arrange your visit or to inquire further. If you cannot come, please consider writing what is in your heart, and know that we will share your words with Janet in her final days. We will keep you and all who have known Janet in our prayers.

In God's Love,
Sister Rose Gracemere

I sit out on the steps on the side of the porch in a patch of sun. The steps lead down the path to the bank of the river. The wind cuts through the trees, and goose bumps crackle up my arms.

What *keepsake*? She spoke of me *warmly*? She must be losing her mind. Katie was her favorite; it was Katie she would ask for. But Katie couldn't go to her; she was under house arrest in Bellingham, so she asked for me? What would Katie have that Sister J. wanted? Neither of them were the keeping type.

"What we hold on to says a lot," Sister J. said once. "But what we let go, sings."

Inside again, I pack a few things for the day. I've been hiking the old logging road to the fire lookout, about two hours up the mountain. There's nobody staying up there this early in the season, so I can be alone. More alone than in the cabin, with the drab furnishings and random objects left by previous rangers. The boarded-up smell that never leaves a temporary residence. The shady intimacy of the trees, crowding around the cabin like very tall people, looking down, watching. At the lookout, the elevation creates solitude, looking down on the trees and across to the rolling hills down onto the plain. I'm supposed to be writing a book, but mostly I watch the river below or sleep on the cot until it's time to come back to the ground.

Carey doesn't know that I go to the lookout, though he could track me, if he wanted. I'm reckless. I bring only enough food and drink to satisfy my afternoon appetite. I make balls of peanut butter and crunched-up cereal — Grape Nuts on the outside keep the balls from sticking together in the baggie, a trick one of the rangers' wives taught me. I pack a thermos of tea and the metal water canister I found when I was up at the lookout one day. Some previous tenant left it there; his family name was written in faded black marker on the side: *Goodkind*. A providential name. Or maybe it's just a reminder to only drink the right water. The *good kind*. I pack the tablets to kill the protozoa when I fill it up in the stream.

Carey takes me on day hikes through the forest on his days off. Out to the lookout and back down the other side of the ridge, nearer the river, and back up to the logging road. We did this several times, until I was familiar enough to take the trail by myself when Carey was at the station. Carey knew I was going out, but he didn't know how often I became disoriented. (*Lost.* Say it. *Lost.*) The first time was after a night of late-season snowfall, in March. I sat on a mossy stump in a clearing drawing a map in the snow, trying to visualize myself from above, high in the clouds, see the whole forest and the river, the logging roads, the stone chimney and whitewashed clapboard of the decommissioned guard station we were living in, the red roof of the ranger station miles away, where Carey was probably heating up leftovers in the microwave for his lunch. There seemed to be three trails, all headed into three plausibly familiar clusters of trees, though I knew that there was only one trail, really. Only one was actually the path that looped back to the logging road, then back down to the Forest Service lane just up from our cabin. When creative visualization failed, I stood and headed up one path, thinking it must be the one, only to trudge into deeper and deeper snow until I was waist-high in a wintering thicket of huckleberry. I followed my footsteps back to the clearing, and by then it was late afternoon and the light was faint behind gathering clouds. I realized I would have to follow my footprints to get back to the cabin. So I did. It seemed so simple, really, just going back the way I came. Following my own footprints is still the most reliable way back home.

Carey said once that taking the same trail in the opposite direction is like walking on the other side of time. Everything looks different on the way back. Same trees, same stobs and snags. Same switchbacks and curves; same vistas, same fallen tree bridge across the creek. But going back the way you came, it's just as easy to lose your footing, but it's harder to get lost. The light shines on things you didn't notice on the way there. The path back, it's the story you tell yourself, afterward.

The fire lookout has windows on all sides. Built by the WPA in 1937, the hand-hewn log cabin keeps watch at 6,013 feet elevation in the Malheur Range. The cast-iron wood stove still works, but now there are also solar panels on the roof. It's not plumbed, and there are strict rules about bodily waste and food, because of the wildlife. Black bears and bobcats, mostly, but wolves have been reintroduced on the other side of the range, and the occasional solitary males and females will split off and wander, looking for mates, looking to start their own packs. I've heard they don't live long alone.

I feel safe here away from people, though I probably have plenty to fear. There's a CB radio I don't really know how to use and an air rifle for sounding the alarm, which makes me feel like I'm in a movie about the apocalypse. Lying on the cot, I let my mind go to the place where mushroom clouds sprout from the distant horizon. And just like that, I'm back on Marrow Island. Sister Janet leading prayer before supper. We all hold hands and bow our heads. It's not a prayer I recognize, but it's lilting like a song. It's about letting go; it's about rebirth. I open my eyes and steal glances at the others. Their cheeks are rosy from cold, damp work outdoors all morning. They look content; stoic. I close my eyes again. I smell the rich, earthy stew steaming in our bowls. The hands in mine are rough and light, like driftwood.

Three

THE ISLANDS

——————

THE LAMP UPSTAIRS still glowed from the window of Rookwood when I set out for the village, so I walked across the lane and up the drive to introduce myself. No one answered my knocks and there wasn't a sound from the house.

Julia Swenson died when I was in high school, and a nephew had taken over her estate for the rest of the Swenson clan, who were in Boston or New York, somewhere back east. If I had ever met the nephew, I couldn't recall. My mother had once called him "an odd one"—some friends staying at the cottage had reported a run-in with him; he had been friendly but extremely drunk.

The curtains were drawn in all the windows along the porch. I walked around the house. There wasn't a car in the drive, so I took my time, looking over the place. I peeked in the door of the carriage house—a half-barn, half-garage structure beyond the house. There was a small car parked inside, covered in dirty tarpaulins, though a faded red corner of the rear gleamed in the dim space. At the back door, I noticed something strange: what looked like a piece of cloth, stuck in the crack. I peered in the window: the door had been closed in haste and caught the edge of a raincoat hanging from a hook on the mudroom wall. I tried the knob—it was barely latched; the door swung open with a nudge.

Having come this far, I knocked on the door and called inside. "Hello? Mr. Swenson?" There was no response. I put one foot inside and half my body, craning my neck to see up the stairs and into the kitchen. There was a distinct odor of kitchen trash, rotting food. I pulled back, carefully closing the door.

He must have been out of town. Bachelors weren't known for their housekeeping. Something struck me as off, but I brushed it aside. Julia was gone; it had been so many years.

I walked back down the lane to my car, feeling the house watching me with one bright eye.

Some people always left a light on when they left home, to ward off thieves.

I drove the long way round the island to the village. If Orwell Island had a primary artery, it would be Hornsea Road, which breaks off from the village's main thoroughfare, Anchorage Street, and circles the island's perimeter almost completely. Almost. Hornsea doesn't actually go all the way around the island. It dead-ends by a small county park with a turnabout. But if you drive on, about twenty yards past the turnabout, the pavement gives out to pitted gravel.

Locals know that after a quarter mile of increasingly rutted road along the shore, there is an unmarked, abrupt left turn into the trees, and a hard-pack gravel road that turns into asphalt just out of sight. Up the slope the fir trees become denser, the woodland changing from straggler pines and madrones to hardy fir and hemlock and Western red cedar. The road continues for almost four miles, where it eventually meets Anchorage Street at the south end of Orwell Village with a rusted sign that says NO

OUTLET. The road is old, but the asphalt is younger than I am. It follows a track that ran around the island before Orwell was even a town, back when it was a trading post for the Coast Salish people and the Europeans who came after Vancouver's expedition. It was our shortcut, those of us who lived on that side.

I drove the grassy, rutted track to the place where asphalt appeared out of nowhere. Then three-quarters of a mile on, at the site of an aborted housing development, I pulled off the road into a weedy patch of gravel. All along the road ahead, between stands of taller trees, were more of the same weedy, treeless spaces: parcels of land, marked and cleared, foundations poured and abandoned, now overgrown with vetch and fireweed.

I parked in what would have been a driveway. There were cans and cigarette butts strewn about the gravel. A potato chip bag in the tall grass. Unimaginative graffiti all over the walls. Half a dozen gangly adolescent red alders stood around the rocky floor like derelicts. Alders take root like this after disturbances to the ecosystem. For generations after logging and fires and other disruptions, the swift and the adaptable take over, not letting a spare inch of earth go to waste. Like the local teenagers who clambered through the nettles to scrawl their secret names into the cement, the alders were opportunists. A couple of the trees even sprouted from cracks in the bottom corners, reaching up to touch the tagged walls. I could almost see spray-paint canisters at the ends of their skinny branches.

I walked around the foundation, found the place where the cement had caved enough to create a few steps—the way in. I stretched one leg down into the space and drew it back. I didn't want to climb down. I knew how the crack came to be there. If you looked closely enough at me, you would find cracks from the same day, the same hour. Minute fissures in my bones. A few half-connected pathways in my brain.

May 1, 1993, was warm, with a taste of summer in the air. The primroses and hyacinth and daphne were blooming. Chartreuse tree tips and pink blossoms. Sunshine on water. All the water: the lakes and rivers and canals; and Puget Sound, the Salish Sea. After weeks of rain, people on the streets of cities and towns in the region were cheerfully stupefied by the glare.

At 9:09 a.m. the ambient noise of the cities and suburbs and seaside towns went mute. A barely recognizable shift, like how the air softens just before a lightning storm. This was the moment when pets became perturbed, barked or squawked or fled under beds. Then almost before registering the difference, there was a rumbling that at first sounded like faraway thunder, then felt like a truck barreling by, then a train coming head-on. Then everything not bolted to the walls, and some things that were, fell. Books off shelves and dishes out of cupboards, food out of refrigerators and art off walls. Lamps, chairs, televisions, toppled. It was loud, not just the city tumbling, but the earth itself. Louder and louder because the sensitive bones of the inner ear register both movement and sound. The ground was rippling, rolling. Witnesses in downtown Seattle described the skyscrapers of the skyline as "doing the wave" like fans at a Mariners game. As the shaking continued, doors fell off hinges when their wood splintered. Foundations cracked and sunk, and houses clattered free of their supposedly solid bases. Streets split like stretched fabric, and parked cars rolled down hills. So many cars scraping and tumbling down the hills and into piles, into the sides of buildings. Bridges wobbled, weak-kneed, and drivers felt like a great wind was blowing across the road; they careened into guardrails and one another. Skyscrapers bowed, dropping whole gleaming pools of window to the ground below. People were in stairwells and doorways and under desks and in the aisles of grocery stores with cans and cleaning products and cereal all over them. Parents and nannies and teachers held children to their chests, covering their heads, practically suffocating them, the shaking going on and on—so much longer than they thought possible. Patrons of the Woodland Park Zoo held tight to the railings and clenched their eyes as the elephants trumpeted and the mother lion froze, crouched with her young, and let out a deep, uncanny yowl, and the polar bears, diving in their pool, clawed at the Plexiglas, wide-eyed, staring into the eyes of the people on the other side who fled as the glass crackled and droplets of water crept through.

All that time, while we cowered—nauseated, crying, waiting for the stillness—a slab of rock beneath the terranes of Puget Sound was shifting, slipping into the mantle of the North American plate along the South Whidbey Island Fault. Tremors were felt as far north as Juneau, Alaska, and as far south as Salinas, California. It was three minutes in which most of the West Coast of the United States and Canada braced itself.

"It's the Big One," we all thought, we all felt in our hearts. The one geologists had been warning us about for years, the one we had been preparing for at school with earthquake drills. There we were, the children of Puget Sound, under our desks, holding on to the legs as they scooted back and forth across the linoleum, doing what we had practiced. I became motion sick; others peed their pants or wailed for their moms.

Meanwhile, all those sparkling waters, displaced by the drop in the seafloor, were drawn back, away from their shores, leaning to the west, and even before the first aftershocks, like an unseen hand smoothing a tablecloth, the waters began their inevitable rush back into their basins. The ten-to-twenty-foot waves washed out waterfronts, sluicing up river deltas, pounding docks, houseboats, locks, bridges, grain and coal terminals, capsizing fishing boats, and scouring the decks of barges. Landslides along the rim of the bays caused more tsunamis, so that the thunder of water and the thunder of earth folded over each other, and our ears couldn't distinguish which death might be coming for us.

Just over three thousand people died, but it wasn't, in fact, the Big One. Three minutes and twelve seconds of a magnitude 7.9 quake. It was a relatively shallow quake, in one of the many tertiary faults within the Cascadia Subduction Zone. But the nature of the sound, with its cities built on wetlands around river deltas and in floodplains, created a sort of echo for the earth's waves, a reverberation of the earth that amplified the shaking on the surface.

The story of the May Day Quake was told over and over again, in different ways, by different people. By scientists and engineers and first responders. By pilots and passengers of planes taxiing into SeaTac who witnessed it from the air. By survivors of the fires that broke out and survivors of boats and ferries capsized and survivors of collapsed bridges and tunnels. Like aftershocks, the stories. To retell it was to relive it. For years afterward, the quake was documented, analyzed, broadcast, and anthologized. I even wrote about it once, on the tenth anniversary, for the *Sentinel*, my college paper. By then, the May Day Quake had been consumed in the popular imagination and nearly forgotten, relegated to anecdote, the way Katrina would be a dozen years later. It hadn't been the Big One, after all; there would be more stories to tell someday.

• • •

I turned my back to the foundation to look at the view. Through the trees across the street and down a rocky embankment was a drop to the strait, where the currents at tide change churned like water in a washing machine. Up the road were other abandoned parcels, barely visible driveways leading to vacant foundations, as if someone had plucked the houses right out of the ground, leaving cavities in the shape of living spaces. I could feel the house that wasn't there, rising out of the gaping concrete mouth. The alders shivered in the breeze, a sound so familiar that I shivered, too.

Turning back to what was behind me — or *not* behind me — I did what most people in my generation do when faced with the ubiquitous and strange: I took pictures with my phone. Then I climbed back in my car, turned on Neko Case, and drove the rest of the cracked road into the village.

Orwell had hardly changed in twenty years. What had been destroyed had been rebuilt or replaced or grown over, but everything still matched up with the map in my mind. Anchorage Street ran the length of the business district. A small-town main street, with the ferry terminal and a shoreline park, a few waterfront hotels and cafés on one side, houses set into an increasingly wooded and rocky hillside on the other. All the old buildings in downtown that had survived the quake were still there — many of them with structural improvements and seismic retrofits. There was a cooperative grocery in the place of the general store that had been condemned after the quake, and next to it a gravel parking lot edged by flowerpots and signs advertising the local farmers' market, every other Saturday, JUNE THRU OCTOBER.

I walked up the street. Tourism had rebounded. Most of the

storefronts were occupied, and there were two shops selling the kind of knickknacks that islanders call "bait."

"How's things?" you'd hear islanders asking.

"Oh, you know. Selling lots of bait," they would say. Or maybe, "Not biting. Need better bait, I guess."

Bait was always at the front of the store and by the register. If the store had a public toilet (most didn't; unreliable plumbing), there might be some toward the back too, for the people waiting to use it.

I peered into the bookstore, at the same storefront it had occupied when we left, though its name had changed to Sound Books & News, and it had been painted, reorganized, with racks of postcards and orca magnets and crab key chains by the door. It was Filgate's Books before, named for the old salt who owned it. My dad and Danny Filgate had been good friends, though Danny was a generation older. He, like my dad, was an autodidact who read everything from the *Wall Street Journal* to Toni Morrison to pulpy airport paperbacks. He had refused to sell bait. He catered to the islanders. You might wander into the shop and find a gathering of fisher-poets: fishermen and -women who spent long hours on the water composing verses—often ballads and other old forms—in their heads. They weren't readings, these gatherings; they were dramatic performances, sometimes with musical interludes on banjo or harmonica or fiddle. The gatherings took place in the off-season, so tourists didn't often run into them. But if one happened to wander into the shop when the fisher-poets were there, it was another of those things that make people fall in love with the islands. The locals set the scene and the mood, like the cast of characters in a Melville novel.

I assumed Danny must be dead. He couldn't have lived to see

his business like this: it looked orderly, sanitized; a display of T-shirts with famous novel covers printed on them on the wall behind the cash register.

I sat on the steps outside City Hall, a newer building that looked like a lot of government buildings—squat and gray and featureless—easily the ugliest building in town. The old City Hall had burned down after the quake. The new one housed a small public library, a state police precinct, and various other municipal entities. It opened in fifteen minutes. Something else that hadn't changed about Orwell was the pace. Nearly ten o'clock and shops up and down the street were just starting to show signs of life.

The sun had burned through the clouds; it was getting warm —dew had started to form between my breasts and under my arms. I pulled my sweater off over my head and thought about taking it back to the car, or putting off the visit to the clerk's office, going up to the cemetery first. A few late-season tourists milled about, looking relaxed. A couple walked by me and said, "Good morning," as they passed. They wore small bemused smiles, their cheeks flushed; they weren't holding hands, but they bumped into each other as they walked, arms brushing intentionally. They had clearly been having sex all night to the sounds of the sea.

I hated them a little bit, for having sex on my island, though I knew that was what people did on seaside vacations. When my mom was a teenager, she spent summers housekeeping at lodges and motels all over the islands. I thought of her stripping one dirty sheet after another. I might've done the same, if we had stayed.

There were two motels, a bed-and-breakfast, and half a

dozen vacation rentals in Orwell. Most people didn't stay on our island. Most people stayed in Friday Harbor or Rochelle, on San Juan Island. Or in the smaller, more expensive places on Lummi and Orcas. The ferries only made a couple stops a day in Orwell. There wasn't much to do here, other than stroll and eat seafood, so it was sold more as a romantic getaway than a family destination.

When Matt found out about the cottage, he had asked why I hadn't told him about it, why I hadn't brought him out here. He wanted to go crabbing and eat mussels right out of the shell on the shore; he wanted to visit the Benedictine nuns on Shaw Island who raised heirloom cattle and sheep. This was just a destination to him, an experience. A place with no context. I was crazy, he told me, for having access to something like this and not taking advantage of it. He was right, that I was privileged in a way most of my peers weren't. Owning property was getting harder and harder in cities like Seattle and San Francisco. The fact that my family had a "vacation home" made me slightly embarrassed.

I had tried to explain to him why I never came back, why I never talked about it. The death of a parent he understood, but the harrowing aftermath of the earthquake was lost on him. He was only a year older than I—he had been thirteen at the time of the quake and had only vague memories of the media coverage. He had moved to Seattle from Brooklyn in 2006. Aside from the tail end of a hurricane or two, he hadn't experienced a natural disaster. He had never felt an earthquake; they were as mythical as Sasquatch to him.

The clack of unlocking doors broke my daze. I wasn't the only one on the stairs waiting for City Hall to open. A tall man stood off to my right, on the top step. He nodded. I smiled back and stood, stretching. An older woman in a pantsuit swung the door open, remarked on the beauty of the day, and held the door for us. I took my time up the stairs so that the man would go through first, but when I reached the top, he had paused to wait for me.

"You were here first," he said, and nodded toward the entrance.

"I'm not in a hurry," I said.

He led the way, and I followed behind, looking him over. He was wearing official-looking work clothes: thick cotton button-up with a crewneck showing at the top, dark, sturdy slacks with a belt, and steel-toed boots. Like a uniform, but not a uniform. No patches or decals. Like it was his day off, but he still needed to look the part. Law enforcement? I wondered. Fish and Wildlife? He was clean-shaven, with trim brown hair, but he'd been wearing a hat of some sort that had flattened the sides and left squirrely waves on top. We both followed signs for the clerk's desk, and the lady bustled along behind us, asked us to take a seat while she answered the ringing telephone.

We sat in two wooden armchairs with a table of magazines and a potted plant between us. He picked up a *Sunset,* looked at the cover, then glanced up and offered it to me. The cover story was "Ten Island Getaways."

"No thanks." I laughed.

"I guess we've made it," he said, putting the magazine back.

"A clean getaway," I said.

"Do you live here in Orwell?" he asked.

"Not really," I said. I looked at the manila envelope in my hands. All I had to do was file the deed, then the cottage would be mine. "I grew up here. I'm just back to take care of some family business."

He nodded.

"Do you live here?" I asked.

"No, ma'am," he said.

"Ma'am?" I repeated, and laughed. He was maybe three or four years older than I.

He blushed, chewed the inside of his cheek. I couldn't tell if he was trying not to laugh or just embarrassed.

"I'm here for work. I'm not sure where I'll be living at the moment."

A sheriff's deputy came through from a back office.

"Hey there, Carey, sorry to keep you waiting," the deputy said. He came around and shook hands with the man next to me.

"Hey, Chris," he said, "no problem."

His last name was embroidered to his uniform: *Lelehalt.* I recognized him. Chris Lelehalt. His grandma May and my grandma Lucia were both Lummi and in a sewing circle together. Many of the old-timers were Catholic, so the sewing bees were always at St. Mary's, in the basement meeting room with folding tables and chairs, plates of cookies, grandkids playing tag in the cemetery. Chris was a year younger, so I didn't play with him much, but his mom worked at the refinery on Marrow, one of the few women at the plant. She made it home after the quake. Mom and I saw them at the church, where the Red Cross was distributing supplies. It may have been the last time I saw Chris — still lanky and pre-adolescent, black hair cut short and neat. Our mothers were standing around while an old lady gave us all typhoid shots. I remembered my mother asking her something — I didn't actually hear what she asked; they were just outside the circle of mothers. Deb had shaken her head and hugged Mom hard. Chris was next in line, wincing as he watched the shot go into my arm.

"We've just got a few things to go over," Chris was saying, tapping some papers on his hand. "The notary will be here later, the normal rigmarole, and you should be all set up by the end of the day. Let's head on over."

Carey, soon to be *all set up* by Deputy Chris Lelehalt and the notary public, turned back to me.

"Have a nice day, *ma'am*," he said.

"You too, *sir*," I said.

Chris Lelehalt watched this exchange, not recognizing me, and turned when Carey joined him, leading him through to the back of the clerk's office.

"Well, it looks like you're all mine." The clerk stood and was staring at me from behind the desk. She was so short that her eyes were nearly level with mine in my chair against the wall.

I told her why I was there, and she handed me something else to fill out, took my deed, and looked at it.

"Bowen," she said, "the cottage out there by the Swenson place?"

"Yeah."

"Haven't been Bowens out here for a long time."

"No."

"You won't remember me," she said after a long pause. "My son Aaron worked with your dad. Lost him the same day."

I stopped filling out the form. She was right; I didn't remember her. I hadn't even noticed her name plate on the counter, hidden behind a box of tissues: MARLA SHARPE.

"I'm sorry" was all I could say.

"So am I, dear."

She was quiet while I filled out the rest of the form, then she took the lot and made copies.

"Are you moving back here?" she asked while we waited, printer humming.

"I don't know," I said. "It needs a lot of work."

She nodded. "It's an old house; survived a lot better than some. If you're thinking of selling, talk to Jacob Swenson first; he wants to keep that side of the island from development."

"I've never met him — does he live at Rookwood year-round?"

"Oh, yes. He's around most of the year. He oversees things, since Julia passed."

I nodded. "Is he an artist like Julia and Maura?"

She laughed.

"An art lover, maybe. Collects antiques. No, I think it's just a man his age, unmarried, living alone in that big old house out there, people will talk. They call him eccentric. But he's no more eccentric than Julia ever was. Keeps to himself, but makes nice with folks when he needs to. Gives out a scholarship every year at the Festival."

"He doesn't seem to be home. Do you know if he's away now?"

"He goes back east around Christmas, usually, and to Seattle every now and then. Comes back with his little red car packed with knickknacks and furniture."

"A red Saab?"

"Yep, at least thirty years old, that car — I don't know how he keeps it running out here."

"I think I saw his car — in the garage. Does he usually leave it here when he goes back east?"

"That's odd." Her brow furrowed. "He drives himself everywhere. I think he parks it at SeaTac when he flies." She waved her hand. "You know, he's probably just sleeping off a late night, dear," she said quietly, and winked, then turned away to retrieve the copies.

My mother had always complained about the islanders' propensity for gossip, but as a journalist I privately rejoiced every time I met a local busybody like Marla Sharpe.

"Try again this evening," she said, handing me the papers. "I bet he'll give you the tour of his collection."

"Sure, thanks."

I gathered up my copies and slid them into my bag.

I walked toward the cemetery. On the way I passed the Co-op and stopped in to buy a clutch of dahlias—ISLAND-GROWN, the sign proclaimed. There were dahlias bursting like anemones around fence posts and front porches all over the islands this time of year. I probably could have walked up to any front door and asked to pick a few. But I paid the six bucks and kept walking up the hill, past the church itself and through the wrought-iron gate and into the cemetery. The ground was soft under my feet, like the thick soft carpet inside the church.

I passed Aaron Sharpe's headstone, untied the bundle of flowers, and put one in the scummy vase at the base. Near the back, just before a broad open hill sloped down, was Dad's marker. WILLIAM WHITMAN BOWEN, his father's name within his own. Grandma Lucia and Grandpa Whit were tucked together next to him. As a child I had pictured them sleeping side by side in a cozy bed, blankets folded under their arms. A grave was just an underground bedroom, where people went into permanent hibernation.

At my dad's funeral, there had been nothing to imagine. There was no interment, just a headstone on soil, waiting. In case he washed up somewhere. In case some bone fragment gave up some DNA we could trace through mine to confirm. We had nothing to bury. Of all the survivors of the Marrow Ar-Pac disaster, none could remember when or where they had last seen my father. One thought he saw him boarding a boat just before the first waves came; another thought he was helping others, inside, just before the explosion. A few men had burned to cinders when the fire controls failed; pipes that carried water to sprinklers were crushed under the weight of collapsed steel, and water glugged uselessly out into drainage ditches and then back into the sea.

Coast Guard boats and fire flights that may have come to help had either been incapacitated in the quake or dispatched to other emergencies before the radio calls reached them. ArPac was the oldest, smallest petroleum refinery in the area — there were two others — and fires were already underway at Tesoro in Anacortes. There were chemical spills all over the sound, from ships and barges washed against pilings or slammed ashore, from paper plants, from railways along the water. The coal terminal in Bellingham had just been completed, and the wave — though less powerful than it was farther south near Everett and Seattle — spread a cubic mile of coal over land and water throughout up and down the sound.

There were people in the water who needed saving, too.

Bodies had washed up for weeks after the quake, along with all the other flotsam. I had been forbidden to beachcomb — a daily routine in ordinary times — but Katie and I slipped away. Our mothers were sleepless and busy with post-disaster chores, easily manipulated into believing the other mother was on watch. We were twelve and shrugged off their worry like wool cardigans. We had walked through the woods between our houses to a rocky crescent of shoreline. I don't know what we expected to find—I don't remember if we went for any reason other than transgression—but there were more dead shorebirds than I had ever seen, cast among the jagged hulls of small boats, rope and fishing gear, fish and crabs trapped and suffocated or starved in the mesh. We had pulled our shirts over our noses to filter the air, thick with sea rot and animal rot, mixed with the eye-glazing fumes of the chemical dispersants they had eventually used on the oil slicks around Marrow. Everything had an oily gloss, a sheen like a puddle in a gas station parking lot.

A feeling had come over me, as we picked through furniture and disintegrating cereal boxes and a pair of eyeglasses. A man's work boot, a hooded sweatshirt, items of clothing so filthy and sodden we couldn't identify them, heaped over driftwood, branches. I remembered reaching out to touch them —wanting to uncover the logs, maybe? And realizing they weren't logs. I had looked at Katie, and her face mirrored the unease that had settled in me. She had climbed up onto a giant downed tree and reached down for my hand. I took it and joined her, staring over the wrecked shore below us, the clouds of flies hovering over the heaps. We jumped down the other side into the grass and ran back into the woods. We never talked about it; but we both knew. We had been breaking a cardinal rule. And it was obvious he was already dead. What could we do to help him? We couldn't tell anyone without getting in trouble ourselves, so we didn't.

The body wasn't my father, who never did wash up, at least not on Orwell or Marrow, convincing my mother that he had been trapped in the refinery by the fire. I laid the flowers across his headstone. There was a plot next to my father, for my mom. She was remarried, so I figured the plot would be mine, someday.

I spent the rest of the day going over the cottage, making lists of things to be fixed or assessed by a professional. The water heater was ancient, as was the electrical panel. I couldn't believe my mom hadn't needed to replace them after the quake—but then she'd probably hired an out-of-work ArPac friend of my dad's who wasn't going to bother with bringing things up to code. It didn't matter what she had done then anyway; a couple decades of island weather and winter vacancy had left peeling paint, moldy cabinets, leaky pipes.

I stood at the screen door drinking a beer, letting the breeze cool me, and staring up through the mesh at Rookwood. I had pulled up the drive when I got back, knocked on the door again. There was no movement at all from inside, no sounds. I felt the hairs on my arm rise and looked down to see a mosquito lifting off, full of my blood. She flew straight for the screen and knocked herself against it, up and down, until she found a hole —probably the hole through which she had come. I turned to the counter and added *screens* to the list.

Evening was coming on, but there was still plenty of light, so I spent it in the yard, wrangling a season's worth of weeds. In the shed were the tools and more notes from my mom to visitors or hired hands: how to oil and clean the blades on the manual mower (*carefully!*); how to plug in the weed-whacker (*run the cord through the bathroom window*); how and where to find the strawberry patch and the raspberries so as not to mow them down (*Follow the birds and the bees in June!*); encouragements to pick the wild irises for bouquets; where to put the hatchet when not splitting logs (*on the wall in the shed*); and random admonishments and warnings (*Wear gloves! Watch for nettles!*).

By dusk my muscles were spent; I had blisters on my hands (didn't *wear gloves!*). I dropped to the ground, fibrous shards of crabgrass stabbing me through my sweaty T-shirt. The lawn slanted steeply, and my head was pointed downhill, toward the water, arms thrown up, watching the tide upside down for a while, letting my mind drift. I rolled my head to the side, where I could just spy Rookwood's long wide lines through the trees. There were no signs of life at the house other than that one light, still burning. No cars had come or gone. I thought about the red car in the carriage house.

I sat up and downed the last of my beer. Eyes tired, or maybe just dusty, I saw everything through a filter of spores. I felt watched, but also called, beckoned by the glowing window.

"You're drunk," I said. I counted how many beers I'd had and how little food.

In the cottage I pulled on a sweater and found a working flashlight. He wouldn't mind, I told myself. No one on the island would mind if a neighbor saw to a light left on. There were probably still keys to Rookwood somewhere in the cottage. I thought of Marla Sharpe at the clerk's office — she knew my family; she could vouch for me. I was a landowner! I let myself follow the drunken logic, emboldened by my legitimacy as a remade local and a newly minted property owner, as I crossed the lane in the dark. I knew enough not to pause, not to think. On Rookwood's dark porch, I didn't hesitate as I reached for

the latch on the door. Like most doors on the island, it was un-
locked. I gave it a shove and watched it swing heavily over the
flagstones of the entry.

I called out a loud *hello*. My voice didn't even echo, lost to the
heavy walls of the house.

"It's your neighbor, Lucie Bowen," I called again, closing
the door behind me and standing there in the silence, flashlight
aimed at a mirror opposite the door. An arch to the left led to
the parlor, an arch to the right led to the hallway and carved
staircase. I felt twelve years old again; I wished Katie were there
with me.

I found the light switch — an old-fashioned one, two Lucite
buttons with circles of abalone inlay — and the chandelier above
me lit up. It made everything beyond its glare seem darker and
more forbidding. Being alone in a half-lit house seemed scarier
than being in a dark one, so I turned it off.

I kept the flashlight trained ahead of me and headed for the
staircase. The house smelled dusty, stale. Unlived-in. I stopped
on the landing and sneezed a few times, wiped my nose on the
back of my sleeve. I looked down at my feet, at the carpet on
the stairway, faded and worn to threads in places.

Above me was Maura's famous self-portrait, lifelike and im-
perious. She was probably in her forties at the time, brown-gray
hair pulled up and back, wearing a pale blue dress, not a trace of
a smile on her face. It wasn't a beautiful portrait, but it was strik-
ing. She painted it between the wars; art had changed then, Julia had told me, because of the shock of modern warfare. I was
ten at the time, in shock myself from the quake. Maybe that was
why she had said it. Because she wanted me to know that there
was a world full of tragedies besides my own.

I continued up the stairs, telling myself I had no intention of snooping, just turning off the light. The adrenaline was killing the beer's soft buzz. A long hallway ran the width of the house at the top, and I turned to the right, following the glow at the end, the last door on the right. It opened on a large bedroom with a perfectly made four-poster, a suitcase open and half-filled with clothes on top. The sight of something in progress like that made me doubt myself: Maybe he was home? Maybe he had been home and I had missed him? But the rest of the room was off: there was a through-breeze; the window of the dormer was open wide, and there were two lamps lit, not just the one visible in the window. The other was tipped on its side on a bedside table, the shade hanging over the edge. I closed the window, noting water stains on the sill and leaves on the carpet below. It had been open for some time. When was the last rain? It had been a few days, a hard rain after weeks of unseasonable warmth.

When I turned to the lamp on the table, my foot bumped what was left of a broken highball glass on the floor. On the bed, the suitcase lay open like a book. Men's clothes, folded neatly. I ran my hand over the cool cotton shirts. A belt, a pair of casual leather loafers, an eyeglasses case, a toiletries bag. I couldn't help myself; I was in this far, wasn't I? I opened it. There were shaving supplies, a toothbrush, contact lens case, and a prescription bottle of Klonopin with Jacob Swenson's name on it.

I swallowed a lump rising in my throat and took a breath. I thought again about walking through the wreckage with Katie, reaching for the remains, realizing what they were, reaching out for her hand instead.

Four

THE WOODS

BABIES EVERYWHERE. This time of year is all eggs hatching and sprouting and slippery bald heads and blind eyes shoving themselves toward the light. Everywhere you step, a birth.

After Carey left for work, I saw one of those spiders that just weeks ago looked ragged and starved. It had survived the winter somewhere under the shitty couch and was hauling itself out of the darkness and making its way across the floor in the direction of the back door. I didn't examine it before I reacted. The door was open, beckoning to the spider, I suppose, so I grabbed the broom and tried to sweep it out onto the porch. But with the first swipe hundreds of babies went tumbling off her back. They were so fast, the specks of them with their spotted translucent bodies like baby octopuses, almost not there at all. They raced off in all directions, spun their immature threads wildly at the broom straw, clung to it. I tried not to step on them, shaking them from the broom, trying still to usher them out the door. But their mother just kept running, all eight legs whirring, a few little ones still holding to her body and dangling off by weak strings.

"Don't leave your babies!" I called after her, but she was faster now that she wasn't carrying all her children. "What am I going to do with your babies?"

But she was out the door.

"Shit. Shit, *shit!*" I sounded just like my mother. I learned to swear by listening to her cooking dinner, cleaning out the cabinets, weeding the garden. Household chores pissed her off, especially after my dad was gone.

I watched the babies scatter, tried to create a breeze that would waft them after their mother, then tried gently sweeping, but I just smeared their delicate bodies across the linoleum tiles. I took the broom outside and thrashed it against a tree trunk to shake off any still clinging, any still alive.

It's my birthday, again. I did the math when I woke up; it was my first conscious act. Thirty-five. I'm thirty-five. I've been losing track, adding years without thinking, or taking them away.

My mom called this morning, just after the baby spiders, but I didn't pick up. She left a message on the old machine. The machine with Carey's voice that says nothing about me, the way I requested it. She knows where I am; I always tell her now. But I don't write or call much. It will be Mother's Day in a few days and I'll call then. She used to tell me that my birthday was her Mother's Day, that she didn't care about the holiday. I remembered this while she was talking through the machine. I'm still in trouble for taking off and almost dying on the same island that killed my dad. She would never put it that way, of course, but I can hear it in her voice. Yesterday was the anniversary of the quake and his death, so I was thinking about it. Every year, the anniversary comes hulking along, its shadow blotting me out.

I considered picking up the phone. But there are no direct conversations with my mom. Only questions underneath questions. No matter how I try to steer it, we seem to cover the same well-trod path around what we won't talk about: that we both lost the first and best man we ever loved, the man who had tied the two of us together in a safe, tight knot.

"How's Carey?" she starts, which is her way of asking if he has proposed or if I've proposed to him. If I don't intend to marry him, if we're not going to make babies, she can't fathom why I would come out here. Why did I leave the city, where I was closer to her and my stepdad, my grandparents, a therapist? She thinks I'm undertaking some kind of self-concocted exposure therapy.

"I sleep better out here," I told her once. It's true: I sleep like there's no earthquakes, I sleep like there's no ocean.

I wiped minuscule spider parts from the linoleum, listening to her wish me a happy birthday. She was on her cell phone in the car, traffic under her voice.

Carey's at work all day. He insisted we do something for my birthday, so when he comes home, we'll make the drive to Prairie City and eat at the hotel restaurant. Some days, when he's been out in the woods, he smells like lichen; a heady boreal sweetness you'd never guess would come from a plant that does not bloom. I smell him every time; I put my face right into the crook of his neck as soon as he walks through the door. After a while he asked me why I did that, and I told him. I want it, that smell. I want it in a way that I can't explain, that goes all the way into my cells. I can't tell if this desire is biological or emotional. The first time he went down on me, here in the woods, in the high mountain winter, he told me I tasted like the sea. I kissed him and tasted myself in his mouth, and it was true—it was like urchin or salmon roe. I had never noticed before, my own taste. I think about the things you cannot know about yourself until someone else shows you, and I wonder if this is how it starts, love, or if this is all it is.

I'm taking the old mining road to the lake today. I leave a note that says "I'll be home soon" on the kitchen table. There's only one note, I just keep leaving it over and over again, then pocketing it as soon as I get back. I always make it back before he finds it. It's on the table today, just in case. If something happened to me out there, Carey would find a crumpled, weathered piece of my notebook paper with deep crease lines from the folding and unfolding. He would hold it in his hands carefully, barely touching it, like a suicide note. If I didn't come back, he would be the one in charge of finding me.

I witnessed a rescue in my first days here, a backcountry skier who didn't report back. Dogs, helicopter, volunteers in the snow with whistles. They let me volunteer, though I didn't have the training. I learned as we went. It was the most exciting thing that happened all spring, the prospect of coming across a mauled, frozen outdoorsman. That was how Carey prepared me for the worst.

"Could've been a lynx," he said. "They follow the sound of the skis from miles away. It's like deer through the snow."

I thought about this and concluded I would always root for the lynx, even if it meant I never cross-country skied again.

But the guy was just lost. He had a dozen protein bars and some emergency matches on him; he melted snow for water. He seemed irritated it took us so long.

Then the snow was gone, earlier than usual. There weren't as many hard freezes, and snowfall averages all around the state were low, despite a late-season fall. When the pack isn't as deep, it can melt completely in just a few warmer-than-average days. Spring arrived suddenly; now everything is blooming and hatching. The conversation around the ranger station is all almanac, all the time. Mosquito year. Blackfly year. Drought year. Fire year.

I asked if that meant the fire lookout would be staffed this year, and Carey said, "Yeah, maybe." Which means I'll have to find another place. My first choice is the lake, since there's a one-room cabin there. Carey said Eagle Scouts built it in the nineties; it's a miracle it's still standing. I've seen it once, from a distance. It looked more like the setting for a horror movie than a place to relax, but I'm going to investigate. Get my scent in the air so the animals there start to know me. If they know me, if they recognize my scent, will they be less likely to want to eat me? Or more?

I spend a lot of time up here thinking of all the different ways people die in the wilderness. There's the obvious: hypothermia, dehydration, hunger. Or the fatal mistake: eating strange plants, drinking giardia-laced water. There's the unlikely, but imminently possible: drowning; bear; snakebite. There's bad luck: rockslide; falling tree; lightning strike; drunk hunter. There's the long exit: tick bite, Lyme disease.

Or when I'm hiking a steep trail and my foot slips in the loose rocks and I catch myself — just barely — on a root or a tree branch, stumble back onto the path. I look down and see a very real vision of my broken body and the headline flashing across the news feeds of everyone I know, the shares on social media: "Body of Seattle Woman Recovered in Malheur Forest." At some point I made a choice to be there, snagged on that shelf of earth and not down at the bottom in a heap. Not just one choice, many choices. Thousands — how far back in my life? days, weeks, years? — they flow back instantly, it's not even conscious; all the choices jolt through the body and some cellular consciousness, some small muscle in my foot that senses the imminent danger, sends up a flare to my brain. So that I reach out at the right moment, leaning just so, throwing my weight back onto the trail. My thoughts stream back. I remember the moment I chose that particular trail, chose to come out alone, at that time of day, under those dry conditions, in those inadequate shoes, not the proper boots, because they would be too hot. Did I drink enough water? Eat enough breakfast? I rested, on that rock in the shade just a mile back, though I wasn't especially tired — did some part of me know? And farther back — the choice to leave Seattle and follow Carey to the woods at all, the choice to go to the islands, where we met, where I could have died. It flashes through my body, with the adrenaline in my bloodstream, the certain knowledge of how tenuous it all is, the web of everything I've done — all leading to this moment: staring down at that parallel life, the one where I/she lies unable to move, in the bottom of that ravine, covered in dust and rocks and the ash of old fires, until I/she dies. Which choice was it? Which one saved me? Which one killed her?

And I then wipe my brow and hike on.

Halfway to the lake, mosquitoes strum the air. The sun angles through the trees and I'm aware of my sweat, along with the chemical perfume of my exhalations that the female mosquitos recognize from yards away. So much for this dry heat; where the air is thinner, you work harder for each breath, and I've been exerting myself. I might as well have a neon sign over my head that says BREAKFAST. The mosquitoes have been exerting themselves, too. They've been fucking and now they're hungry. They need energy to lay the thousands of eggs they will deposit in the first still pool of water they find. Through the pines to the lake, they feed on me like children. I don't catch them till they're flying away, full of my blood. Male mosquitoes, the dandies, survive on wildflower nectar.

I smell the water before I see it. Water lifts all the smells around. The mist rises; the vapors carry particles of resin and pollen and fungi spores. As I climb the last fallen tree and the lake comes into view, I connect a low murmur to the sound of it: not waves lapping, but the deeper, subtler sound of movement beneath the surface. I close my eyes and inhale, trying to feel the course of the vapors through my body, the whole invisible forest in my sinuses, my lungs, my blood. Everything right down to my cells and further: to the mitochondria, the tiniest lungs, where respiration continues after the death of the brain, the heart. The last breaths of the cells happen there, as the body decays, releasing all that stored energy at last. Hot sacks of cells, our bodies, like compost heaps, steaming with everything we take in, unsure of how to let go.

When I open my eyes, I focus on the ground near my feet. A shrug of fallen needles and leaves that seems to be levitating, and I know that underneath I will find the fruits of the mycelium. I carefully lift a corner of the leaf cover with a stick to reveal the pale young bodies of the mushrooms. I squat to get closer, and a smell like maple syrup wafts up out of the duff. I pluck a specimen from the rim of the colony. A fat, opalescent beetle scuttles into the vacancy in the soil. I hold the specimen in my palm and gently examine it. It looks deceptively delicate, almost feminine, something out of a fairy tale: thin white stem, slick, round, lilac cap; but it is firm and unresisting to the touch. I look at it lying in my palm and think of Sister J., shroud-pale, plucked from her island, cell walls breaking. Sometimes I hear Katie's voice in my head, answering questions I haven't really asked. I hear her now, telling me to put my hands in the soil, like I did on Marrow, to feel the threaded white mass netting my fingers.

"Mycelium takes everything we give it," she says, "and transforms death into life. It communicates directly with the soul of every living thing that touches it."

"But I probably shouldn't eat it," I say, to Katie or whatever's listening.

You're supposed to talk or sing when you're alone in the wilderness, to alert the wildlife that you're there, that you're coming, to startle them away. I usually sing. A woman in Colorado fended off a cougar by singing opera to it. When I'm not singing, I talk to Katie. At first it was awkward—I was afraid I'd encounter another hiker who would overhear my half of the conversation and think I was crazy—but now I'm so used to it that I find myself talking to her in the cabin or at the lookout.

The birdsong continues all around as if I'm not there; Katie's gone quiet. I want to eat the mushroom. I test it with my teeth. I take a small bite out of the cap. It's slippery on the outside but almost powdery dry inside. I hold it in my mouth long enough to know it is vegetal, almost spicy but not unpleasant, then spit it out. I pick another and place them in a small paper bag. Tuck it into the top of my pack, so it won't be crushed. There's a book back at the cabin for taxonomic classification.

The scout cabin is another mile around the west side of the lake. I take a small, almost-disused path and have to scrape my way through a curtain of branches to find it, a half-fallen tree barring the way. The door is off the hinges and leaning horizontally across the threshold. I use a large forked stick with clusters of lichen to remove the spiderwebs from the door frame. Not taking any more chances with arachnids today. When the doorway is clear, I poke my head inside. It's dark, with only one window (broken out), and it smells distinctly like piss. There's a shiver in a dark corner, and I'm certain there's a nest of snakes there, so I step back outside and walk along the trail until I find a path down to a small stretch of silt and rock shoreline.

It won't do for a retreat. At the fire lookout, I float above the trees. That's where I'm most at ease—in midair, like a cloud.

I plant myself on a dry boulder and grab a can of beer from my backpack. As I open the can with a pop-crack, I wonder what kind of meal I sound like to the lynx. The cheap lager foams all over my hand. My mouth and throat are parched, so I drink half of it in one slug. It buzzes through me. The cereal and peanut butter balls go down fast, and the rest of the can after. Then I'm stripping off my boots and socks, without a second thought, opening another beer, and wading into the water. It's so cold I gasp, but force myself to breathe through it. The days have been warm this spring, but at this elevation the nights can still fall close to freezing. In the winter, the lake was frozen over, and it hasn't been that long since it thawed. It's ice-clear; I see all the pebbles in the bottom, stretched several feet in front of me, where the bottom dips into a darker blue. There are layers of color, in the lake, just like in the sea, when the water is still. The water is denser where it's coldest near the bottom, so the colors become murky and shaded, and the fish and rocks down there distorted.

The second beer goes down while I'm up to my ankles, kicking one foot then the other to acclimate them. The sun is directly overhead now, shining hard on me, shining straight into the water. I look out across the whole of the lake as a breeze stirs it up and the smallest whitecaps I've ever seen wave at me from the deep, dark center. I drink the rest of the beer, feeling the blood thump in my feet.

I look out several feet in front of me and catch a strange glimmer in the water, threads of light, dancing like weeds from the lake floor, at first just one, then I count three, four, six. I blink, let my pupils adjust. Still there, a trick of the light. Burning on the back of my eye. Like the filaments of incandescent light bulbs. Like old-fashioned tinsel from a Christmas tree. I look away, but when I look back, they are still there. When I move my foot, they move with the ripples but stay more or less in the same place. They are farther out than I planned to go, but I want to get closer to them.

I back out of the water, watching them, letting the angle of light through the trees change my view, but I still see them there. I try not to take my eyes off them as I drop the beer can, take off my jeans and unbutton my plaid shirt. I pull my tank over my head as quickly as I can, and they are still there, glowing elements, shocks of lightning, though they seem slightly farther out than before. I consider leaving my bra and underwear on, but it seems weirder, somehow, to wear them, so I take them off, too, and drop them on the pile of clothes.

Naked on the shore, I watch the filaments underwater. The lake surface quakes in a breeze. It beckons me, with its crisp little waves, so I walk into the lake. When the water reaches my navel, I take a breath and dive under. My eyes close on their own, and when I force them open, they burn and everything blurs. Then ribbons of light streak through the water, and for a moment I think I can see the filaments again, but then they are gone.

I surface panting, water dripping over my face, off my eyelashes, scanning for the filaments, eyes skimming the water all around me, raking my arms to stay afloat. I swim back toward the shore, and that's when I notice the larvae, skirting the warmer, weedy, silted edges of the lake: thousands of them, translucent, writhing, their mosquito mothers hovering over them. I think it's another trick of the light, but I can almost feel their hunger; I am sure they can smell me. I find the rocky floor and stand hip deep, swaying. When the air hits me, I feel the tug of cold water on my numb limbs and scramble ashore.

Five

THE ISLANDS

——◆——

ORWELL ISLAND, WASHINGTON
OCTOBER 10, 2014

I CALLED THE sheriff from the cottage. My voice shook a little as I explained to the dispatcher that I thought my neighbor was missing. She told me to file a report at the station in the morning.

"I can do that, but there are signs of—a struggle, I guess, at his house."

"What do you mean, ma'am?"

"Overturned lamps, a half-packed suitcase with medication left in it. His eyeglasses. I haven't seen him all day."

"Do you see him every day, ma'am?" She sounded young but jaded—a world-weary eighteen-year-old.

"No—" I decide not to tell her that I've never met the man. "But this seems unusual, for him."

"Do you have any reason to believe he's in danger?"

"Not really, no. But I'm alone on this side of the island, and he's my only neighbor. I won't be able to sleep."

She sighed.

I hated how frightened I sounded. She was right; it could wait till morning. It was an unnerving scene, but so were lots of odd scenes in strangers' homes—I had no context. Maybe an emergency called him away from his packing? Did I really want to explain to a sheriff's deputy why, in the middle of the night, I had snuck into the house of a man I'd never met? I could hear her typing.

"All right, ma'am. Looks like there's a deputy who can come out." She took down my name and address.

I had toast and coffee and listened to the radio while I waited. After a while, I heard the wheels of a car coming down the lane and pulling in the drive behind my car. Chris Lelehalt stepped out.

"Shit," I said. I took a breath and met him at the door.

He nodded at me. "Hi there, ma'am." He pulled a notebook from his pocket and read, then looked up again. "Lucie Bowen?"

"That's me." He didn't seem to remember me. He nodded again and looked over his notes, then half turned and looked over his shoulder toward Rookwood. He was a handsome guy —clean-shaven, so you could see his features—broad-nosed, dark-eyed, high cheekbones. He looked like he drank plenty of beer and probably had been doing so since he was fourteen, like a lot of the kids on the islands, but he still looked like the boy I had known, too. He looked back at me.

"You've gotten older," he said.

"You, too."

He shrugged.

"Actually, I wouldn't have recognized you, but Marla Sharpe told me you were back to check on the place." He indicated the cottage.

"Ah." I nodded. "She's the lady with the low-down on Orwell, I guess."

He smiled. "She means well. The old-timers, you know. They keep track."

I let him inside and offered him coffee, but he declined. It was

almost ten o'clock. He was working a split shift; another deputy was on maternity leave. So I walked him across the road to
Rookwood. On the way he asked me questions about when I arrived on the island, how long I was staying, how my mom was
doing. I couldn't tell if this was an official interrogation or just
small talk.

When we reached the door, he raised his hand to knock, then
stopped himself and asked, "Why did you go in, again?"

I explained about the light, about not seeing any sign of Jacob
Swenson all day. I played up the family connection: my grandparents had been caretakers of Rookwood; I had run in and
out freely as a child. He seemed satisfied with this answer and
knocked hard, opened the door, calling inside.

"Mr. Swenson, it's the Sheriff's Department."

The second visit went more or less as the first visit had gone,
except that we turned on the lights. I led Chris on the route I
had taken up the staircase, along the hall, and to the bedroom
where the lamps were still lit. Chris looked over everything in
the room, then he asked me to stand in the front entry while
he looked over the rest of the house. It was a large house and I
stood there for twenty minutes, listening to his footsteps, doors
opening and closing. He had stopped calling out Jacob's name.

When he came back through the entry, turning off lights behind him, he said, "He's not here."

We walked back to my cottage.

"Does it look suspicious to you?" I asked.

"I can't say," he said. "But I'll make some calls tomorrow and
try to track him down. We'll come back over if we need to."

I wasn't satisfied, but I knew I wouldn't get a better answer.
Even small-town police were tight-lipped about investigations.

• • •

I spent the next day at the coffee shop on Anchorage Street with my laptop, looking for information on Jacob Swenson. I found out more about the Swenson Trust, Maura's foundation. She had donated land all over the San Juan Islands to the state and county for parks, for wildlife conservation. The foundation still held private acreage on several islands, including Marrow and Orwell, which could be accessed for study with a letter of interest. The address listed was a PO box in Orwell Village. There was a picture of Jacob Swenson on the foundation's website, a polished and combed man in a tweed suit, younger than I had imagined, in stylish tortoiseshell glasses. He looked like the template for a male humanities professor. But as for personal information, I found little. Two articles in the *Island Times* mentioned him in relation to cultural events on Orwell. He had been on the town council for a time and was referred to as "the dapper councilman" and an "inveterate bachelor." (Code for *gay* in the passive-aggressively discreet vernacular of small towns.)

When I tried to research Marrow Colony, I found only passing references on the blogs of Northwest environmentalists and Evergreen students. A few cruising guides mentioned that the Colony welcomed day visitors on their shores but discouraged campers. Their small harbor couldn't accommodate anchorage for many boats. Their lavender goat cheese was a favorite at the Orwell farmers' market.

I called the number for the Colony that Katie had written at the bottom of her letter and was sent directly to voicemail. The soft voice of a young woman with a Canadian accent told me that Marrow Colony messages were checked once a day, but that calls might not be returned immediately, due to the intermittent reception.

"This message is for Kathryn Paley," I said. "Please tell her

Lucie Bowen is on Orwell, and that I'm coming to see her as soon as I can find a boat."

That evening I packed my backpack and an overnight bag with clothing for three days. I found after some inquiries in town that Joshua Coombs, an old captain from my dad's days of working at the refinery, still ferried people to Marrow. I called his number and spoke to his wife, who told me the boat was already going to Marrow in the morning and I needed to be at the marina at 6:30 a.m.

I didn't hear back from Katie. I barely slept all night, knowing I had to be up early, thinking about seeing her again, half worried that she wouldn't be there, for some reason, that she had left in the time between her letter to me and my arrival.

Joshua Coombs squinted at me as I handed him my bags. It was just getting light.

"What'd you say your name was?" he asked.

"Bowen," I said. I knew this was the name that interested him. "Lucie," I added.

He stowed my bags but said nothing.

I looked up at the tops of the trees on the shore. Just standing on the dock made me queasy. I had forgotten about seasickness. Smaller boats had always set me off, my internal ballast shifting with the waves. I had thrown up on every boat my parents ever took me on as a kid. It was a family joke to hand me a sick bag with my life jacket and see how long I lasted before my breakfast came back up.

I had been so absorbed in my thoughts about seeing Katie again, I hadn't thought about taking a pill for the boat. Katie's visits to see me in Seattle during summer vacation had always brought on anxiety—an acid ache in my guts—my mind and body absorbed in the anticipation: What would she look like? How would she have changed? Would I still feel the same about her? It was the same every time; I was never sure if I wanted that heart-punched love to have vanished, or if I could stand to carry it around for another year. Every time I saw her again after some time, it was the same, though: she lit me up inside. It was a feeling I wouldn't know again until I met Matt, though that fire had burned out within two years. What could ten years have done to my feelings for Katie?

Coombs gave me a hand, and I stepped up into the boat, a twin-hull catamaran, smaller than the older monohull he had captained to ferry the ArPac workers but decent: big enough for eight to ten, with a galley, some bunks, and a head below decks. I wondered whether the seasickness would still be a problem—casting my mind back over the years, looking for times when I had been on anything smaller than a commuter ferry since I was twelve, when we left the islands. I hadn't been on a fishing boat; I hadn't been sailing.

I was watching the shore, trying to get my sea legs, when Coombs handed me a cup of tea from a thermos.

"Going to pay your respects to your pa, are you?"

I looked at him blankly, not as surprised by a local with a long memory anymore, and said nothing. He poured himself a cup. I sat down and sipped the tea; it was scalding, faintly minty. I took deep breaths to calm rising nerves and blew them out over the steaming cup.

"My wife makes this tea from herbs in her garden," Coombs said, pronouncing the "h" in *herbs* and drawing the word out. He took a swig from his enamelware mug, though it must have burned as it went down, because he coughed.

"*Oswego tea,* she calls it. Settles the stomach," he said, after choking down the rest, somehow managing to sound both skeptical and proud of his wife's command of folk wisdom.

"Thank you, I appreciate it," I mustered.

"I remember your dad," he kept right on. "I remember every one of the nine who didn't make it, but especially the few I didn't ever bring back."

"There were only three," I said, and he grunted. "You brought most of them back."

I looked away. There was a man walking up the dock now, with a pack and a sleeping roll. It took me some concentration to recognize my companion at the clerk's office.

"Is this our other passenger?" My voice caught in my throat on the word *passenger.* I took another sip of tea. I felt forlorn: I didn't want to be on this boat with him, making small talk while I tried not to vomit. Why would he be going to Marrow?

Coombs hollered down to him, and Carey tossed him the sleep roll and hauled in the bag himself. When he saw me, he looked surprised and looked to Coombs—for an introduction, maybe. But Coombs just handed him a cup of steaming Oswego tea and went about pulling up anchor. Carey looked at the cup in his hand as if he wasn't sure what to do with it.

"Good morning," he finally said to me.

I lifted my teacup in acknowledgment and took a deep breath as the anchor came up. Carey sat down next to me. He was wearing a uniform this time, and the patch on his nylon parka said FOREST SERVICE. A park ranger. There was a park on Marrow Island, Fort Union, closed since the earthquake. We watched Coombs alternately whistling and cursing, carrying on a conversation with the boat's various instruments.

"This is strange," Carey said after a minute.

"It is," I said. "You shouldn't sit so close to me."

"Oh—I'm sorry." He moved to the bench opposite me. "I didn't mean—"

"No—that's no good either," I said, imagining losing it on the deck between us or, worse, right onto his official khakis.

He stood up, but the boat was moving now, and he looked around, unsure of where to go. I could feel a rise in my throat every time I swallowed. My chest felt heavy.

"I'll just sit up here." He gestured to the cabin. "I apologize—"

"It's not you," I managed to get out. "I get seasick."

He stopped and looked at me.

"Oh. That's not strange," he said matter-of-factly.

"If you say so."

"I understand. Don't worry about it," he said. He was earnest, but there was a languorous undertone to everything he said, as if nothing could surprise him. He stood looking at me, then sat next to me again, but with about two feet between us. I didn't object.

"It feels like the water knows I don't belong on it, and it's trying to toss me back on land," I said. I closed my eyes and tried to concentrate on words, on talking to him and talking myself out of the feeling.

The engine picked up speed as we left the harbor, and the forward motion became more rhythmic. When the wave of nausea passed, I realized that I had been leaning over at an awkward angle, with my head practically between my knees. I straightened up and leaned back. Carey stared off into the distance. After a moment he glanced back at me. I must have looked green, but he had the decency not to notice. He offered his hand. I switched my cup to the other hand and took his with my warm one.

"Carey," he said. "We didn't meet properly yesterday."

"Lucie," I said. His fingertips were cold, but I felt an urge to hold on to his hand. Tethered to him for that moment, my insides calmed, steadied by another body.

"You're a park ranger?" I asked as I let go of him, hoping he hadn't noticed my hesitation, the way my hand fell to the bench between us, bracing.

"Yeah," he said. "What about you?"

"Journalist," I answered, watching his expression. He seemed undeterred, which wasn't always the case with government employees. "I write about the environment."

He nodded. "What are you doing out here?"

"An old friend lives out here, at Marrow Colony," I said. "Have you heard of it?"

"It's a farm collective or something like that, right?"

"Something like that—we'll see. This is my first time."

"Strange place for a farm—given the history. I suppose the land came pretty cheap . . . ?" He trailed off. He seemed to expect me to fill in the blanks.

"I guess so." I shrugged, but I was thinking about it myself. How the Colony had ended up on Marrow, and how they had managed to live on the island for so long, after the devastation that occurred there.

Orwell was getting smaller and smaller in the wake behind us. My eyes started to tear up from the early morning chill, my cheeks and ears burning. I was wearing a wool sweater under my life jacket, and under my jeans and cotton T-shirt, an old pair of silk long underwear that had belonged to my mother. She had loaned me the long underwear for a camping trip in high school, and I had kept them, remembering how she used to wash them by hand and hang them to dry in our little bathroom on Orwell.

Coombs hollered something over his shoulder, but I couldn't hear. Carey went to have a word and came back. He sat down and leaned down, closer to my ear.

"He said it might be rough ahead. Almost there."

The swells hit. I felt it in my lungs first, in the cavity of my chest. A sudden vacancy, then a swift welling up. Empty, then full. Brimming. I broke a sweat and my vision perforated into thousands of pricks of colorful light, like pixels. I managed to turn and lean as far over the edge of the boat as I could to throw up. We hit another swell and I lurched forward. I felt Carey's hands on my waist, holding me in the boat while I puked.

When I was empty and the worst passed, Carey helped me back to my seat and put his coat around me. He poured me more tea from Coombs's thermos. Then he sat right up next to me and started talking, like a voluble stranger at a bar.

He was new to Washington, he told me. He had been in Montana before, at Glacier. I leaned over with my elbows on my knees, and he did the same, so that I could hear his voice, right next to me, over the motor. I sipped my tea and listened, tried to concentrate on what he was talking about: wildland firefighting, forestry school, working for the government. Chris Lelehalt had deputized him that day at the clerk's office; most park rangers are deputized; many carried firearms.

"But not out here," he said. "People love their public lands here. No anti-government fanatics shooting at rangers, setting tripwires and spikes on service roads."

The state wanted to reopen Fort Union State Park, he told me, on the other side of the island from the Colony. I nodded that I knew where it was; Katie and I had gone to summer camp there. It was a decommissioned military base and historic site from the Pig War in the 1850s; the campers had all slept in the old barracks.

"How much do you know about what happened here?" I gestured to the ruins of the ArPac Refinery. We were coming up close to it. The docks were wasted; the charred, weathered cement of the remaining walls and smokestacks looked like a monument to something—a terrible war, maybe, something violent and manmade—not an earthquake. There were plants growing out of them now, taking root in the cracks, in the dust. I looked back to Carey.

"I know a lot about the disaster itself," he said, "but not about what's happened to the island in the last twenty years. That's the reason I'm here."

"Me, too," I said. We looked at each other. I felt calmer. It felt uncomplicated, admitting it to him.

The boat had ripped past the ruins of the refinery at the southeast edge of the island, pulled north-northwest around a forested ridge where the Colony's dock in the rocky harbor finally came into view. Coombs hollered back that he had radioed ahead to the Colony. He brought them mail and supplies when he was coming their way. There would be someone there to meet us.

We were seniors in college the last time we saw each other, but I knew the woman standing on the dock was Katie. I wiped my eyes and blinked into the wind to watch her getting closer, becoming real to me again. She was tall, taller than I was by two inches, slender, but with broad shoulders and long arms, a narrow neck, like a goose. She had never been graceful but had always seemed at ease with her body, confident and deliberate in her movements. She stood at the end of the dock, hands in her pockets, perfectly still, watching our approach. Or at least she looked serenely in our direction; maybe she was looking past us, over the water, to the islands, to the mainland. Her dark curly hair squiggled out from under a knit cap. She wore knee-high rubber boots with jeans tucked into them and a thick canvas jacket over a long wool sweater.

Behind her, small wooden houses were tucked into the hillside above the harbor, the occasional rounded roof of a yurt in the trees, almost camouflaged, and closer, at the pinnacle of the first rise above the dock, the pale weathered chapel with its steeple rising like a treetop. Against the landscape, Katie looked like an icon, a modern saint: she was beautiful and austere; she owned the landscape. I was almost terrified of her.

Carey and I looked to the shore silently as the boat neared the dock. He would disembark there and hike up to Fort Union and the old guard station. The park and the Colony were so close, the only signs of human intervention on the north side of Marrow, separated by a single paved road that ran down the center of the island.

There had once been a few residents—homesteaders, fishermen—and summer inhabitants of the rustic, roughing-it variety. Unmarked gravel and dirt roads passed between houses here and there. Some had private docks; others used the harbor near the chapel as moorage. The chapel dated back to the 1840s, to the Catholic missions. A village and trading post had sprung up near the chapel, for the white settlers, with a one-room schoolhouse for the settlers' children and baptized children of the nearby Coast Salish tribes. My grandmother's parents met at the school: a Lummi girl and an Irish boy who married when he was eighteen and she was sixteen. The schoolhouse was long gone, along with most of the other original buildings, in ruins or torn down by the 1920s and '30s, replaced gradually by vacation cottages and rustic cabins. There had been a house or two on the western slope of the island, south of Fort Union, northwest of the refinery, but they were destroyed by a landslide after the quake. What was left of the makeshift village near the chapel to the northeast was now Marrow Colony.

After so many years, I didn't know what to expect from Marrow. The refinery fire had burned for days, and its smoking ruins were all we could see from our shores. The communities on all the islands had been affected by the quake, but the petroleum and the flame retardants and oil-dispersing chemicals had toxified Marrow's groundwater, its soil. Everyone living on the island had come to Orwell or gone to one of the other islands. There had been efforts at cleanup, then settlements with property owners, but when we moved away the following winter, Marrow Island had been abandoned.

Before Katie decided to join the Colony, the ruins and abandonment were how I thought of the whole island. I had nightmares for years in which I was there, searching for my dad, who was somehow still alive but lost, unable to find his way out. I was the only one who knew he was still there, but I was unable to save him—he was always just a few more feet away or under rubble I couldn't lift. In my waking life, I pushed the islands out of my thoughts.

Coombs cut the engine and threw a rope out to Katie on the dock. I watched her tie us fast. She seemed as worn as the pilings, patches of dirt and holes here and there in her clothes, weathered hands. When she stood up and looked at me, her eyes shone, her cheeks were rosy under her freckles. She had crow's feet, deep lines in her forehead—it was obvious she worked outside—and strands of silver in her auburn curls, like her mom, who had also gone gray in her late thirties. Still beautiful, but more confident, stronger, as if she had filled into her potential self. She radiated joy.

"And here's the welcome party," Coombs said. "Hallo, Miss Kate! I brought you the Orwell folks I promised you. They smelled fresh when they came aboard, but this one"—he gestured to me—"might need some airing out."

Katie laughed. "You could never hold your breakfast, could you?"

"I didn't eat breakfast," I told her.

"Never go to sea on an empty stomach, Lu. You know that."

I shrugged Carey's coat from my shoulders and handed it back to him. He looked like he needed it. His cheeks were bright red, his nose running. I reached in my vest pocket for a tissue and handed it to him.

"Thank you," I said to him.

He took the tissue and nodded, wiped his nose.

"You'll come back on Monday morning to pick me up again?" I asked as Coombs helped me down to the dock.

"I'll be back for the both of you. Be down here at sunrise." Then he turned to Katie. "I have mail for you, Kate."

Carey and I looked at each other. We would be going back together, too. How much of me could he handle? I'd probably puke on the way back. I couldn't tell if he was picturing the same scenario.

"Are you sure you don't want to find another boat?" I said.

He shook his head. "I don't know what you're talking about."

I dropped my bags on the dock as Katie took two large parcels from Coombs. She scanned the return addresses briefly, then set the boxes down next to my bag.

"I can't believe you're here," she said, and hugged me tight.

Her body was warm. I squeezed her back, feeling the strength in her limbs and the bones of her sternum and spine. The dock swayed; I squeezed harder, for ballast.

When we pulled apart, she said, "You look like you."

"You look like a new woman," I said.

"Thank god," she said. She looked askance at Carey, who had been pretending not to watch, shrugging his coat back over his shoulders, warming up. "Excuse us," she said to him, "we haven't seen each other in a long time."

"Carey McCoy." He put out his hand. He seemed to shift into his uniform. His smile stiffened, became official. I compared it to the smile he almost gave me at the clerk's office: his smile had been deputized. He seemed on his guard.

"Kate," she replied, taking his hand firmly.

"Carey and I are new friends," I said. He might have blushed. I cleared my throat. It was still raw from the vomit, my mouth full of saliva.

"I see you're from the Forest Service," Katie said, trying to sound nonchalant, but with an energy that told me she might be on guard, too. "It's been a long time since I've seen a ranger out here."

She looked back and forth between us, gauging our familiarity. Her smile never disappeared, but there was a wariness in her eyes. I knew that whatever her outward expression, she was scrutinizing every detail. Carey apologized and explained he was new to the post, but that he'd be out more often over the next few weeks and bringing colleagues from Fish and Wildlife eventually. Katie nodded.

"Well, I'm sure you'll have a lot to do at the park. You'll have to let me introduce you, first," she said.

"Introduce me?" Carey asked. He looked at me.

Coombs was setting off again and gave a shout and a wave. We watched him and waited for the sound of his motor to fade.

"This way." Katie set off up the dock onto the shore and we followed.

Climbing up the bank behind Katie, I tried to get my bearings. I could feel the torpor from my lack of sleep, the early boat ride. I was desperate for a cup of coffee and some toast. Carey asked how I was feeling.

"Better," I said, and tried to believe it.

We tramped up a gravel path, winding through boulders weedy with vetch and bird-scattered mussel shells, the rocks slick with last night's mist. The sun broke through the clouds and lit up the tree line behind the chapel. Gulls wove in and out of the long early morning shadows.

At the top of the embankment, I looked out over the water we had just crossed. Orwell wasn't visible from here, only Haro Strait, and the distant mainland. Inland, beyond the chapel, a rooster crowed, sparrows called, and the tide flowed symphonically. Otherwise, it was quiet; no sounds of people, machinery, industry. Inland, the landscape was serene, prosaic. After all the nightmares, all the years evading thoughts of Marrow, it might as well have been the island I knew before the quake. I wanted to feel relief, but I couldn't, quite. I knew better. I knew that beneath the surface, tremendous changes had taken place.

Carey made small talk with Katie, and I listened to her responses, to her voice, the same voice I had always known.

"Nineteen ninety-six," she was saying, to the question of when Marrow Colony started.

"And how long have you been here?" Carey asked her.

"Since 2005," she said. She looked back at me. "I dropped out of Evergreen without telling anyone. Lucie went all the way to Olympia on the train to surprise me for my birthday, and I wasn't there. My roommates gave her all the stuff I left behind."

Carey glanced back at me.

"Do you still have any of that stuff, Luce?"

"Nope," I said. "I burned it all."

"She's kidding," Katie told Carey. She could always tell when I was lying.

"We don't have coffee around," Katie told me. "Not unless someone trades for it at the farmers' market or something."

I stared into the cup she had handed me. The steaming brew looked like coffee; it smelled smoky and bittersweet. I had poured goat milk and honey into it immediately. But it wasn't past my lips before I knew it was not coffee. Carey and I sat at a round wooden table in the kitchen of the larger cottages, which was a sort of communal space for meetings and record keeping. Through an archway in the living room was a small office with a very old computer and dented filing cabinets.

"It's roasted chicory and dandelion root," Katie said. "Like the Civil War soldiers used to drink. It's nutritionally dense: magnesium, potassium, phosphorus. You won't miss the caffeine."

I told her I doubted that but drank anyway.

She laughed, her back to me, cutting bread from a dense little loaf on the counter. Carey had already swallowed half his cup. He seemed anxious to get on with his work.

"Sister J. will be here any minute," Katie said. She put a plate of bread and a crock of soft, pale butter on the table. I helped myself, spreading the butter thickly over the bread. It was toothsome and sour, like a Danish rogbrød, dark and moist and flecked with seeds, and the butter was briny and tart. I ate the small piece in three bites and washed it down with the chicory brew. Carey watched me, sidelong, and I pretended not to notice.

I looked out the small window next to us. People passed on the worn path between this house and the fields, the woods. They carried tools of various sorts, buckets. One woman carried a chicken under her arm, stroking its head. At one point she leaned down to whisper something to it. The room was barely lit; no one noticed us peering at them from behind the dark glass.

"You seem worn out. The boat did you in, huh?" Katie asked me.

"No," I said. "It's not that. I just didn't sleep much last night."

"No?"

I hesitated. I was still uneasy about what I had found at Rookwood.

"I guess I'm just too used to the city now."

Katie narrowed her eyes, scrutinizing me, like she knew there was more. But she smiled.

"You'll get used to it before you know it. Then you'll go back to Seattle and have to put in earplugs."

There were loud stomps at the side door—boots shaken of soil or sand—and a deep, laborious cough and clearing of throat. In the morning quiet, the sounds amplified, reverberated through the wood of the door and the plaster walls; the table shook lightly on its uneven legs. I had the uncanny feeling of a child who has woken a sleeping grandfather, a surly, unappeasable patriarch. As the door opened, I was looking at the top of the door frame, waiting for someone tall and burly to enter—like a lumberjack. But Sister J. was short—maybe five feet two inches—and solid, but gaunt, swallowed by an enormous gray hoodie.

She closed the door and stood with her hands clasped behind her, gazing brightly at us, looking intently at Carey, then me. Then she closed her eyes and took a long breath, seeming to breathe us in, her nostrils flaring a bit and her chest rising to meet her oversize clothing. When she opened her eyes, she looked to Katie and nodded firmly.

"It's a good day," she said, her voice deep, marled by time. She might be mistaken for a man over the phone or on the radio.

Sister J. sat and reached for one of my hands and one of Carey's. Her hand was warm just up to the tips, then icy cold at the fingernails; she squeezed. It was a sort of handshake. Neither Carey nor I looked away from her or spoke at all. I didn't know how to speak or what to say. Katie introduced us, but the usual greetings and niceties seemed unnecessary. Sister J. looked at us intently, this small, compact woman, with alert blue eyes and large, stained, crooked teeth offered in a narrow smile. She didn't seem surprised to see a park ranger sitting at the table. Coombs had said on the dock that he and Katie had spoken last night. He must have told them we were both coming.

"I've invited Ranger McCoy to Sunday dinner, Sister," Katie indicated Carey with a nod and wiped her hands on a towel. "He'll be on the island through the weekend."

She gave Sister J. a cup of chicory coffee and sat down in the fourth seat at the table. But then her face went still, and she stared out the window, like she was suddenly somewhere else in her mind—past or future? Possibly someplace present but not *here*.

"Call me Carey; I'm not sure I'll answer to Ranger McCoy." Carey shuffled his feet under the table, pulled his long legs in under him. He was gathering himself to go.

"*Carey,* do please come share a meal with us anytime, and let us know if you need anything. The state of things at the park isn't . . ." Sister J. trailed off, looked upward like the words she needed might be somewhere near the ceiling. "Marrow's still a ragged place. We've been the only ones here for so long. It is a daily practice, an hourly practice, in loving. Marrow must be loved to be known."

This last word, spoken with some consideration, seemed to wake Katie, whose eyes focused on the room again, looked to Sister J.

"You'll see," she said, speaking to Carey and me, but still looking at Katie. The two of them locked eyes and Katie smiled, but faintly. She clearly wanted to say something but held her tongue, either for us or Sister J.

"You picked the perfect time to come. We have our harvest supper on Sunday," Sister J. said, looking at us again. "After all your work in the park, you'll need a good hot meal and some company. And we'll keep you busy, too, Lucinda."

"Lucie—" I said.

"Lucie." She nodded.

Carey said of course he would come on Sunday and thanked Katie and Sister J. Then he pulled on his pack and picked up his sleeping roll and took Katie's directions out to the road and on to the park. I watched him hike the distance and disappear into the trees.

A migraine was circling my right eye.

Every morning at Marrow Colony began with work prayer. They prayed not on their knees in the chapel, not beside their beds or before breakfast with head bowed, but working at the chores of the farm, with their hands and bodies. Everyone had different tasks that rotated day by day, so everyone was intimately involved in the various labors of the Colony. Today was Katie's day to milk the goats. She was taking me with her, though she was already an hour late.

"Everyone rises at dawn or before," she told me. "Unless they're sick. We don't really follow clocks; we follow the circadian rhythm of the island. When the birds wake up, we do too. It takes some getting used to, but after a while, you just wake up at the right time."

She was talking as she looked me over in the mudroom and, grabbing a pair of rubber boots, squatted down to fold the tops down for me, shoving the leg of my jeans in. I felt like a child, like the mornings when my parents layered and outfitted me at the kitchen door before school, back before global warming had set in, when we still had harsh winters on the islands, when every day was a different kind of wet. It wasn't like that in the Northwest anymore; rainy seasons came and went in weeks, not months. Warmer temperatures reigned. It had rained hard last week, dropping an inch of rain all over Puget Sound, but only for about twenty-four hours. Just enough to saturate the soil and send up the petrichor for a day, remind us of the earthy musk we used to take for granted. I looked outside: the day would be pleasant by 11 a.m. Katie handed me a hat and a pair of fingerless wool gloves and led me out to the goats. I left the rest of my things in the meetinghouse. We would collect them after breakfast and she would walk me to the cottage, where I would sleep for the next two nights.

From the house we walked away from the shore and the chapel, up a worn footpath in the grass. Katie pointed out the Colony's different buildings and features.

"That house over there, the plot it's on belonged to a woman whose husband died in the Civil War. She came all the way across the country, then got on a boat to the islands and staked a claim on Marrow while Britain and the U.S. were still fighting over who owned the San Juans. If any man—British or American—crossed the fence line, she'd come out of her hut with her dead husband's musket and shoot his hat off."

We looked over the cottage, which was clearly more sophisticated than a homesteader's hut.

"What was her name?" I asked.

"Martha Glover," she said, looking at me. "She eventually remarried, had several children who took over the farm."

We kept on. To the left behind the chapel on the broad sunny hill was the orchard—apple and pear, mostly, but a few oddities like quince, mulberry, and persimmon—and among them, the beehives. Katie explained that the beehives were one of the most important parts of the farm.

"Establishing a healthy bee population was a struggle for years. Now we finally have the colonies going strong, pollinating the crops and the native plants, producing enough honey that we sell it at co-ops around the islands. In the summer I go to a couple of the farmers' markets. I'll show you what we do—I'm sure it'll be a really modest operation, compared to things you've reported on."

"I'm sure it's more than that," I demurred, feeling I didn't really need to. She seemed confident, proud. Not at all unsure that what they were doing was impressive.

There were more hives near the largest of the vegetable gardens—where they grew squashes, beans, corn, amaranth, and hay. Beyond those, closer to the trees, were three cottages like the one we'd just left, separated by quarter-acre plots, weathered but tidy, with foxglove and echinacea still in full bloom, herb gardens between, along with large driftwood and flotsam sculptures—most taller than me—in the shapes of animals and people.

"My husband is the artist. His name is Tuck."

"Your *husband?*" I felt my cheeks burn. It had never occurred to me that she would be married.

"Not legally. We had a ceremony here. My parents didn't even come. I tried to write you, to tell you, but the letter came back to me."

"When was this?"

"Four years ago." She looked at me with concern. "I'm sorry."

I tried to imagine the man she would marry—she had always said she didn't believe in monogamy, let alone being someone's *wife*.

"I've missed a lot," I said.

"You'll meet him soon. I think you'll like him—he's a lot like some of the people you've written about. The activists." She smiled, forgetting that I had never appreciated her taste in men.

Other colonists, men and women of varying ages, were here and there, silently working, backs bent, arms laden, pushing wheelbarrows, using hoes, baskets in hand, some of them bundled up against the morning air, others in shirtsleeves. No one spoke, but anyone we passed looked me in the eye and smiled.

"Tuck and I share a house with Elle and Jen. Elle is our herbalist. She runs the apothecary and assists Maggie, the midwife. Jen's our compost and soil expert."

"Everyone has a specialty?"

"Everyone has an assigned job, yes, but we all take part in the various jobs around the farm with our morning work prayer."

"What's your job?" I asked.

"I'm Sister's assistant," she said.

"What do you do for Sister, exactly?"

She paused and looked out at the fields.

"I keep track of the things."

"What kind of things?"

"Physical things. What we buy, what we sell. Money. I communicate with the outside world." She looked at me and shrugged. "It's not very sexy, but someone has to do it. We're not separatists, we're still *of this world*, and I'm the one who deals with it."

The path forked and we took a mossy hill toward the fenced pasture and the barn, up against a stand of firs. It was still shady in places and mist lingered. Behind the trees I could see the smokestacks of the refinery, like dead old growth, ancient stobs from giant petrified trees. Katie followed my gaze.

"Is it strange being here?" she asked.

I shook my head.

"I don't know. The smokestacks make me think of Stonehenge," I said, "or Easter Island, you know? Places where manmade monuments outlived their time, their usefulness, their meaning. Hundreds of years from now, it'll be mystical. If this place still exists, if humans are still here, they'll think oil was our god."

Katie was quiet for a moment, then she squeezed my arm, trailed her hand down to mine, and took it in hers.

"I'm glad you're here. I wish you had come a long time ago." There was a warmth in her voice I recognized. But something else, too. Something winnowing through her words, a charged current of feeling. Like she had a secret.

She let go of my hand and we walked on.

The towers disappeared from sight as we descended the path

to the pasture. The damp chill clung to me, and I curled my fingers into my woolen palms in my pockets.

There were two others in the barn already — an older woman with curly silver hair and a man no older than thirty — occupied with feeding and milking the goats, raking the dirt floor of droppings.

"Usually, we don't speak to each other during work prayer," Katie said. "But we sometimes have visitors, so it'll be okay. Just don't be offended if no one talks to you."

Katie led one of the goats toward a stool near the doors.

"This is Penelope," Katie told me, dumping the contents of a cloth sack — some bread heels and apple cores — into a bucket hanging from the pen. Penelope sniffed out the food and shoved her nose in the bucket.

"Have you ever milked a goat?" she asked.

"No, but you know I'll try anything."

"Here," Katie said, gesturing to the stool. I sat.

"Hold your hands like this," she said, showing me the form, making a funnel of my right thumb and finger. "And squeeze like this, with your other fingers, careful to aim the milk at the pail."

Katie squatted behind me, an arm alongside mine, helping to aim, squeezing my hand in hers so that I could feel the pressure. Occasionally Penelope looked back at us, chewing, flicking her tail, scuffing the dirt with a hoof.

"The idea of the work prayer," Katie explained, her breath warm on my cheek and her curls bristling against my skin like wool, "is that we let our bodies move in the world before our minds get caught up in analyzing everything. I go from sleep to work easily now, but at first I had to stop thinking."

"You have to stop thinking?"

"We don't have to stop being intelligent or aware. I had to learn how to stop analyzing everything. We try to let thoughts come from our immediate actions. From being present and experiencing. So much of our thinking is involved with things we've already done and things we have yet to do. It's almost impossible not to be thinking about some future moment or some past mistake or tragedy."

I looked up at her, but she kept her eye on the milking.

At first I thought we'd never fill the metal pail. It seemed so big, and Penelope's udder not especially large. It was strange, feeling the milk pass through, seeing it steam in the morning air. But the level rose steadily. Katie let me go and patted the goat with a gloved hand. I kept on, less sure of myself without her hands on me.

"First thing in the morning, we try to be truly present in one thing, in one action, and consider it a prayer. It's the practice of being in our bodies, our bodies in the world, our awareness on what is in our hands. Penelope has a work prayer, too. All the animals do. They endure a lot every day, to help sustain us. They give so much in their short lives."

She leaned down and whispered something to the goat, and I remembered again the woman who seemed to be talking to her hen earlier.

"What did you say to her?"

"What?"

"What did you say to the goat just now?"

"Oh." She seemed startled. "I said, 'I love you.'"

"Do you tell all the animals that you love them?"

She thought about this a moment, looked around the barn at the other goats. The silver-haired woman walked by with a pail of milk and smiled generously at me, my hands working awkwardly at Penelope's teats. The tips of my fingers were warm again.

"Yes. I do," Katie said.

We hauled our pails of milk out of the barnyard and up to the dairy house, Katie silent this time. I wanted to ask about her parents, about her husband, about what it was like being married, what other chores she did for work prayer, but wanting to observe the rituals, I was hesitant to break the silence for what amounted to chitchat. The dairy house was one of the newer cottages at the top of the hill. It was a squat, angular building with straw-bale walls and repurposed windows of varying shapes all along the south side. We walked round to the north side, where the roof slanted down and disappeared into the slope of a hill. The dairy was back there, cool, away from the sun. Katie helped me pour the milk into a stainless-steel vat inside the back door.

We stepped inside to meet the silver-haired woman from the barn.

"Good morning, Maggie," Katie said, breaking the silence. "This is Lucie."

"Here's our visitor," she said, shaking my hand firmly. "Welcome. I saw there was someone else on the boat this morning? A friend of yours?"

"A forest ranger," I said. "We weren't together; we just happened to be on the same boat."

"Ah." She nodded and glanced at Katie. "People cruise by the island all the time, sometimes even stop on the shore, but it's rare anyone wants to stay. People stayed away completely for a long time." She paused, looked out the window toward the rise where the trees hid the smokestacks from view. "A long time," she said again, and surveyed the work in front of her.

"Is this where you make the cheese?" I asked.

"The cheese?"

"That they sell at the co-op on Orwell."

"Yes. We do it all here. Cheese, yogurt, kefir, butter . . ."

The room looked like an ordinary kitchen, but there was a long worktable down the middle with a sink at one end that drained into a tub below.

Katie saw me examining the sink and explained, "It's for catching the whey. We use it for drinks and baking."

"We don't waste anything, if we can help it," Maggie said.

She showed me around, pointing out an old metal suitcase with a few holes drilled in it, wires emerging from the holes. She opened the top of the suitcase to reveal jars of yogurt nestled in wool hats, with heating pads beneath.

"We don't actually use the refrigerator much, since most of our dairy is cultured and consumed quickly," Maggie told me.

"The electricity—it's all solar?" I asked.

"It is. We have to regulate temperature, for culturing, mostly in the winter months. When we first started out here, I was making yogurt near the wood stoves, the pellet stoves. We tried constructing a special cupboard above the cookstoves—which did *not* work, smoked yogurt, can you imagine?—consistency was much harder then."

She led me to the farthest corner of the north wall and opened a heavy wooden door revealing a long, low, cave-like storage area for the cheese, dug directly into the hill. The shelves were full of cheeses in various stages of ripeness; the smell bloomed into the room, yeasty and acidic, with notes of hay and shit, like the barn. I whistled and Maggie smiled.

"The magic of microbes. Where would the human race be without them?"

"I know some food writers who would crawl all over each other to see this place. It's very Old World, very European. You've never had anyone come out to write a profile?"

Maggie chuckled. "I'm sure they don't know we exist. Do they, Kate?"

Katie joined us. "Food writers? No, not in my time."

"How long have you been selling at the co-ops and farmers' markets?"

"Only a few years now," Maggie said. "We used to barter with it, but Kate convinced us to start selling, too."

"It's useful to have cash" was all Katie said.

"But"—I was thinking of the fields, the gardens we had passed, the bread and butter I had eaten earlier—"how are you able to raise food and animals here, without risk of contamination from the refinery site?"

"That's why you're here, is it?" Katie asked, head cocked, half smiling. "To find out how we did all this?"

She didn't sound upset, but I felt accused of something.

"You invited me. I came to see you *and* the island." We looked at each other for a moment.

"Yeah," she said. "Of course." She looked away.

Maggie ducked into the cave, hunched slightly to avoid hitting her head, and returned with three small wheels of ripe cheese. She took them to the table and wrapped them in squares of striped cloth that looked like they had been cut from a men's dress shirt. Katie pulled a basket from a wall hook.

"It'll be first meal soon," she said. "The food is safe, don't worry. And there's solid science behind it. But it's complicated. I want to show you."

She pulled four quart jars of yogurt from the fridge and put them in the basket, along with the cheese, and handed it to me.

We walked a long path through the trees and along the bluff. I asked Maggie how long she had been on Marrow.

"Since the beginning," she said. "I met Janet—Sister J.—after the earthquake. I lost my house in West Seattle—slid right down the hill and into the house below. Two years later I was still living in temporary housing. I was working for the county at the time, as a public health nurse, working with mothers and babies. I'd met Janet at a community meeting and we'd become friends. She asked if I wanted to help with this project on an island in the San Juans. I thought I had seen it all, at that point. The city was noisy, dirty, traffic worse than ever, and people in need, everywhere you looked . . ." She stopped, breathing heavily (the hill was quite steep), looked around, took the basket on her other arm. "An abandoned island sounded like paradise."

"Weren't you worried about being exposed? You're a nurse— did you ask what you were exposing yourself to?" I was remembering the days after the quake when the fire just kept burning, its soot everywhere, the chemicals they dropped from planes over the trees, dumped into the water to disperse the oil slicks. Marrow was a smudge on the horizon that burned our eyes.

"All the islands and the coastline, the waterways, everything was contaminated with something. Everything the water touched. You were probably scared; and your mom, too, after seeing it happen. She did the right thing, taking you away. But—" Maggie stopped short and squinted into the sun to look at me. She opened her mouth to answer but reconsidered, looking away. "No, I wasn't scared. I could see what needed to be done," she said, and walked on, a determined smile on her face.

I let her go ahead a few paces and reached out for Katie's arm.

"How did she know about my mom?" I asked.

"Nobody just shows up here. I knew you were coming. I told them you were coming."

"Told who? Everyone?"

"There are only thirty-six of us; word gets around."

Most of these thirty-six souls were headed to the Gathering Place on the bluff north of the chapel. The sun was full in the sky now, midday bright, warming the higher elevations of the island. We filed past the whitewashed chapel, gleaming with sunlight, more lighthouse than church. Some walked together, chatting; others were solo. From all directions, in the clothes they had been working in, some of them looking weary, others bright-eyed. It reminded me of lunch hour on a college campus, how the bodies travel worn grooves, in rhythm. There's an orchestration of movement when everyone follows the exact same clock, day after day.

In decent weather, the first meal was usually served on the bluff. Up the slope I could see the roof of the outdoor kitchen. I asked Maggie more about the early days.

"It was just like camping for a long time. There were about fifteen of us at first, with a few interns Janet picked up at Evergreen who came and went. We cooked everything over wood fires for a year or two, knowing it wasn't sustainable in any way but not knowing what else to do—until we heard about a man in Oregon who was building solar ovens. This was before you could look up everything on the Internet—or at least, we couldn't, you know, because we'd have to go to the library in Friday Harbor to do it—so a couple of the students we had then went down to Oregon to find out how to do it. They came back with the man himself. He wanted to see what we were doing here—wanted to see how we were managing . . ."

She trailed off, out of breath, as we crested the hill and met the full view of the bluff and Bone Cove, named for the bleached logs the tide carried in and left scattered over the shore. I set my basket down and stepped closer to the rocky embankment that spilled down to the shore.

"An orca washed up down there that first summer," Maggie said.

"Washed up—dead?"

"Nearly dead. We couldn't do anything for it. I got used to dead birds washing up, the fish, the crabs, the sea stars, even seals. But that whale, she did us all in. We had a goddamn funeral for her."

"That seems reasonable to me. Did you send her back out with the tide or . . . ?"

"Oh, we sent her home." She patted my back and picked up the baskets. "We hauled her up to the field with a tractor and let her rot. She's still fertilizing our crops, that one."

I must have looked dubious, but Maggie just smiled. "Her bones are still up there."

"Did you ever find any human remains?" I asked. They both stopped short. "Washed ashore or on the island?"

Maggie looked at Katie, then back to me.

"No, we never did," she said, her smile gone. "I'll take these on up to the tables." She hobbled a little as she walked, and I called after her.

"Do you want some help?"

"No thank you. You girls take your time."

I looked at Katie.

"She never tells me those stories," she said.

"No?"

"Not often. Must be your gift for getting the scoop." She raised an eyebrow at me and smiled.

"I don't know about that." I leaned into her. "I got fired."

"What?"

"Laid off, technically, but it doesn't matter. I don't do it anymore. Or, I'm not working right now. I'm sort of —adrift, at the moment."

She didn't say anything, just watched me sidelong while I stared out at the sea. The sunlight off the water made it look like it was on fire. Pain angled through my eye, and I could feel myself tightening around it. A gust of wind hit me, and I took in a lungful of it, closed my eyes. Arrows of light burned inside my eyelids. I felt Kate taking my hand. My body relaxed, a conditioned response to her that should have been lost years ago. The memory of a younger Katie next to me. The way our sweaty hair stuck together as we huddled under a blanket, the peaked tent it made stretched between our heads and our drawn-up knees. The way I could feel both of our hearts beat through the aftershocks. The way we listened to the waves reaching up and out of the sea. We had heard them all, the cold fists of water pounding the shore. We had counted them under our breaths.

We stood like this for a few silent minutes, and I was sure Katie was there with me —not there on the bluff, but *there,* under the blanket on our classroom floor.

"Kate." A man's voice came from behind us, and she dropped my hand as she turned to answer. Maggie had moved on up the path, and a tall man stood in her place. He was our age, with a patchy red beard and dirty blond hair, face scuffed with dirt from work. Katie met him and they spoke softly, his head bowed to hers. She looked into his eyes and kissed him, then took his arm, leading him my way.

We ate at a long picnic table under the open-air lodge-pole structure that served as both dining hall and outdoor kitchen. There was one straw-bale wall that buffered the prevailing southwesterly winds and protected the cooking and prepping areas. A rain barrel full of potable water, a stainless-steel worktable that looked like it had been lifted from a morgue, with two women working away at peeling potatoes for dinner. The solar ovens, three cubic feet of Mylar and wood that looked like little satellites, were out from under the trees against a whitewashed straw-bale wall that reflected more light back into them. Under cover in the kitchen were three rocket stoves made from repurposed beer kegs. Tucker told me these were fairly new—the kegs donated by a brewery in Friday Harbor—inspired by the prototype of a Scottish guy who had been living off the grid for several years and blogging about it.

"So he's not completely off the grid," I said. "If he's blogging, he must plug in sometimes."

Tuck and I were sitting across from each other at a long picnic table, bowls of a thick amaranth porridge steaming between us. He was thoughtful, well-spoken, with a sadness in his eyes and a smile that was disarming, like he hadn't always been handsome or smart or well-spoken but had earned it over time, after years of not giving a damn. He had taken my hand like a vise when Katie introduced us, and I found myself wondering what she had told him about me. The way they all looked at me—curious, not unkind, but not exactly warm—I had the unsettled certainty of someone who knows less about everyone than they know about her.

"It's not what it used to be, 'going off the grid,'" Tuck said, setting his spoon back in his bowl. He spoke softly, a languid Pacific coast lilt, with gravel underneath. "Everything's on the grid. Or *under* it," he said, gesturing to the sky. "It's longitude and latitude. It's radio waves and cell signals and drones. The grid is *us*. Everything on the planet touches everything else. There's no such thing as 'off the grid.'"

"You're the one who used the term," I said. Katie was sitting next to him with her hand on his leg under the table. She didn't say anything.

"You're right," he said, taking a bite and wiping his mouth with a bandanna from his pocket. "I meant something else by it. It means living as far off the industrial food supply chain as possible. Avoiding fossil fuel consumption . . ." He went on, but I tuned him out. I made eye contact and nodded occasionally, but I didn't hear what he was saying. I had heard it all before. Even men who should've known better—overeducated, progressive types who probably considered themselves feminists—had no compunction explaining things to me. I learned early on to use their inclinations against them when I was reporting. I got the best quotes from men like this; they loved to tell me *how it is*— whatever the subject was, as if I didn't live in the world, didn't do research or even read. They wouldn't even know they had said something damning until it was in the paper.

Women were different; women told me as much with their silences as their words.

I glanced at Katie; she was devouring a bowl of greens while Tuck made his point. She looked up at him as if she were listening, but her gaze was glassy and distant. Her brow furrowed when she looked into her bowl of kale, like she was divining the leaves, then stabbed and carefully inserted a bushy forkful into her mouth, chewing thoughtfully, thoroughly. Tuck seemed about done, spooned porridge into his mouth.

Folks around us at the table had been listening. I could feel them, tuned to our conversation. I waited for someone to say something, to offer some other thought. A few toward the ends chatted with each other, but those near us kept eating, quietly, watching the two of us. They were watching me, waiting for my response.

"That sounds about right," I offered. I added a thoughtful nod for good measure.

Tuck leaned back, looked up the table to Maggie. They made eye contact for what seemed like an awkward amount of time.

"You should try these." Katie passed a bowl of greens across the table to me. "So good this time of year," she said.

I had finished my amaranth, so I scooped the greens into my bowl. They were wilted and glistening, dressed with something tart and pungent. I passed the bowl to Jen, the woman next to me, thirty-something and covered in tattoos, her short hair almost completely gray. Katie had introduced us and I had liked her instantly.

"Thanks." She smiled and served herself some greens.

"So, Lucie," she started, "I read an article you wrote for the *Pacific Standard*." I shoveled greens into my mouth. "Do you write for them a lot?"

"No, not really. That was a freelance gig."

"Well, it was good. It was the one on gentrification and the housing crises in West Coast cities."

"Yeah, that was just a few months ago."

"I liked that you emphasized the post-quake bubble. Not a lot of people talk about that."

One of the older colonists asked what "bubble" she was talking about.

"The demographics of neighborhoods changed when developers"—Jen's cheeks went red, like *developers* was a profanity she couldn't stand to hear come out of her own mouth—"came in and bought up swaths of property from homeowners who couldn't afford to rebuild. Insurance payments were slow in coming or they were denied, and people had these HUD vouchers for temporary rentals, but I mean not ideal living situations. So people took these offers of cash for their houses, either to move out of the city altogether or try to find somewhere else to live. But because of the lack of livable housing, the displaced were forced into less desirable parts of the city, and those neighborhoods, that should have been temporary, just stuck. Created new ghettos.

"We lived in South Park at the time, which was very working class. Our house survived the quake, but the Duwamish River flooded—our whole neighborhood was two blocks beyond the hundred-year flood mark, and we had water three feet up the walls—that's how far it came. We didn't have flood insurance. A developer paid cash—half its value before the quake—for the house, along with most of our neighbors' houses. Over the next ten years, we looked into moving back, but they leveled the whole place and rebuilt from the ground up: lofts, a yoga studio, a Whole Paycheck—the full nine yards. It's this wealthy bohemian enclave now. And you know what the sick motherfuckers renamed the neighborhood? Duwamish Plains."

There were murmurs of commiseration. It was a common story for those who had lived anywhere on the West Coast in the last twenty years.

Jen looked at me. "Sorry, I should've let you explain. I get all worked up about it. You tell a lot of stories like that in your article."

"No, you're right: those wounds haven't really healed for a lot of people. The gap between people who can afford to own their homes and those who can't is getting bigger, so the cities themselves—the land, the resources, the access to open spaces, to things like the amazing vistas of Elliott Bay and the Olympics—all of those things are owned by fewer and fewer people, leased out at enormous rates to the rest of us. And it behooves those people to lobby for the status quo with elected officials, so the bubble never went away; it's like it—" I paused; the sun was shining directly in my face and my head tingled, felt airy. "It's like it grew a thicker membrane."

"With help from people like your stepdad," Katie cut in. She said it casually, but there was something brittle in her voice, its edges crystallized. The table went quiet again. I stared at her, the pulse behind my eye throbbing a little harder. I blinked.

"You're right. He's a developer. My mom married a motherfucker." I half smiled. "Not a neighborhood-leveling motherfucker, but I'm sure he did his share."

"Hey, my folks are Silicon Valley millionaires," Tuck said, getting up from the table. "We can't help where we come from."

I almost liked him for a minute.

"Shit, I'm sorry. I shouldn't generalize," Jen said.

"Don't apologize." I touched her arm. "I'm really glad that article spoke to you."

It had been my last big published piece; my editor at the

newspaper had rejected it, then I was laid off. *Pacific Standard* had picked it up two months later.

After that, we talked about the weather — the longer dry seasons, the disappearance of the rain the Northwest was known for — it was what everyone talked about through the heat waves of every summer. The rains last week had done little to fill the two small streams on the island.

After lunch, they decided that Tuck would take me to the edge of the Colony, to show me something they referred to as "the project." It was something started in the early days of the Colony and carried on ever since. Katie had work to do with Sister J. in the Colony House, their office. I wasn't thrilled to be alone with Tuck, but he was Katie's husband, and I was curious about him and about "the project."

We started from a hidden path behind the barn. For a while, I could still hear the younger goats playing on the mossy roof and bed of an old pickup truck that had been slowly rotting away in the pasture for years. But soon all I heard was the wind in the tops of the trees, birdsong, and the water — always the low murmur of the waves.

"How long have you been here?" I asked him.

"About ten years."

"That's a long time. You're what — thirty-five?"

"Thirty-six."

"What made you come out here, at twenty-six?"

"This," he said. "I wanted to do some good, somewhere."

He stopped and looked around him, over the ground — there were leaves all over, yellow and red and brown, normal fall foliage — then he put his hands on his hips and tilted his head back, surveying the arch of trees over us. The tops of many of the firs were rusted on the windward side, though not quite dead; new growth had sprouted from the old, the desiccated. Lichen clung to the rusted patches where branches had fewer or no leaves or needles at all.

"Noxious gases released during the refinery fire," he noted, pointing for me. "And the fire retardants ArPac sprayed from crop dusters to keep the fire from spreading."

"That was two decades ago," I said. "You came here ten years after the fire. What did it look like then?"

"Still pretty dead. The Colony itself was well-established. They were cleaning up the soil in the fields, using water filtration, graywater systems, composting toilets, but the rest of the island was still suffering. The heavy metals and chemicals they use in petroleum extraction and production stick around. As long as the rest of the island was still sick, the Colony was sick."

As we started walking again, I looked up every now and then, watching the bald, singed areas increase the farther we were from the Colony. He kept talking as we made our way. He grew up in the Bay area with middle-class parents who happened to get rich in the tech industry. He had been a disaffected skateboarding youth who dropped out of Berkeley in his junior year to work for Greenpeace. His parents weren't pleased, would never understand why he gave up a formal education for a life of activism.

"Why *did* you give that up?" I asked.

"My first protest on the Berkeley campus: divestment from oil. Something about being in the crowd, feeling the strength in our voices, urging the university to do what was right. Then seeing how the university ignored us, shrugged us off. It made me more determined."

He turned to look at me, trailing behind him.

"Why do you write about the environment?" He seemed to be trying to compare us, somehow.

"I'm sure you already know my dad worked at ArPac."

"Katie told me a lot about you."

"My dad was in environmental compliance. He had warned the company about potential violations to safety regulations before the earthquake, but ArPac was dragging its feet about making the necessary upgrades to equipment. The explosions, the fire, all of this might have been prevented."

Tuck didn't say anything.

"My mom didn't talk about him much. I came across information about the settlements by accident when I was eighteen."

"But you didn't want to come back here until now?"

"Has Katie ever talked to you about what it was like—the earthquake? the aftermath?"

"Yeah, of course," he said, sure of himself. He was confident that his wife wouldn't keep anything from him.

But she wouldn't have told him everything. How we slept in the school gym that first night, yes. How we were always within arms' reach of each other, or how we concocted a plan to trick our harried teachers and find our own ways home, maybe. But how her menses had started the week before, how she worried the earthquake might make it start again? Or how we had our first kiss under the blankets in the dark, my hand on the small of her back, her hand on my cheek? She wouldn't have told him. No one would ever know. My father was missing in the burning refinery; her house had been crushed under a hundred-year-old cedar. It would always be our secret, the things we did to comfort each other after the quake.

"Without Katie, I don't know how I would've coped. My mother was in shock. Everyone was in shock."

"I understand that it was traumatic." He sounded less confrontational now, more sympathetic. "I'm just wondering why now? Why not ten years ago? Weren't you curious? About Kate? About the house?"

I swallowed. "I guess enough time has passed for the—" I stopped myself. *Guilt.* I was going to say *guilt.* "For the trauma to subside," I finished.

Half a mile from the barn, we came to a paved road: the only one on the island, laid by ArPac when they built the refinery; used by almost no one then and absolutely deserted now. Perhaps ArPac once had development plans for the rest of the island, after the costly investment in the refinery; in any case, the road, much like the electricity, was never viewed by islanders as the gift it was purported to be. The earthquake had wrinkled and warped the blacktop, leaving a deep cleft down the center through which weeds and saplings thrust their bodies. Tuck stepped onto the road and placed a hand tenderly around a fir sapling that barely scraped his knee.

"Conifers take their time," he said. "A human year is only a few weeks, a month for a fir tree. I'll never see the day this tree is taller than me."

An airplane droned overhead, a small one, loud and low. I wondered what we looked like standing there on the reclaimed blacktop. We watched it fly away toward Vancouver, then crossed the road and picked up the trail again.

We both fell silent for a while. My headache waned, then returned, several times along the walk. It made organizing my thoughts difficult. My head felt clearest when we were just walking or stopping for water. I noticed fading blazes on some of the trees and the occasional cairn trailside. I asked how old the trail was, but Tuck didn't know—he guessed it predated the Colony, though, because it was a favorite of the few deer on the island.

"How are there still deer on the island?" It seemed crazy to me that they could have survived when the island was covered with oily ash and chemical flame retardants.

"We think they swam over from Orwell."

"Bullshit."

"I've seen them swim at super low tides."

"I grew up on these islands, and I've never seen a deer swim that far."

"They survived, they swam—whichever: they mate. They have young. They love our berries and veggies, so we watch them. Right now we think there are around six to ten on the island. We don't know much about the health of the population —maybe your park ranger friend will look into that—but we have found dead deer around the island over the years. No natural predators on the island though, so right now we hunt one or two a year, in season."

"The dead deer—the dead animals you find—Maggie mentioned them. Do you know how or why they've died? If it's not predators, is it toxicity?"

Tuck didn't answer at first.

"You're eating the deer, right?"

"It's as safe as eating factory-farmed hamburger regularly, I'm sure."

"No, it's not. The two are not analogous. Hormones and antibiotics in farmed meat might contribute to disease in humans, but they're not directly tied to carcinogenic activity."

"Contribution to disease and carcinogenic activity are analogous." He seemed irritated. "You can find levels of carcinogens and endocrine disruptors and neurotoxins in all the farmers' market heirloom produce and grass-fed cattle you eat in Seattle. There's aluminum and mercury in breast milk. There's no escaping it."

"But proximity to contamination increases toxicity to more immediately dangerous levels. I get that a couple generations of 'better living through chemicals' has affected the food chain everywhere and concentrated in human bodies, too, but you *chose* to come here, where it's not just possible but *verifiable* that the level of contamination is higher and more of a threat."

Tuck's jaw tensed; he wanted to argue, it was obvious, but he held back. Why? Why not let me have it?

My temple throbbed and my hand went on its own, massaging the vein there. He handed me his water bottle and I took a swig.

"You will see," he said, quietly. "Just follow me."

The forest of the outer island became denser and the undergrowth more diverse, Oregon grape, salal, sword ferns, and hillocks of dense mosses and liverworts. The recent rain, followed by a stretch of unseasonably warm days, had combined to bring out the fungi—many more of them than I ever remembered seeing in the woods on Orwell. The topography of the island was like Orcas, with variations in elevation as the rocky, uneven shoreline rose to small peaks, sometimes with vistas of the entire sound. We climbed steadily up the forested hillside, and I asked more questions about the island's plant and animal life. I asked questions that I knew the answers to, just to see how Tuck would answer them. I couldn't tell if he was putting on a show for me. His answers were confident and not economical, so that there were large spaces of time when I tuned him out entirely. He had studied the ecology; he had spent his few years on

Marrow building better graywater and waste systems, studying the way forest health affected the well water. He had earned his confidence but not his patronizing tone. I was more and more disgusted that Katie had ended up with a guy who was so deeply a chauvinist.

He quickened his pace up the hill we were climbing, seeming anxious to get to the other side. I heard running water ahead and climbed after him, following as he crested the hill and stepped aside at the top, stood on the stump of a fallen tree. When I arrived, he reached out his hand. I stared at it for a moment, then took it and let him pull me up, joining him on the stump, stepping over the ebullient orange fungi that oozed from the edges. We were looking down into a gully. Every tree still standing on the hills around us was rusted to black over the trunk and branches. The ArPac smokestacks loomed, almost as tall as the trees here, but farther down the creek. The fire—or at least the oily smog of it—had been funneled into this gully. The long, narrow impressions of fallen tree trunks—the ones that would have fallen in the quake, as the topsoil was shaken and roots unearthed—were prostrated over the opposite hillside, pointed straight down into the creek bed. But the forest floor was alive; up and down the hillside, ferns, mosses, grasses, and young trees issued from the singed earth beneath, a vivid chartreuse layer over the decay.

I almost didn't see them at first—what Tuck had brought me there to see. I stepped down from the stump and carefully made my way down the steep path to the creek. I slipped, skidding down the embankment into a fallen tree, my boot gouging into the red-tinged soil, revealing underneath a network of spidery white threads exposed. I sat up to get a closer look, and there they were, right in front of me: mushrooms—buoyant clusters of chocolate caps on slender, eggy stems. From the ground I could see them everywhere, up the hill behind me, off the trail, farther into the undergrowth. Tuck came down to help me, but I shooed his hand away. I crawled along the ground. Grasses and weedy, spent flowers towered over them, sheltered them, in many places, but lifting fern fronds revealed dozens of them, hundreds. I climbed up and scanned the forest floor all around me. Now that I knew to look for them, I could see them everywhere. Across the creek they grew in the slender trenches of dead wood laid by the fallen trees, like rows of vegetables growing neatly in a garden.

"Holy shit, Tuck, what is this?"

"These are wood-eaters. *Psilocybe azurescens,*" he said. He squatted down next to me, carefully lifted away old needles around some of the mushrooms, and showed me what they had been growing from: the wood of fallen trees, now almost dust, almost soil, but with that same silky white web running throughout.

"*Psilocybe?* They're psychedelic?"

He shrugged, gestured around the forest floor.

"That's one use for them. They also happen to be miracle workers," he said. "The mushrooms are just the fruit that grows from the mycelium. They can go on for miles just under the soil, taking up what's there—vegetation, animals, mineral—breaking it all down, leaving soil the plants can thrive in. We've been inoculating different parts of the forest with different species, watching to see which species naturally occur, which to add. But it all depends on the rain out here. We've been waiting for a good rain to start the fruiting season. You came just in time."

He wanted to show me more. I followed him across the creek and on for a quarter mile, toward the refinery, until we were within sight of the old chain-link and barbed-wire fence at the property line. He walked up to a cedar, the bark no longer umber and fibrous but scraped away, ashen. But at the base of the trunk were large white tufts of another mushroom, like sea sponges tossed under the tree.

"*Sparassis crispa*," Tuck said. "Cauliflower mushroom. These trees were some of the first inoculated. Sarah Chen, one of the research scientists Sister J. convinced to come here, she and her students from Evergreen started the experiment. They wanted to see if they could expedite the soil restoration with the help of mycelia. Mycelia don't just digest vegetation. It can break down bone, fur, feces, and—it's been known for some time—plastics, petroleum and crude oil, industrial chemicals like hexane, even heavy metals like arsenic and mercury, cadmium, vanadium . . ."

While he talked, Tuck stooped down and ran his hand through the duff below the trees.

"They started with soil at the Colony; hauling in inoculated sawdust and wood chips from a mushroom farmer on the Nisqually Indian Reservation. They built mitigation fields one by one, layering dead, contaminated trees and plants, the mycelium starter, soil. The mycelium breaks everything down, creating new soil, *clean* soil."

My phone was in my back pocket. My battery was low, but I started taking pictures of the mushrooms, the trees, the revived plant life around the creek. I turned and the refinery appeared on the screen, through the trees. It was a beast. Concrete slabs and metal pipe works, now charred and broken, rusted, scattered over a grassy expanse of a few acres between the fence and the blacktop surrounding the refinery itself. I thought I could see the path the fire took, over those two days that it burned, from the shattered machinery at the hot center, out through the corridors and windows, along the weedy edges of blacktop, through the fence.

I couldn't take a picture of it. I looked past it, to the water. We had hiked half the island to get here, and I could see Orwell, Waldron, other islands, hazy in the distance.

"Living trees burn slowly," Tuck was saying. I had tuned him out again. "Many of these trees you see, the ones that are blackened, they were still alive inside for some time. Eventually they suffocated, with no way to photosynthesize."

I turned away from the refinery, looked up to where the tops of the dead trees met the sky.

Suffocation, the word wrote itself over and over inside my skull.

Six

THE WOODS

_____

MALHEUR NATIONAL FOREST, OREGON
MAY 2, 2016

WE'RE EATING FANCY burgers and drinking craft beers at the hotel restaurant in Prairie City. It's still my birthday for a few hours.

We talk about work for the entire meal. It's not unromantic; we're interested in the same things: ecosystems and how humans use and interact with them. Public lands attract all kinds, mostly the decent people. But all populations have a fringe. For park rangers, the fringe is everything from well-armed anti-government militants and poachers to nature-worshipping spiritualists and Bigfoot enthusiasts. But day to day, the bulk of Carey's work involves preparations for the next "big one"—the next big fire. In the last five fire seasons, every one of them has seen a fire that was larger and harder to fight than the previous season's worst. The pattern has put them on notice.

He tells me stories about being a smokejumper, parachuting into remote, roadless locations to fight fires. I have seen his scars, the burned patches of arm and leg that look like topographic maps. Some of these stories I've heard before, but I like listening to them. I can run my hands over his scars, feel the texture the fires have woven into him, but the stories come from a part of Carey I can't touch.

I'm supposed to be working on my own story. I have an editor waiting for new pages. And I do write—I tell Carey—I am writing. But I'm not writing about *then;* I'm writing about *now.* I write what we had for dinner the night before and how we both farted all night and opened the window though the screen was shot and the mosquitoes came in. So we closed the window and swore we'd go a month without eating any beans at all.

"That's what you write about?"

"It's what I want to write about," I tell him. "It's like this: every day I start in the present, and I think back, one day at a time." I'm drawing in the air, as if I'm connecting dots on a line, right to left. "But I'm also cooking oatmeal, or hanging laundry out on the line, or hiking up a mountain. I'm tired of looking back."

I drink my beer. Carey's waiting for me to continue, but I'm waiting for him to catch up and come to the conclusion on his own.

"Okay," he says, chewing, swallowing, "so, the story of today just keeps heading off into the future, and your story is in the past."

I beam at him. *You get me,* I'm about to say.

"But"—he puts up his hand—"and I'm asking because I'm curious, not because I'm objecting to what you're saying. But doesn't writing require pausing, sitting in one place? You can't stop time, but you can be still."

I chew a mouthful of burger.

"I'm having trouble being here and there at the same time."

After the check, Carey tells me we are going to stay the night at the hotel. He booked a room, not just dinner reservations. I didn't pack anything, but Carey has: toothbrush, paste, a pair of jeans and a shirt for the next day. The only thing he didn't pack for me was clean underwear.

In the room there's a bottle of wine, a huge piece of chocolate cake, and a gift, wrapped neatly in newspaper. It's a watch with GPS tracking.

I sit on the bed, looking at it. I feel chastened.

"You don't have to wear it every time you leave my sight," he said. "It's just to be safe. When you're out there alone."

I can't look at him.

"Thanks, I guess."

"Luce."

"It's a tracking device, Carey. Like I'm an endangered species you're studying."

"Jesus, I didn't mean it that way. I have one for work, Lucie. You could track me down in a tornado. I don't know where you are, ever."

He wants to touch me, I can tell. But it will hurt him so much if I recoil or, worse, if I don't respond at all. I know this about him, I can feel this about him, as I sit on the bed, three feet away. I am like a wild animal.

"I go to the fire lookout," I say.

"The fire lookout?"

"Or Mosquito Lake. I went there today."

"Where's Mosquito Lake?"

"The lake up by the old scout shack."

"It's called Cougar Lake."

"Well, I've only ever seen mosquitoes."

"You won't see a cougar or hear it, but it can still snap your neck."

"A lot of good GPS would do me."

"At least I'd be able to find you."

"Parts of me."

"Luce."

We still aren't touching. He's still afraid.

"I can think of worse ways to die," I say, and wonder as the word *die* crosses my lips if this will be the last time, the last thing, the last push I give him before he gives up and walks away. He shakes his head, his jaw set.

I jump on the bed and take off my shirt, my socks, my belt, nearly fall off, trying to kick my jeans from my ankles. He watches me, bewildered but pissed. I take off my bra and fling my panties at him. They hit his chest and drop at his feet.

"Which part would you eat first?" I ask.

"You've got a sick sense of humor," he says. But he reaches for my hand, draws it up to his face, and rests his cheek in my palm.

I tell him on the drive back to the cabin that I am going to see Sister J. in Spokane. He doesn't say anything at first, just nods. A young buck appears at the edge of the trees. I see it first, coming out of the woods on my side and getting ready to leap the ditch, jumping onto the berm. We're going about fifty and I holler, "DEER," and Carey slams on the brakes. The buck stops in the middle of the blacktop and stands like a statue, like they do when death has come to a screeching halt in front of them. They don't even blink. There are no other cars. We wait, hearts rattled. He stares us down while a doe scampers across the road behind him and takes off into the woods on the other side. A logging truck turns the corner ahead, coming at us. The buck doesn't take his eyes off us till Carey lays on the horn and revs the engine. Then he follows his mate into the woods. The truck barrels by, the driver flashing his lights to thank us for chasing the deer off the road, bark and lichen flying onto our windshield from the bundle of trees on its bed. I wonder whether the buck would have stayed there, staring us down, while death came at him from the other side.

When we start driving again, I'm holding his right hand on the seat between us. We're quiet, but the air in the cab feels heavy. Finally Carey says he thinks I should wait until he has a weekend off, so he can drive with me to Spokane. It's not about protecting me, he says. He knows I can take care of myself. It's just better to be traveling a distance like that with someone.

I traveled farther alone to come out here from Seattle.

"The letter came weeks ago," I say, "and she's not dying any slower."

Seven

THE ISLANDS

———◆———

"SPAWN?" I ASKED.

"Spawn." Jen nodded.

We were in a nursery of sorts. A Quonset hut among the trees behind the barn, where Tuck left me with Jen to get back to his work. It was partially dug into the ground, earthen-floored, unlit, and ran at least thirty feet, with a door at each end. The doors were open, making boxes of light on the dirt, but we wore headlamps. The air was cool around my ankles and warm and heavy around my head, like in a greenhouse. There was a sweet, pungent, yeasty odor in the air, like fresh bread and soil. This was where they stored their spawn — young mycelium colonies of various species.

"I've been mushroom hunting," I say, "and I've seen growing kits for oysters and shiitakes, but I've never seen mushroom cultivation like this."

"So, mushrooms are just the fruiting bodies of the much bigger organisms," Jen explained. I nodded. I knew this. "Before they're mushrooms, they look like this." She held up a gallon-size freezer bag full of what looked like moldy brown rice, small specks completely overtaken by soft white fuzz. "That's alder sawdust from downed trees, inoculated with *Grifola frondosa*

—maitake mushrooms. We inoculate the medium—sawdust, wood chips, sometimes cardboard or burlap or straw—and the mycelium overtakes it, rapidly, tiny white threads hundreds of miles long in some cases, bound up together. Spawn."

"And this is how you—the Colony—has been remediating the soil?"

"Yeah."

"Mushrooms?"

"Mushrooms. When they're not trapped in a bag like this, when they're in a forest, say, or a field, the organism can stretch for miles right there under your feet."

"I've read about the use of microorganisms in oil spills—bacteria especially—but they work too slowly for broad commercial use after big spills."

"How slow is too slow for the planet?" Jen asked. "And how much more harm did ArPac do when they threw dispersants all over the oil in the sea out here?"

"You're right, obviously, I agree with you," I said, walking down a row of stacked burlap sacks. "But, I mean, how many years does it take? And how do you even know that it's working?"

"We regularly send soil samples for testing. Obviously, the entire island isn't okay, yet. I mean, we're not *done*. But given the right spawn, in the right conditions, we can create healthy, viable soil in six months. Sometimes less."

Jen took me outside to show me a mitigation field at the bottom of the goat pasture, where they covered waste runoff with layers of inoculated sawdust, straw, and bark. The whole was covered with burlap to protect it from the hot sun and watered if it started to dry out.

"It's like a giant compost heap, but working three times faster to create soil," she said. "We start with sterilized medium, inoculate them with the variety of mycelium best suited to the medium and conditions. We turn the pile every so often, until the materials are soil, ready to be added to the fields and gardens. The mycelium is then acclimated to the climate, the conditions; it infiltrates the existing soil, and the remediation process continues."

"How?" I asked. "How *exactly* do mushrooms remediate? Are they digesting the heavy metals, the toxic chemicals?"

"Sort of. Yes. Some mycelia can break chemicals down into their elemental parts, rendering them less harmful. Mycelium produce enzymes to decompose plant and animal matter, and some of those enzymes also break down petrochemicals, plastics, complex chemical compounds created in a lab and unleashed on the world. Others can absorb heavy metals into the mushrooms themselves, so they can be removed from the ecosystem. It doesn't all happen at once, but over time, with different applications and different mycelia, gradually the natural balance of interdependent plant, insect, and microbial life can return. It all starts with the mushrooms."

"So you don't eat these mushrooms?"

"No, not the ones directly involved in restoration."

"So, what do you do with them?"

"We put the mushrooms through the process again, in the soil, with a fresh batch of spawn from some other species. Mycoremediation isn't new and neither are the methods. We've learned and borrowed from others who have been studying them casually or on much smaller scales for decades. No one has ever had the opportunity to try something like this."

She took me back to the hut and showed me more mycelia. Varieties they cultivated for food and medicine, and experimental species donated or exchanged with mycologists around the world.

My right ear was ringing; my headache hummed, and the light coming in from the far door made me turn back toward the recesses of the hut, where the bright white mycelium spawn, in their bags, in long wooden bins, seemed to give off a light of their own.

"Are you all right?" Jen reached for my arm.

"Yeah, I've just had this headache all day."

Walking the path under the firs, I asked Jen how she first heard of Marrow.

"One of my professors at Evergreen had come out here. He was an ecologist, really into the microbial relationships. He was all charged up about soil remediation when he got back. And God. He said he felt God here."

"God? This professor is a scientist?"

"I know. I'm an atheist," she said. "I think he was somewhere in the Intelligent Universe camp, but he came back talking about God. I wanted to see for myself. Sister J. inspires different feelings in different people—for me, it's not G-O-D. You've met her, right?"

I nodded. "I grew up Catholic; my dad's parents were devout. They're both gone now. And when my dad died, my mom and I just stopped going to church. I went to parochial school, an all-girls' school. But I was never confirmed, and we don't practice. I call us absentees."

Jen shook her head. "Yeah, I can see how you might lose faith after losing your dad. Mine's gone, too. But I was an atheist before then."

"Are a lot of the colonists Catholic? Or were they?"

"Only about, maybe, a quarter of us. In the early days, there were more. There was a sort of radical environmental movement afoot in the Diocese, and Sister was the leader. She held meetings and gave talks on 'earth ministry.' When the archbishop told her she had to stop—you know, when the Church was investigating all the nuns for being social activists?—she walked away from her order. She said she had a higher calling to minister to the earth, not men. She gained a lot of supporters that way—outside of the church, too. Followers and benefactors. *'Saints don't follow orders,'* they say." She turned to look at me, raised her eyebrows.

"Saints?"

"I don't really believe in saints, but if anyone qualified, it would be Sister J. She put herself on the line. She did something she knew would get her kicked out of her order and her church, her whole life and community for twenty years, to try something no one had ever tried before."

"The mycoremediation was her idea?" Wind snaked around our bodies and rattled fir needles onto the path and into our hair.

"She met a man who told her it was possible to clean up toxic soil with mycelia, and she knew of an island that needed to be cleaned up. It became her mission."

Jen left me with Elle at the apothecary. We sat on the stoop, and she took my pulse at the wrist, first on one side, then the other.

"Does it have a center, or is the pain evenly spread?" she asked.

"It's here," I said, tracing the line of pain from my eyebrow to the bridge of my nose around to the inner socket.

She took my pulse again, her steady hands on my wrist,

her head cocked to the side this time, like she was listening to my pulse.

We hadn't met earlier; Elle wasn't at lunch, no one mentioned why. She had been standing in the grass near the apothecary when we walked up, staring at something in the distance. She was tall and reedy, with short dark hair that curled over half her brow. She wasn't what I thought she would be. I had had visions of an earthy woman in layers of flowing skirts and scarves, like a young Stevie Nicks. But Elle was boyish in a worn-out T-shirt and jeans, beautiful and androgynous in a way that both men and women probably found attractive. A small sea-worn shell, suspended from a silver chain around her neck, landed at her sternum. My eye was drawn to it, the chalk-white of the shell against the thinning white of the cotton.

"You didn't sleep much last night?"

"No."

"Okay. Come with me." She stood up and disappeared behind the screen door, and I closed my eyes. The porch was shaded, but the meadow before it was blazing in the midday sun. My eyes prickled when I looked anywhere near it.

The cottage was cool and dark. I waited at the threshold for my eyes to adjust. There was a small living room with a wood stove, furnished with soft armchairs covered in pillows, a wooden table, and a bookshelf stocked with volumes on folk remedies and herbalism and Chinese medicine and nutrition. An amethyst geode the size of a human face rested in the center of the table. I squatted down to look and traced the crystal formations with a finger, rested my palm over the glassy curves. Elle appeared in the arch that led to the kitchen.

"I've just put the water on," she said, not smiling, but not unkindly. She had a direct, gentle way about her.

In the kitchen, sunlight slid around the edges of a blood-red cloth in the window, but a cool breeze blew through the back screen. I walked around the room while Elle put herbs into a mortar and pestle at a worktable and the water simmered on an efficiency burner. In the place of a stove and refrigerator, there were dehydrators and drying racks, bundles of herbs hanging from them, mushrooms laid out to dry on sheets. The cupboard doors had been removed, and the shelves were lined with jars of herbs, labeled with names and dates. Each shelf had a label, too, indicating the family of herb stored there. There was an indentation in one wall that had once held a folding ironing board. The ironing board was gone, and the space now held small brown and blue dropper bottles of tinctures and flower essences.

"How long have you been here?" I asked.

"Almost eight years." Elle looked up and out the back door, which led to the edge of the meadow and the start of the trees.

"You're Jen's partner?"

She nodded, continued her work. Jen was loquacious, outgoing; Elle was more reserved.

"Did you two meet here?"

"We did. I came to apprentice with Margaret—Maggie. She's our midwife, our medicine woman."

"I met her this morning," I said. "She was milking the goats."

"We all do, sometimes." She nodded. "Even Sister J."

The water was starting to boil. She poured it over a jar full of the herbs she had prepared for me, screwed on a cap.

"It just needs to steep. Do you often get headaches?" she asked. She wanted to turn the focus away from herself.

"Just in the last few years."

"Stress, maybe?" she offered.

"Stress?"

"Are you stressed?"

"No."

She looked at me and nodded like I was full of shit. I turned away.

"Can I touch?" I was standing over a tray of dark blue fungi. Elle looked up. "Of course."

"What are they?"

"*Cortinarius violaceus*. Violet caps. About a week after the fall rains, we start collecting them."

"What are they for?" I picked one up. It looked like a mushroom you'd buy in the grocery store, but it was the color of a varicose vein. I sniffed it.

"We're not exactly sure about those."

I looked at her curiously. She smiled for the first time.

"We only work with edible varieties in the apothecary. But part of what I'm working on for the Colony is understanding what each individual has to contribute to the health of the whole. In the beginning, we work with a combination of what we know and what we can intuit from what we know. We know, for example, that *Cortinarius violaceus* fruits in the early fall after warm rains. So, we might start by wondering whether they would be helpful for ailments induced by wet warmth, like certain kinds of rheumatism or influenza. Or we might wonder the opposite: if it might ameliorate ailments that are exacerbated by dry, cold climates. *Cortinarius violaceus* grows near conifers, but not just any conifers: it prefers the amabilis fir, *Abies amabilis*, which are rarer than noble and Douglas firs on the islands—and perhaps that has something to do with the sweet sap the amabilis exudes. Maybe the violet cap digests the sugars of the sap, and maybe it could be indicated for blood sugar regulation."

"But there aren't that many people here—how often do you actually get to test these hypotheses?"

She poured the tea through a strainer into a mug for me.

"It's not an allopathic model; I'll never be able to write a peer-reviewed paper or anything like that. But I don't really care."

She pulled a jar of honey from a shelf and set it in front of me with a spoon.

"Stir a good tablespoon of honey in the tea."

I did and watched the honey dissolve into the murky liquid. I took a mouthful and felt the heat and scent flow to the back of my throat and bloom up into my sinuses and around my eyes. It wasn't spicy, exactly, but it had the effect of a hit of horseradish, opening my nasal passages and making my eyes water. I swallowed and felt it cool my entire throat as it went down.

"Jesus Christ." I started laughing. The sensation passed, and I was left with the honeyed, herbaceous flavor on my tongue.

Elle raised an eyebrow. "Just take sips."

"What's in it?"

"The strongest flavors come from the rhizomes of garlic mustard. It's an invasive species but almost impossible to get rid of, so we found a use for it. We weed it from our fields and the wild spaces—when we can—and it becomes part of our medicinal collection here. There's also wintergreen, yarrow, skullcap, fireweed . . . It's a useful blend."

"How sick do people actually get here? How often do you need to try a new treatment for rheumatism? Everyone seems relatively young and healthy." I thought of Sister J. and her cough, but didn't mention it.

"The average age here is forty-two. So, it's true, we don't see a lot of diabetes or rheumatism or things like that. Flesh wounds, insect stings, strains, and sprains. There are almost a third more women here than men. So, migraines—yes. Menstrual irregularities."

"Birth control?" I offered. "I notice there are couples here but no children."

She paused and looked thoughtfully at me. "Yes. There's a long tradition of wise women using herbs for birth control. You'll want to drink lots of water, too. The tea's diuretic and diaphoretic." She gestured to my mug.

She poured off a jar of water for me from an old Tupperware pitcher, like the kind my mom made lemonade in when I was a kid. The water was perfectly clear, catching the light from the window. I took a drink, conscious for the first time that I was drinking well water, that I couldn't taste anything but water. I held it up. I don't know what I expected to see floating in it. Lead? Cadmium? Sulfur? Little skulls and crossbones?

Elle saw me.

"It's as clean as water you get in the city. Probably cleaner."

"How?"

"Filters, for drinking and cooking water."

She showed me a lidded bucket with a spigot and a tube in the corner behind the door.

"Six layers: gravel, sand, charcoal; gravel, sand, charcoal. Muslin at the bottom." She handed me the pitcher and gestured toward the end of the hose, turned the spigot. Water flowed into the pitcher.

"We probably don't need to use them anymore—it's been a while since everyone was religious about it. I boil, then filter twice. I don't want to compromise the treatments." She nodded at my tea. "It works best when it's hot."

I watched her work for a while, as I sipped the tea. Feeling it
burn its way down my throat and into my head, my chest. Soon,
I was sweating the headache out of me.

Katie came to collect me. The pain in my skull was waning, but
my eyes were still sensitive to the light. I borrowed a straw hat
from Elle, who told me to rest awhile and handed me a lidded
jar of water with a sprig of mint in it. Katie walked me through
the medicinal garden and out to the meadow. We made our way
over a dirt and grass path through the trees to the central cluster of cottages. They had the look of a prewar summer camp,
with a name for every house, painted in bright colors on a sign
outside each door. The first colonists named the cottages, and
though they must have been struggling in those early years just
after the quake, they seemed to have brought a sense of whimsy
to Marrow. There was Oysterville and The Pequod, Valhalla and
Atlantis, The French Quarter and The Royal Fernery. My cottage, which was set aside for guests—visiting scientists, ecol-
ogists, family members—was called the Helix Nebula. There
were flower beds and herb gardens around some; others had
gone to seed with whatever would grow there—grasses and
flowers and young trees, but with birdhouses rising out of them
on stilts, or piles of wood alive with mason bees. It was all habi-
tat, Katie said. The only requirement was that a conscious decision had been made by the inhabitants. There were laundry
lines slung with sheets and underwear and jeans. Wind chimes
answered every breeze.

The vault toilets were not like the typical outhouses of camp-
grounds. They had built them to look like regular buildings, little shacks and cabins made of salvaged wood and windows and
doors. The inner walls were made of a clay composite—a per-

fectly insulated material that kept them warm in the winter and cool in the summer. Tuck was the one to innovate on the design, a model he perfected after studying at Yestermorrow in Vermont. It became an artistic challenge, improving on the toilets. A couple had retractable sunroofs so that you could shit under the open sky. Each was planted round with native herbs and wildflowers.

"Where did the salvage come from?"

"Some were from cottages here—the ones that collapsed after the earthquake—they took them down piece by piece and reused everything they could. In the time I've been here, we've had quite a few donations of materials, too. There's a network of folks around the islands who keep us in mind when they have something taking up space. Like that, over there." She pointed off through the trees.

"Is that a boat?" I peered through the trees to an open space where I could just make out the blue-and-white hull of a cruiser —probably a fifty-footer—the V-bottom buried in the dirt, like it was sailing through the forest. We were at least a mile from the dock. "That's incredible. How did you get it up here?"

"Tractor. It took some doing, though."

"Does someone live there?"

"It's the lab." Katie started walking again and I followed.

"That's a lab? What kind of lab?"

"Soil and water stuff, mostly. It's where they process the samples."

"Who's 'they'?"

"Tuck and Aaron. Zadie and Jen. The occasional student— they come and go—you know the types. I was one of them once."

"I'm surprised more of the students don't stay, honestly." I was taking in the view, the quaint cottages with the Salish Sea beyond, the gentle swaying of the trees. I looked at her, expecting agreement. But she looked troubled.

"We attract a certain type of person, for sure. Young, interested in environmental issues, social justice, minimalist living. But there's usually a point, after six months or so . . . Either it's something you can give yourself to, or it's not."

"But you stayed. Tuck, Jen, Elle — ?"

"We were the last newcomers. We had a little cohort — along with Andrew and Tom, who had been at Yestermorrow, in Vermont; Carly and Angela, the sisters from Alaska who run our fishing boat now; Zadie and Luke, who were part of the organic farms exchange. We were all looking for something meaningful that we couldn't find out there." She gestured toward the mainland. "We were all in it for the long haul, from the beginning, so with Sister's blessing, we started making the Colony ours. Most of us never had the chance to make homes for ourselves out there. It wasn't this trendy thing yet, to be raising goats and bees, and fermenting vegetables or whatever, you know?"

We sat on the hillside in the breeze and looked out at the water.

"I can't explain it. Things have changed. For a while after the earthquake, when we were teenagers and going into college, it seemed like there was energy around dealing with big problems. Reconstruction, earthquake mitigation, energy efficiency, affordability, and quality-of-life issues. There were people willing to do the work. But something shifted in the consciousness a few years ago. It was like people had reached this level of comfort and didn't want to give it up. They stopped wanting to fight and started to accept that we would never win the fight. That the forces against us were too great, the problems too out of control. People smart enough and caring enough to see the danger the planet was in, but too—I don't know—too over-whelmed? too complacent? to do anything about it. We started losing benefactors."

"What do you mean by 'benefactors'? Jen mentioned them, too."

"There were some liberal Catholic supporters of Sister's mis-sion who donated supplies—solar panels, yurts, goats, farm equipment, money for mycelium spawn—which doesn't come cheap when you're cultivating them large scale like this. Every-thing, at first, came either from benefactors, bartering, salvage, or voluntary labor. It hasn't been easy, keeping this level of sup-port for the last decade. There are sexier movements out there."

"Maybe," I said, thinking about my ex and his orchards. "But I'd write about it."

Katie looked at me like she was measuring the distance be-tween my eyebrows.

"How does a nun get into mushrooms?" I asked.

Katie left me at my cabin to rest while she finished her chores for the day. Of all the houses, all the buildings I had seen so far, this one was most like an old summer cabin. Logs for walls, stone fireplace, one room with a kitchen at the far end and a door out to the privy and shower. The door to the left off the living room led to a small bedroom, a door on the right to a screened-in porch just wide enough for a twin bedstead, no cur-tains. It was simply furnished, like all of the buildings I had seen so far. A rug in the main room, but otherwise bare floors, swept clean, a love seat, and a coffee table. In the kitchen, a wooden table and two mismatched chairs, a ceramic jug of fireweed and meadow rue in the center. I leaned down to smell them and saw that pollen and black aphids had fallen all over the table. An earwig shimmied under the pottery.

I plugged my phone into my solar charger and put it in the window. I had a message I couldn't retrieve because of the shaky signal. Chris Lelehalt, maybe, with news about Jacob Swenson.

I opened the windows of the sleeping porch, took off my shoes, and laid myself down on the bed. The sun was low in the sky. I hadn't felt so weary in a long time. My body sank into the soft mattress; the heat sank into the room. The breeze lifting the thin muslin curtains, a bee throwing its body at the screen. *Hum-tap. Hum-tap-tap. Hum.*

I should let it out, I thought. But I felt weighted to the bed, wooden-limbed. What was in that tea?

Training my eyes on the trees outside, the way they seemed to bend over the cabin, over the bed itself. I thought my eyes were open, but the way my thoughts turned, I knew I was starting to dream. I was falling backward through the day, details large and small, floating forward. I was searching the cabin's kitchen for a jar, a cup to capture the bee. I was at the window, cupping it in my hands. When I opened my hands at the back door, it was gone. I walked into a field of fireweed, listening to a lecture by a famous ecologist—I knew she was famous—on the first plants to return after a fire. *That's why it's called fireweed.* It looks like a fire on the hillside, those waist-high red fronds licking at the wind; it's the ghost of what came before it. *It brings the bees back, and they make the best honey from it,* Katie was saying to me, holding a stem of it up to my face even though the bees were all over it. I was trying to take notes for an article or a book —a book I was going to write about Marrow Island resurrected. I could see my hand scrawling notes, but the words made no sense. I tried again: *furweed, friarweed, friendweed.* I can't get the *fire.* I write it over and over again. My hand numb, my letters loopy, drunk. In the pictures I've taken, the lens is buttery soft. *Is it the camera or my eyes?*

Muscles twitched, my hand reaching, but only my fingers lifting, and I was aware, for a moment, that I was still lying on the bed and the sun was lower in the sky. I heard singing somewhere nearby, like a choir, that sent goose bumps along my arms. *But I'm dreaming,* I told myself. The distant conversation of ravens, harmonizing with the wind chimes. I pulled the blanket over me and sank, again, into the bed. An unkindness of wind chimes.

Asleep in the broad window seat at Rookwood, the one that looked out on the wraparound porch, on the lawn, and the view of the sea. I knew I wasn't supposed to be there this time. Someone would find me and I'd be in trouble. They couldn't know that I knew. But I was so tired I couldn't move. I forced my eyes open, and out the window there's a man, walking down the steps, across the yard. I could see everything beyond him: Marrow, ArPac, the cottage, the Salish Sea, rising in huge waves under a bright sky. And there was Jacob Swenson, getting into a boat as the tsunami approached. He couldn't see it. I dragged myself up from the window seat. One leg wouldn't move; my voice was muted, a whisper though I knew I was screaming. My eyes dropped shut like curtains—I ran my hands along furniture and walls to get to the door. *I'm dreaming*—I knew I was dreaming—but I had to make it to the door. I had to stop him. *What happens if I stop him?* I wanted to see what happens when I save a life. So I say to myself: *You're dreaming. You can fly, you're a ghost.* So I willed myself to fly through the wall to the porch and around to the other side —but he was so much farther away than he seemed. I was floating over the lawn, over the drive, down to the shore, but slower, slower. *But I'll never save us both.* The wave rose; it washed over everything. *Breathe!* so I did. And the wave washed away. There he was at my feet, beached, like a seal; he was dead. More than dead. He was leftovers for the rooks. And I wrapped my arms around him and wept because it wasn't Jacob Swenson; it was my dad. My dad's face, falling apart all over the beach. I clutched at his clothes as his body dissolved.

I jerked awake, sweating, hair stuck to my face. The day outside was almost unchanged, the sun still bright gold, angled low through the trees, casting shadows on the walls of the sleeping porch. I heard the creaking of the front door—I had left it open wide for the air.

I took my phone from the charger and checked the time. I had slept for less than two hours. Why did I feel like I was clawing myself out of a season of hibernation? My eyes wouldn't adjust to the light, my insides felt drained. I was parched and ravenous. A breeze rustled through the trees outside and through the screens. The air smelled like everything—wilderness and the sea and life and decay. It was almost enough to revive me. I kicked off the blanket and let the air through the screens blow over me, let my eyes adjust to the light outside, stretched out between the trees. I listened to a bird calling in the trees, a long, complicated refrain, trying to pick out its different parts. I slowly became more conscious, forcing the synapses to spark, feeling different parts of my brain waking. The bee was on its side on the window ledge, dead.

Dinner was oysters, greens and roasted potatoes, and loaves of sourdough. I hadn't enjoyed oysters as a girl, no matter how fresh, but my hunger made them delicious to me now, steamed at the fire pit, a dollop of butter dropped in the shell and chased with dry herbed mead.

We ate outside, on the bluff, like we had earlier in the day. Talk circulated about the indicator clouds streaking across the radiant sunset; rain would come soon. Without water, there are no mushrooms. I was becoming aware of how much of the colonists' conversation revolved around water and the paucity of it, the drought that was descending on the West. It was difficult to imagine, looking out at the sea, that there could ever be an absolute end to the rain in the Northwest, even with all the stories I had written about the subject. I sucked oysters from their hot, calcified bowls while one of the old-timers, Jack, told me about the oyster, its importance to the wild waters it lives in, the way it filters and diversifies the ecosystem, how their populations have increased as their natural predators have dwindled, especially after the sea star wasting disease that swept through the year before. No one knew why the sea stars had died, only that their limbs had begun to shed, then become palsied. Then they detached themselves one by one, creeping away, leaving their bodies to die. Jack said they had to thin the oyster beds off Marrow's shores every now and then, for an oyster bake like this. And they would smoke and jar them for the winter, too. The cooks brought more oysters from the fire, every table steaming with heaps of them, their shells burst open from the heat of the wood coals.

I began to feel sick, like my belly was full of seawater. I had eaten too many, too quickly.

Katie and I sat close together, as Tuck helped with the oyster shucking. A spirit of the celebration drew people to the fire. The mead was stronger than I had guessed, and I was warm in the cheeks, less connected to my body, and freer with my conversation. More people were introducing themselves to me, sitting nearby and asking me questions about where I was from and what I did back in Seattle. Some of them asked about the current state of politics at large; they didn't all make it off the island very much and didn't have much time — or chose not — to tune in to radio broadcasts from Canada or the U.S. As the night wore on, the questions became more personal. Jen, who had obviously warmed to me more than anyone else, asked whether I was seeing anyone. So I told her about the breakup, the two successive layoffs, the attempt at freelancing. And then I started talking about the cottage on Orwell. How it looked after twenty years: the same, but falling apart; how memories of those years sifted through every minute of the present there.

"Are you thinking of staying?" Katie had been sitting back, quiet, letting me hold the center of the conversation. She leaned toward me, examined my face in the firelight. I couldn't tell which side of the question she wanted me to come down on.

"I don't know," I said. "I just can't imagine selling it, unless Jacob Swenson, my neighbor, will buy it so it goes back to their family."

There was a lull in the murmur of conversations, and I felt the focus of the group shift to me. Mostly the younger folks, the ones Katie had referred to as "the cohort."

Jen was the first to speak. "Yeah, definitely. Jacob would be the best person to buy it, if you wanted to sell. No chance of him developing the property. But if you wanted to hold on to it for a while, and you weren't going to stay on, Tuck could look after it for you. He's been Jacob's handyman for years."

"Really?" I said. I looked for Tuck, but he was nowhere that I could see. I looked to Katie.

She nodded. "Yeah, Jacob's been a friend of the Colony since the beginning. We try to give back when we can."

"I should talk to Tuck, then," I said. "I think Jacob's missing. The police were out the other night." Katie became still, tense. The mood shifted around us.

"What do you mean, 'missing'?" Jen asked.

An owl called in the woods not far off. I looked around the fire at the faces in the flickering light.

"I mean, I tried to get in touch with him. There was a light on in an upstairs bedroom for two days, but he wasn't home. So I went in and found his glasses and medication and stuff, in a suitcase. And another lamp knocked over. Windows open. It was really unnerving. So I called the police."

Jen and Elle exchanged looks, but no one spoke. It did nothing to alleviate my fears that something had happened.

"What?" I asked. "You're freaking me out."

"It's just not unlike Jacob to disappear for a while, without a word," Katie said.

"Do you know where he goes?"

"We're not sure," Katie said. "But you shouldn't worry about it. I'm sure he's around somewhere." She squeezed my knee.

There was an awkward silence on our side of the fire, then Jen said she was on kitchen duty in the morning and needed to hit the sack. Elle followed. Katie and I sat around the fire while others came off kitchen cleanup and filled in. Tuck brought us a blanket, and we wrapped it around our shoulders. Some of the older folks were telling stories about the early days, the mishaps and minor disasters. I listened, but felt colder and colder as night settled over us, more alert to the sounds of the waves.

I leaned over to Katie's ear. "Where's Sister J.?" I hadn't seen her all day.

"She's been helping Maggie," Katie whispered.

"Where's Maggie?" I whispered back.

"She's with Sarah."

I gave her a beseeching look. I hadn't met everyone yet.

"Who's Sarah?"

She kissed my cheek and leaned closer to my ear.

"She's dying."

Katie walked me back to my cabin through the dark, arm looped through mine. Clouds covered the moon and stars. She knew the way, but I stumbled along, catching my feet on unexpected roots.

"Do you want to come in and talk?" I asked. My teeth were chattering. "You could sleep over here. Like old times?"

"That's sweet, Lu." She sighed, using her pet name for me. She stopped suddenly.

"Listen!"

"What?!" I was looking around in the dark. Was something coming?

"Shh."

Then I heard it: wing beats. Hundreds, maybe thousands of them, somewhere between the trees and the clouds, in the black sky. Migrating birds, flying south through the night. For such delicate creatures, it was a haunting sound: thousands of wings battering the air, coming in like a wave, a slow rush over our heads. Then the chorus of their nocturnal song, the way they call from front to back, short high notes, one bird to the next, to lead each other on. We tipped our faces to the sky and listened. A minute, maybe two, and they were gone.

"I always feel like I've captured something precious, when something like that happens," Katie said. She took my arm again and led me on across the field.

"Can you tell what kind of birds they were?"

"Vireos, maybe? I don't really know. Smaller birds. The geese and the cranes, their calls are lower, harsher."

"I had forgotten about the night migrations. I've missed these things about the islands, without realizing I was missing them."

"I've missed you, Luce. I didn't realize until I saw you on the boat. I was so nervous about you coming until I saw you there, seasick green." She laughed.

I laughed, too. But it made me uneasy, talking about the past, talking about our feelings for each other.

"Katie, why was everyone so strange when I mentioned Jacob Swenson?"

"Because there was an incident with Jacob not too long ago. He has an alcohol problem, and Sister J. called him on it. He left town suddenly."

We were coming up to the cabin, and I pulled away from her arm.

"What was the incident?" I thought about the pills I had seen in the suitcase, the empty whiskey bottle. "Was he suicidal?"

She paused, calculating.

"No, nothing like that," she said. "He has helped us over the years, but he has been less and less reliable in the last year, paranoid. He thought his family was after him, then he thought we were after him. We tried to help him, but it's tricky. It's always been understood that if something happened to him . . ." She paused again, choosing her words very carefully. "His family would take over the Trust, and we could lose the Colony."

"The Swensons own the Colony?"

"Who did you think owned it? The Swensons own the whole island, Luce; they always have. Except for Fort Union—Maura gave that portion to the state back when they made the ArPac deal."

"Why would Maura have leased the island to ArPac? She was an artist—"

"The Swensons were major shareholders in ArPac. Where did you think their money came from? Maura's paintings? They had a long-term lease on that land that Julia nullified after the fire. How did you not know this?" She sounded almost angry at me. "You really have been checked out, haven't you?"

"I haven't been 'checked out.' I've been living my life." I was bewildered at her bitterness.

"After Julia died, the family sent Jacob out here to get him out of the way, keep him busy with the Trust. He has been lying to them for years about the island. They think the land is too polluted to be of use and too much of a liability to sell. They don't know we're here."

"How do you know all this?"

"Because Jacob was like family to us, like Julia was to you. She was devastated by what happened here, and he knew it— the disaster sent her to her grave, Lucie." Katie's voice rose a pitch. "Sister knew Julia; she offered her a way to—do penance, or whatever, for the damage, for the loss of life. The deal was already in the works when Julia passed and Jacob took over."

She looked away from me, fuming. I said nothing.

"She was like a grandmother to you. She took care of you. You didn't even come back for her funeral."

"It was only two years after my dad's funeral; I was fourteen."

"But you never wondered what's been going on here all these years?"

"Why are you so angry at me?"

"Because you could have come back any time, Lucie. You could have reached out to me, once."

"I couldn't come back."

"Not even for me?"

"I'm sorry. I was never the brave one."

"That's bullshit." But her voice had softened.

We were stopped, her face lost in the dark. I didn't know what to say, so I wrapped my arms around her. She stiffened, then re-laxed, pulled me in closer. We stood like that for a while, sway-ing, drunk. Then she took my face in her hands and brought her nose to mine.

"So what's different now?" she whispered. "Why did you fi-nally come back?"

"I don't know." I shook my head, shivered. "You wrote me."

Katie pulled away.

I closed all of the flimsy curtains around the little sleeping porch, but the gaps were many and wide. I felt the dark watch-ing. I undressed like a girl in a locker room, pulling my bra off under my shirt and out through the sleeve. I climbed into the bed and switched off the metal lamp clipped to the bedstead.

Katie went back to her cottage, to her husband.

I lay there thinking about the island and what I knew about industrial contamination from Superfund sites and oil spills and open pit mines. At old copper mine sites, the leaching fields of arsenic and cadmium and zinc leave water unpotable for miles and for decades, soil so acidic it isn't good for food or grazing cattle or anything. What can't be seen is dangerous, the smallest particles of heavy metals in the soil, in the water, for decades, for generations.

Marrow was six square miles. One-third had been burned or chemically polluted to a noxious heap. The rest had been contaminated enough to warrant abandonment.

In my senior year of high school, I was helping my mom clean out the basement. Her new husband had built her a house on Lake Washington; they were moving, and I was going to college. In a box marked for shredding, I found the reports from the lawsuit, the case against ArPac and the settlement they had reached with the families. I had seen the list of toxins that had, in my father's case, and in their words, "accelerated the immolation so that remains could not be verified, identified, or recovered." They had fought my father's death, claiming that the severity of the fire and the near annihilation of the remains they had found meant they could not be certain that "one or more of the missing employees had not been swept away in the tsunami." Later I would write about another of ArPac's disasters —an explosion on a platform off the coast of Alaska—noting every name of every one of the same damn chemicals.

Everyone—even the state—had abandoned Marrow. Everyone but Sister J. and Julia Swenson, and Jacob, and all the others who had come and stayed. They had built their homes, their community, here, even when it wasn't safe to do so. Sister was with the dying woman, Sarah, keeping vigil for her. Sarah was one of the early colonists. She had been here in the early days, drinking the water, going to sleep at night with soil under her fingernails and in her nostrils. She ate food grown here or harvested from this sea. Was she burning to death, but slowly, from the inside?

• • •

A knock on the cabin door woke me. I guessed it was 6:30, the sun not quite risen but the sky a creamy blue.

I was following Katie on her work prayer again. She met me outside, a large burlap bag slung over her shoulder. I said, "Good morning," but she put her finger to her lips and kissed me on the cheek. She looked tired, her eyes sandy and swollen, her hair still mussed from sleep. Sheets of fog clung to the sea like a big unmade bed. We walked through the trees, mist hanging in the air before us. You could open your mouth and eat it.

I had assumed we would be milking again. I almost turned in at the gate, but she took my arm, nodded her head toward the fields. She held my arm fast; she rested her head on my shoulder, the top of her head pressing into my ear. I tried to hear her thoughts, to communicate telepathically, like we used to do sometimes as girls. But she only raised her head and sighed, gazing ahead, and led me on to the field of root crops and greens.

We made our way to the far edge and continued walking slowly along the fence line, Katie scanning the barbed wire and ground. After several yards, she touched my arm. I looked up at her, and she gestured to her feet. A rabbit, neck snared by a trap, hung from a trap in the fence. She pulled a pair of leather work gloves from the sack and put them on. Then she released the trap, looking up at me to make sure I was watching, and pulled the rabbit up by the legs to show me. The rabbit's head dangled, its eyes and mouth open, rectangular teeth jutting out. She pulled out another sack, handed it to me, gestured for me to hold it open, then dropped the rabbit into it.

I stared into the bottom of the sack. The rabbit's broken neck folded up, its milky eyes looking somewhere above me. Was this what she was thinking about when she rested her head on my shoulder?

She reset the trap and we walked on.

Not all of the traps were the same, and not all of the rabbits were dead. For the living she had a BB gun, also in the sack. I tried not to look alarmed when she pulled it out. She raised it and aimed squarely between the terrified animal's ears. I forced myself to watch the life twitch out of them. Katie closed her eyes briefly after each one, looking less pained by the act of killing than I would have expected. How many rabbits had she killed?

One trap had only a back leg left in it—a fox had eaten it, maybe. Or it had torn itself free. Katie freed the furry little foot, a grim, satisfied smile on her lips.

We took the rabbits to the kitchen, where Katie, one man, and another woman showed me how to cut off the heads and the back legs at the joint, skin, and gut them. The sound of the skin tearing free made me feel my own skin in a way I never had.

Washing blood from my hands in a basin full of stone-cold seawater didn't feel like praying. It felt like penance.

Eight

THE RIVER

HANFORD REACH, WASHINGTON
MAY 7, 2016

IT'S OVER SIX hours from the Malheur to Spokane. I told Carey I would wear the GPS watch the whole time, and here it is on my wrist, tiny red light flickering in the dark. I imagine him watching it beat like a tiny red heart on a screen somewhere, in the middle of a digital Palouse.

As I crossed from Oregon to Washington, I gassed up in Kennewick. There were signs for the Reach—this long stretch of the Columbia River near the Hanford Site. It was twenty miles out of my way, but I wanted to see the place where the retired nukes go.

A broad expanse of river on a plain, a wetland alive with birds and insects, a distant cluster of concrete buildings, an alien city surrounded by volcanic hills as desolate as the surface of the moon. It surprises me, how beautiful it all is; how calm I feel, sitting on the banks of a river rumored to harbor radioactive effluent. No one believes in containment, despite the Department of Energy's official statements. But people still live here, raise children downstream.

I think about how we keep making these beds, and the only real choice is choosing which one to sleep in. The one with the loveliest view? The cheapest cost of living? The vibrant nightlife and culture?

Sister J. is lying in her bed over a hundred miles from here, still alive.

My hand is in the pocket of my sweater, resting on a small metal tin. In the tin are a dozen dried wavy caps, *Psilocybe cyanescens*. They're the only things I could think she might want from me.

Nine

THE ISLANDS

———

"WE'RE ALL STILL waiting for the 'Big One,' aren't we?" Sister J. was walking the shore with me before midday meal. We gathered seaweed, which they washed and dried and stored for food and medicine. The tide was low and the beach widened into mud flats.

"The big earthquake? I guess we are," I said. "Or any other earthquake, with all the faults we're living on."

"Your father died here, didn't he?"

"At the refinery, yes." I wasn't sure where these questions were going, but it didn't feel like Sister was just trying to get to know me.

"And it took you some time, but you came back. To see the place where he died, to be here."

I didn't respond. I busied myself cutting a bunch of bladderwrack from a rock. She tromped over to me with a bunch of her own and put it in the basket beside me.

"Does it feel safe here to you, now?"

"Not when I'm being interrogated by women religious," I said.

Sister cackled and slapped her knee, then fell into a coughing fit. I put a hand on her back and held her arm to steady her. We each had a small, sharp foraging knife in one hand. She finished her deep hacking and chuckle-coughed some more. When she was done, she was out of breath. I settled her on a rock and sat beside her, dropping our tools in the basket. She seemed older than her fifty-seven years.

"I admire your boundaries, Lucie," she said when she had regained her breath. "I know it's not easy to talk about loss, even years afterward."

"I don't mind talking about what happened, but I feel like there's a riddle here, like this conversation isn't really about me coming back," I said.

"I apologize. Sometimes I don't know what I'm saying until I've talked my way around it for a while."

We sat for a moment, watching a pair of gulls squabbling near the water's edge.

"What does my father's death have to do with earthquakes? Besides the fact that he died after one?"

"I've noticed, over the years, that people are much more comfortable talking about the tragedies that have passed than the tragedies that are to come."

"That's probably true."

"After the May Day Quake, people rebuilt, despite knowing that there would be other earthquakes, even bigger ones. Why? Why, when you know untold danger is imminent, do people stay? Invest time and money in a city that may crumble again?"

I thought for a moment and said, "I think we trick ourselves into believing we are safe, that we've learned from the past and can survive what comes, so that we can continue to live in the world, have relationships with each other."

"What if we're not tricking ourselves at all, though? What if we choose to take great risks so that others can continue to live in the world and have relationships with each other?"

"You're talking about the Colony?"

Sister J. took a deep breath and let it out.

"Smell that air," she said. "When I smell that air, I think, *God is good.*"

She lifted herself from the rock and picked up the basket.

"Sister, is the island making you sick? Has it been making others sick?" I stood so that we would be face to face.

"The island sustains us as we have sustained it." There was sadness in her eyes, though she smiled faintly. "And that is what we want the world to know."

Sister J. didn't join us for midday meal. We parted ways at the fork in the path; I headed up the hill to meet Katie, and she went down to meet Maggie. The colonists seemed subdued at the lunch tables; conversations were quiet and contemplative. No one mentioned the dying woman.

Katie and I sat alone at the end of a table. I told her about the conversation I had just had with Sister. She chewed her greens and stared at a knot in the woodgrain.

"What do you think she was trying to tell me, Katie?"

"When I wrote you — four months ago? — things here were a little different. We were feeling confident that our method had been successful, that after twenty years, we might be able to share what we had learned. I thought that you might come and write about us — about Sister J.'s mission — and that maybe it would bring some donors our way, so that we could expand the cleanup to the refinery site itself."

"So you do want me to write about the Colony?"

"I thought that you might."

"If you wanted me to come to write a story, why didn't you just ask me?"

"I wanted to see you, too. We haven't seen each other in so long, I didn't know, I guess, if this would work. And Sister wasn't sold on the idea."

"She didn't want me to come?"

"She didn't want anyone to come. But I thought if she met you, if she understood what this place meant to you and the work you have already done — and what drives you — she would change her mind."

"Has she changed her mind?"

"About you, I think so. But she's still worried about what publicity would do us. It might make things difficult for us, legally."

"What do you mean?"

"Technically, we're squatters."

"But you have an agreement with Jacob Swenson?"

"Nothing in writing."

"Nothing?"

She shook her head.

"Squatters have rights, Katie. Especially after so many years and so much investment in the property."

"Right." She nodded.

"With publicity, you might gain widespread support among activists, you'd probably get the attention of more donors . . ."

"Yeah, that was the thought. But there are complications with that."

"Like what?"

"Like taxes. We haven't been filing."

"Okay. I mean, you could become a 501(c)(3) and file retroactively. There are tax lawyers who can fix these problems."

"This just . . . it isn't what we're about, is all. We don't want to be a business; we just want to keep doing what we're doing."

"If the park reopens, there will be a lot more traffic on the island, Katie. People are going to become more aware."

"I think we just need time to figure out what we're going to do. And it's not the best time for us, at the moment."

"Because of the dying woman?"

Katie nodded.

"I understand. I do. I guess I just don't know what you want me to do with all this. It definitely complicates things for me, if I were to write about the Colony. I can't tell the story you want to tell. I have to tell the story I see."

"Let us get through Sarah's passing. We'll figure it out."

I spent some time in the kitchen helping to prep vegetables for the harvest supper, until Jen shooed me out, saying I was a guest and I should enjoy the last of my time here before I left in the morning. The kitchen was bustling, and many had suspended their usual activities to help with the preparations. Katie had vanished.

So I set off for Fort Union. It was about a mile to the park through the trees to the northwest. I took my time, noting the way the landscape changed as I approached the western side of the island, how it dried out and the trees thinned, leaving wide-open spaces of mostly summer-spent grasses. But I also noticed how each step away from the Colony showed an island whose recovery was less and less visible. There were more dead trees, still standing, but leafless and gaunt, hollowed out. And the trees still living showed less new growth. They weren't thriving like the trees around the Colony. This time I took pictures along the way.

Carey wasn't in the old ranger station — really just a one-room

hut near the shore; it was empty of everything but dust and spiders. There was a sturdier structure for the ranger's quarters, a
cabin up the hill past the barracks. The decaying building was
uncanny, with nothing but trees and sea behind it. It seemed
shrunken, with warped, peeling cedar-shingle siding, windows
boarded up like empty, lidded eyes.

I was taking pictures when I heard footsteps behind me.

"You here for an official interview, ma'am?"

"I could be. I'm not sure at the moment."

"Would coffee help?"

"You have coffee? Jesus, I'd love some coffee."

"Come on." He gestured toward his cabin.

He was cooking on a camp stove, so heating the water took
some time. While we waited, we sat on the steps of the cabin
talking. I asked how his assessment was going; he asked how my
visit was going. Watching him pour the water into a cup of instant coffee, I thought about the well at the park.

"Have you tested the water here?"

He looked up at me, curiously.

"Haven't yet. I'm just here to check out the camp and set things
up so the biologists can come in and do what they need to do."

"Did you filter that water?"

"Nope." He handed me the steaming cup.

"What if it's full of hexavalent chromium?"

He shrugged. "We're not living here. Short-term exposure,
almost twenty years after the fact . . . The human body's pretty
resilient."

Not willing to wait much longer, I took a scalding drink from
the metal cup.

I moaned. He laughed.

"Does it taste like poison?"

"It's perfect."

We talked more about the difference between remediation and restoration. Working for the Forest Service, Carey was more accustomed to restoration—after events like fires, floods, landslides—than remediation, which involves removing toxins from the ecosystem. It was one of the reasons—that and the remoteness of the site and the projected costs—that Fort Union had been closed for so long.

"That's what baffles me about your friends over there at the Colony," he said. "They've been exposing themselves to—whatever's here—for a long time. Have they got million-dollar filtration systems? Did they have a barge unload a few metric tons of fresh topsoil to grow their food in?"

I took a mouthful of coffee from the bottom of the cup to buy myself some time. I didn't know how much I should tell Carey, as much as I liked him.

"You can talk to them about it," I said. "Or, once I figure it all out, you can read the article. If I write one."

I spent the next couple of hours wandering around Fort Union —through the buildings, along the western shore of the island —taking pictures until my phone died, while Carey finished up some work. Then we walked back to the Colony together, for the harvest supper.

We talked most of the way, about where we had gone to school, where we had traveled, where we had lived, where we wanted to live. I told him about the situation with the cottage, my job, my finances. How I didn't think I could live in Seattle anymore. He talked about growing up in Bakersfield, where his dad worked for an oil company, and knowing he never wanted to live in California again. The sun was setting behind us, casting our shadows onto the path before us. It started to feel like a date, and we fell into an awkward quiet as we neared the last hill down to the Colony.

The chapel below was lit up, with lanterns lighting the path to its doors. A procession of people carried dishes from the fires on the bluff and the various kitchens in the cottages. We passed the fires, and Andrew handed us dishes to carry, too.

The entire chapel was rearranged, set up like a banquet hall, with the old bench pews turned alongside the tables. Beeswax and tallow candles burned in the windows, on the altar, along the lengths of tables. Katie was there, setting dishes on tables, counting to make sure they were evenly distributed. Someone was in the corner, playing an old upright piano, and voices filled the room — as they always do in churches, the chattering voices of the congregation reverberate and hum. The room radiated warmth.

Sister J. touched my arm. Her eyes flashed in the candlelight, full of tiny flames.

"I am so glad you're here," she said.

She took my arm and Carey's and led us to a table in the center of the room, seating us across from each other, near the head. The she slipped into the crowd and led others to their seats. Maggie entered, looking weary but dressed in a fancy blouse and flowy skirt, and sat near us.

"Maggie," I said, reaching a hand across the table to her.

She grasped it in her left and covered it with her right. Her hands were as soft as kid gloves, with delicate wrinkles and bones like stays, thin and strong.

"Lucie," she said, and smiled. "I'm so sorry I haven't seen more of you."

"This is my friend from the boat, Carey," I told her.

She released my hand and shook Carey's.

The places were filling quickly around us, Katie and Tuck, Elle and Jen, Maggie and others. Each table covered in dishes. Katie told us what everything was as everyone settled: the rabbit soup, crab chowder, salads, sauerkraut with dulse, bread and cheese and butter, sweet roasted squash custard, bottles of dandelion and elderberry wine. Carey looked calm but out of place in his uniform.

Sister stood at the head of our table and soon the room fell quiet. She nodded and smiled as she scanned the room, taking time over the faces of those gathered.

"Here we are," she began, "once again under a harvest moon, on our great green island. Among friends, new and old. All family. We gather to celebrate the work we have done, to give thanks for another year." She picked up a glass and held it aloft. We all did the same.

"Another year!" she called.

"Another year!" came the response.

We drank. I caught Carey's gaze over his glass.

There was a long pause while we set our glasses down.

Sister began again: "I saw my first shrike of the season this week. I was pulling garlic mustard from the potatoes at the field's edge. We here—"

Sister looked at me, then at Carey.

"—we here have come to know the shrike, who shows up in the fall. The migration. Thousands of birds gather and fly in the night, by some inner coordinates, never questioning, never asking *why?* Just following the call: north or south. They land in our trees at night, feast on our mosquitoes, our horseflies, or they pass us by, urged on by the call. You might hear their wing beats under the stars and wonder whose spirit has flown this island. Yet some of our winged friends spend the winter among us. The hardier ones"—laughter trickled through the group. "We welcome them, we accept them as our own for as long as they choose to stay. The shrike is one of these: a winter guest. The shrike has an unmistakable song: a cheerful trill, uplifting, like a ladder of light, when your hands are in the dirt. This morning I heard her song and I knew she was among us again. I listened to her for a good while, thinking of the work we do to survive and the songs we sing. Soon the shrike was done with her morning call, and I heard the smaller birds again—they bounced from branch to earth all around me, the sparrows diving to and fro, and the nuthatches in the trees. Then there was a thrashing in the brush beyond the field and the mewling call of the rufous-sided towhee, foraging in the undergrowth, her feet in the earth—as mine were—her head to the ground, as mine was, working for her food, toiling for sustenance. What a blessing, I thought, to find myself in this time and place, among the creatures—*one of* the creatures of this island, our island, this *Earth*."

Sister looked down at her hands.

"I worked on, prying out those garlic mustards root by root. After a while, there was another curious call from the towhee, and another thrashing in the brush, and a flock of sparrows scattered, lining up along the fence across the field, watching as a chase commenced in the bushes before me, the sounds of wings and a struggle in the leaves. Then all was quiet, and I heard the call of the shrike again. I couldn't spot her. Her soft gray crown and her black mask. I returned to my work; I listened. The bird chatter resumed. I gathered my tools and headed for breakfast. Coming back along the fence line, I looked for the shrike. I wanted to see her, the first of the season. I never found her. But

I did find *her* morning work: a rufous towhee fastened through the neck to a barb in the wire—"

The silence in the room deepened—so still I could feel my heart beating at my rib cage. Sister's voice deepened, her words coming slower, heavier.

"The shrike, of course, though her song lifts the soul at work, will also mimic the calls of her cousin birds, luring them to her table, darting from her hidden perch when the songbirds begin to feast. She strikes with her fierce beak, carries her prey to a thorny bush, or in this case a barbed wire, and she impales the creature and eats its flesh. She saves the remains, safely snagged above the ground, for her mate. In this way, she survives the winter among us. Of the rufous towhee, the sprightly grub-eater, the industrious nest-builder, we may say that she was un-suspecting, that when she heard the shrike mimic the towhee song, she did not hear the arrival of her own death. So why did I weep for the towhee? Released of its flesh, the soul flies. Why weep for the towhee? Why did I not rejoice with the shrike?"

Sister J. bowed her head. Others bowed or stared into the middle distance, solemn. Tuck still had that trace of a smile on his lips, his eyes moist—was he crying? Carey glanced at me; he seemed unnerved. I could see the sweat on his brow. He shifted in his seat and met my eyes again, holding my gaze this time. He seemed uncomfortable, from the parable of the shrike, maybe, or the closeness of the bodies around us.

Sister continued in a brighter tone, and I looked away from Carey.

"Ignorance is God's greatest gift to us," she said. "Ah, you would say, but we have learned so much on this earth that is of use, that sustains us, that sustains those who come after us. And yes, I concur! It is the ignorance of what is beyond this moment that I'm thinking of. We know only what has come before and what is now, but not what is to come, and that, *that* ignorance, it is a gift. And then there is all that we think we know, but which is yet to be further illuminated. The mysteries of the stars, the cells, the cosmic dust we came from and into which we will dissolve. What we don't know, what we are incapable of seeing, hearing, smelling, touching, and tasting—indeed what we see, hear, smell, touch, and taste but cannot comprehend—this is the gift that allows us to sleep at night, to dream, to love each other, to sow and reap, and to build, to bear—"

She stopped short and held back. Elle inhaled sharply next to me.

"—to bear the burdens, the losses," she continued. "We sleep at night because we don't allow ourselves to believe that the murderer does not sleep, she stalks us every moment, behind every shadow, under our fingernails, from the forest canopy, in the depths of the sea, out of cracks in the earth, between colliding atoms. We dream because what we have seen, heard, smelled, touched, and tasted has filled us up with life and there is no room: our bodies, these organisms we inhabit, cell by cell, spend every second of every day trying to make sense of this, *this*—"

She slapped her heart, opening her arms to the room, hands cupped around some weighty, invisible substance.

"Look at what we have built! Could ignorance build this? Could ignorance take this burnt, poisoned crust of land and make it green again, and make it live again? We have witnessed a resurrection! We are living a resurrection!"

Her voice lowered to a whisper, but it carried down the table and up to the rafters in the still space.

"And yet. And *yet*. Death waits. Death watches. Death sings from the branches while we work, lifts our unknowing souls, calls us to fly."

She bowed her head again, and the entire room seemed to exhale. Heads down or eyes closed, some tears, some blissful smiles. Sister lifted her head and signaled to Maggie and Katie, on either side of her. Everyone rose and joined hands around the tables. Maggie hummed the key and started to sing. Voices around the table joined in:

> Come thou fount of every blessing, tune my heart to sing
>   thy grace.
> Streams of mercy, never ceasing, call for songs of loudest
>   praise.
> Teach me some melodious sonnet, sung by flaming
>   tongues above,
> Praise the mount, I'm fixed upon it, mount of thy
>   unchanging love.

The singing was energetic and robust; full-throated, simple harmonies that were nothing like the dispassionate singing of the Masses of my childhood. I sang along with the melody, not sure of my place in the song, pausing to breathe when I couldn't remember the words, but compelled to sing by the tension rising in my chest that told me I would cry if I didn't let something out of my throat. Katie sang next to me in her raspy alto, eyes closed, her hand delicate in my sweating grip. Carey stood with his eyes closed and head bowed, not singing, his body upright as ever, and still as a tree, with a softness to the bend in his neck, the slope of his shoulders.

Everyone seemed to have a part, every note memorized.

Occasionally I could hear a particular voice, distinct from the rest, a higher harmony, a vibrato. At other times, certain phrases and notes—*prone to wander, Lord, I feel it, prone to leave the God I love*—then every voice seemed combined into one. Once or twice I suppressed a shiver—all of our bodies connected, the rhythm flowing through us, rising and falling in waves. I felt something move in me. It felt like joy and also like surrender.

When the song ended, the reverberation through the room remained and no one moved until it had passed, until we could plainly hear the waves again, the wind picking up outside. We held hands a moment longer, then released and sat. That sound of the congregation sitting, the shushing of all the clothing folding into limbs, the shuffling of feet.

We passed tureens of the mushroom stew around the table, and chunks of the bread, still warm, soft goat cheese with herbs, a salad of berries and greens, the rabbit stew, and bottles of wine. There was little conversation at first, just *here you go* and *thank you*, but the faces and bodies around were warm and glad. After we had taken our first bites, our first tastes of the briny stew, the bitter greens, the quiet lifted and there was conversation, laughter. The lines around Carey's eyes had not softened, but he held my gaze and smiled.

I listened to the wind, watched it blow clouds past the moon through a break in the trees. I tried to convince myself I didn't have to pee, that I could wait until morning. I had to be up early again, to meet Coombs at the dock. I had drunk too much elderberry wine and my head was heavy. I threw the blankets off and grabbed my sweater and slipped on my sandals.

The moon was bright, but there were more shadows than I

anticipated. Even with a flashlight, it was easy to become disoriented. I walked nervously down the path to the little vault
toilet between my cabin and the next two. It was still warm in
the loo, even with the breeze coming in an open window, flowered muslin curtain billowing. Frantic wind chimes. I heard
voices, too, but coming from the woods behind me. As I walked
back, ears tuned to the murmur of the voices, sometimes carried, sometimes obscured by the wind, I saw lights, deep in the
trees. I turned off the flashlight and I crept back to the cottage
door, watching them. Many lights, but not beams, more like the
flames of candles. Oil lamps?

On the walk back from the supper, Katie had told me they
had a ritual for the dying, that they gave them a tea of herbs and
mushrooms to help them on their way.

"On their way?" I had asked.

"To the lights," she had said.

"What does that mean?"

"Maybe you'll see, someday," she had said.

"Have you seen them?"

"We all have."

"How?"

"We open our minds to them." She had sighed, like she was
tired of my questions.

I watched the lights move between the trees, listened to the
occasional strand of voice. Were they performing a ritual out
there? I didn't want to let them out of my sight, but they flickered and vanished.

In the morning Katie woke me at dawn. She handed me a cup
of tea and a cloth napkin with some bread and butter wrapped
in it. She didn't speak but indicated with a silly pantomime that I

should eat before the boat so I wouldn't get sick. The water was always worse on an empty stomach.

We made it to the dock as Coombs was pulling in, Carey already waiting. He was unshaven, clothes more rumpled after his second night at Fort Union. Neither of us had showered in two days. I was looking forward to a hot shower and flushing toilet. Katie handed me a note on the dock and kissed my cheek. We pulled away and I watched her walk up the dock, getting smaller.

The note said, *I'll call you soon. xo, K.*

Ten

THE PALOUSE

SPOKANE, WASHINGTON
MAY 7, 2016

THE SISTERS KNOW I'm coming, but when I get to the Provincial House and tell them who I am, whom I have come to see, they tell me *Janet* needs to rest for the night. She's been given a sedative. I turn to leave—to find a motel closer to town. Maybe a bar. And the sister puts a hand on my arm.

"You are welcome to stay here." She's already leading me through the entry—polished brick floors that I think must be very dangerous for elderly nuns with canes and walkers. "We know you've traveled a long way, and Sister will be so glad to see you in the morning," she says, patting my arm, not letting go, so that I wonder who is supporting whom.

She's afraid of these floors, too, I think.

Though she looks younger than some of the others. They walk alone through the halls. All gray and silver and white-headed. Some mostly bald. A couple wear short blue wimples with rough cotton smocks. Old school, pre–Vatican II attire. Maybe they just like not having to brush their hair or choose from their three dowdy flowered dresses or blouse/elasticized poly skirt outfits for the day. They shuffle along to the chapel from all directions for evening prayers. There's a black box—like a giant mailbox—at the start of the drive to the Provincial

House, where people can leave their sorrows, their problems, for the sisters to pray on their behalf. But this is where the retired Sisters of the Holy Family go, when they can't physically be out living the Gospel in the world much anymore. Put out to pasture here, in this building on the Palouse above Spokane. Part convent, part senior center. Staffed entirely by other, slightly younger sisters.

I might get a little thrill out of those notes, if I were the sisters. Glimpses of life's dramas outside these walls.

We turn down a hallway, through swinging wooden doors, the polished brick giving way to linoleum, also polished to a gleam. The lights are low here, like in some high-end grocery stores, and I wonder if this is another trap, like the shiny floors, intended to steal a few minutes here and there from life by slowing a body down.

"What's your name?" I ask my guide.

"Oh, I'm Sister Rosemarie," she says, and then, face turned up to my ear, as if it's a secret, "But you can call me Sister Rosie."

"Okay," I say, and she nods and laughs like she knows something I don't know.

She leads me out a door and across a walkway lined with roses and a courtyard with a tall marble statue of the Blessed Mother, surrounded by flowers—and I realize that they would have celebrated May Day recently, crowning the Mary with flowers. I crowned Mary in the May Day Procession in high school, no longer a virgin myself (not that anyone knew). Down the path we come to a ranch-style house, set back in the trees, and Sister Rose releases my arm. I follow her inside, and she leads me down some stairs into a carpeted lower level that smells exactly like a church basement: dustless, vacuous.

"You can sleep here," Sister says, showing me a small furnished bedroom off a sitting room with windows that look out onto the forested hillside. There are crosses everywhere, made of straw and wood and brass and macramé. On every wall.

"Usually the visiting priests stay here," she tells me, "but there aren't any right now. Father Thomas comes up from the university for services these days." I look at the twin bed, made up neatly in a patchwork denim quilt like a little boy's room.

She shows me to a bathroom nearby, and there is a cross above the toilet. She opens a cabinet to show me a clutch of generic toothbrushes in cellophane wrappers and a tube of Aim.

"That's very kind," I say.

"Breakfast is at seven, after sunrise service. Please come. The sisters would love to meet a friend of Janet's."

"Has she had many visitors?" I ask.

Sister Rosie smiled and took my hand, squeezing it fiercely. "You're the only one, dear. And we're very glad you've come."

I'm lying in the bed the priests sleep in, in my underwear and one of Carey's undershirts. I took it out of the laundry bag before I left. He had worked all day in it, under his uniform—the unseasonably hot spring, early fire season on the way. He wore it at least two days ago. It's slightly rank, but soft.

I smell him and count the lithium pulse of my watch till I sleep.

In the dining room I say hello to every sister. This is the journalist in me: talk to everyone, make eye contact. I can't help it, anyway; they are either watching me as I go through the cafeteria line or they are blind. I am taller than the women in front of me, a head above their delicate, veiny skulls. Someday, I may be this old, my body shrunken, translucent.

There's a toast station and I wait with one of the sisters, my bread in one side of the toaster and her bread in the other. She doesn't know who I am or why I'm here. Her name is Sister Rosemary.

"Rosemary," I say. "There are so many 'roses' here."

"Yes, yes," she says with a dismissive wave. She is at least ninety years old.

"What year were you born, Sister?" I ask. I want to know if I'm right.

She doesn't blink an eye: "Nineteen twenty-two," she says. "And I still do the *New York Times* crossword every day."

She offers to butter my toast—I forgot to take a knife. I accept and watch as she slathers a tablespoon over four square inches of wheat bread.

I sit with Sister Rose and Sister Rosa, born in Mexico City, 1930. I want to keep them all straight, but I don't know how I'll do it, so I decide to call them all "Sister" no matter what. Like they did with Sister J. at the Colony, as if it were her given name. Soon we're joined by Sister Michael, who tells me she's a Kennedy.

"Really?" I say.

And she says: "It's not as glamorous as everyone thinks it is."

"Oh, no?" She tells me how many cousins there were, how many divorces, how many illegitimate children, how she was the last of four girls to wear the hand-me-down shoes. I nod and eat my eggs.

Sister Rosa asks me what I am doing with my life, like my own grandmother might, if I were sitting at her breakfast table on a bright spring morning. I tell her I'm living with a park ranger in the Oregon wilderness, writing about Sister J. and what she did on Marrow Island.

She burps behind a napkin and leans across the table. I prepare myself for a lecture on living in sin.

"We're not supposed to call her 'Sister' anymore," she says.

"Oh," I say. "Well, *Janet*, then."

Then she shakes her head. "I don't care what she did, she'll always be a Sister to me."

I think about telling her who I am. That Sister J. went to prison because of me. Or because of what I knew. Even now it feels tenuous—the case against her and all of them. But Sister Rose asks me, mouth full of oatmeal, what it's like living with a park ranger and whether he wears a uniform. And I tell them about Carey. Of course they love a man in uniform as much as —if not more than—other women.

Sister Rosie finds me at breakfast and tells me that Janet is awake and asking for me. They've told her that I'm here. And she seems very alert, very lucid, Sister Rosie says. I say goodbye to the sisters and listen to them talk about me as I walk my tray to the dish bins. They're hard of hearing, so they don't bother to whisper. They believe I'll marry the park ranger and have a baby. A little babe of the woods. It's the sort of nativity they can believe in, even if I can't.

Sister Rosie takes my arm, as before, and leads me across the polished entry again, through a different set of doors and into another wing. This one has a distinct nursing home smell, though it looks just like the other wings with its linoleum and crosses and a sort of absent-minded silence, as if it didn't occur to anyone to make a fuss, to make any noise at all.

"Janet wouldn't come at first," Sister Rosie tells me. "She wanted to stay in Walla Walla. The women there—in the prison

—they liked Janet, you know. It's not often they get somebody like Janet."

"A nun?"

"Oh, no. We're *sisters,* not nuns. Such a funny word. *Nun.* Like *nothing at all.* No, we're *sisters.* Nuns are cloistered. We live with the rest of you, believers and unbelievers alike. We don't just pray—we fight the good fight. We go to jail more than you'd think, and we die like soldiers, sometimes. Even so, Janet is an original. She was always . . . her own woman."

"Did you know her before?"

"I 'knew her when,' as they say. She was always asking questions. Always wanting to change people's ways. Even if it meant putting herself in the path of power . . ."

We stop at a door in the hallway, blinds down over a window to the side.

"Prepare yourself," she says. "She's very near the end."

As prepared as I think I am to see this woman—I practiced by picturing the mummified remains, the ones in South America that have been taken over by fungus as the climate has changed —I am not prepared. She's alive, but she doesn't look human. She looks like an insect, folded into the bed, yellow and desiccated.

The eyes don't shrink, but the flesh does, the body does what it can to keep the heart beating. It takes the meat first, the muscles and their coats of fat; collagen under the skin, in the lips, swallowed up by hungrier cells; the skin falls, shedding like generations of wallpaper. But the eyes—however well they actually *see*—are cartoonish orbs, accented by the bones of the brow that do not recede with the plump cheeks, but hang over the eyeballs like angry gargoyles, like architectural admonishments.

But I see her enormous eyes recognize me, and I cross the room.

"They call it 'the Inland Empire' out here," Janet says, stopping to swallow every several words. It's sharp, the swallowing. I can hear the esophagus creaking. She'll let me moisten her lips by holding a small paper cup of water to them, letting the water drip over them, but she won't drink. "The mountains, the rivers, the Palouse, all the way down to the Columbia. It doesn't feel right. Using a word like *empire* in this day and age. As if we could ever own any of this. It owns us." Speaking exhausts her, but for the moment, she wants to get out whatever comes into her head. I sit next to her bed holding her hand, careful of the portacath at the top of her wrist.

"It's too quiet here; I miss the sea," she says, and falls asleep.

They're giving her regular morphine injections for pain now, and she sleeps intermittently. I walk around. There's nothing of Janet's in the room, but then she didn't have any possessions to begin with. I thought there might be books, but she can't read anymore. A picture of the island, maybe. If ever she felt ownership for anything, it was Marrow Island. Her island. A picture of Maggie wouldn't have surprised me, but she would probably hide it, keep it close to her body. Maggie is still in prison.

I don't want to leave the room, in case she wakes, but I'm getting a headache from the smell—like isopropyl alcohol and feet. I step out into the hall to ask the sister at the nurses' station whether I can open the windows. She says she doesn't see why not and follows me back into the room. I crank the windows open, and the smell of the rose garden comes wafting in. The sister places a hand on Janet's wrist to feel her heart rate, and after a moment she leans down and tells her, in a voice so

soft I can barely hear, that it's time to change her "trousers."
This sister is younger than the others — maybe my age, maybe
younger — and she has a Spanish accent; her name is Monica. Janet grunts and looks confused to see both of us.

"Your friend Lucie is here to help us," she tells Janet, and she
continues to speak softly, telling her that we'll be done soon and
she can rest again or eat, if she's hungry.

Sister Monica reaches into a drawer under the bed and pulls
out two purple latex gloves for me. I put them on while she
gathers the supplies from below and pulls a trashcan near. She
pulls down the blankets and carefully pulls up Janet's gown and
unfastens the diaper, folding it down on itself. Watery yellow
stools leak out onto the bed pad, and I hold my breath auto-
matically, but the smell isn't overwhelming. It's sour, milky, almost like a baby's. Janet has been refusing solid food for a few
days. Sister Monica asks me to hug Janet to me and rock her to
her side. She passes gas with the shift of body, but Sister Monica
doesn't move away or make a face. She keeps working, steadily,
gently. She disposes of the soiled diaper and pad quickly and
cleans Janet's backside while I cradle her upper body, her breath
rattling out into my neck, sour and cold, my breasts pressed into
the crater of her chest. I feel each of her ribs with every inhale,
the vibrations in her trachea.

"Lucie will lower you back to the bed now," Sister Monica
says, and I do. "And now we clean the front."

Janet closes her eyes as I slip my arms from under her shoulders. Sister Monica carefully wipes the pale, wiry hair clinging
to the mons pubis, ashen pink labia pressed out, the crevasse
below the hipbone, the inner thighs. I watch, listening to Sister Monica's voice, the romantic tilt of her accent on odd syllables. I roll Janet again, to put on clean "trousers," and when

we're done, I release her to the bed and pull her gown back over her knobby bird legs, pull her blankets back up, lift her arms so that they can rest atop the bedding. Sister Monica offers me the trashcan for my gloves, and when I turn back to the bed, Janet is staring at me.

"Have you been here the whole time?" she asks.

I look to Sister Monica, who just nods and smiles as if this is usual.

"I just got here," I say. "How do you feel?"

"Has there been an earthquake?"

"I don't think so."

"Do you think they'll remember to let me out when it happens?"

"I think so," I say. I'm not sure what she means. Sister Monica has left us, and I'm not sure what I'm supposed to do.

"I hate it here." She has a look of disgust I've never seen on her before. On the island, she looked unflappable, joyous. In court she looked beatific and calm.

"I like it all right," I say.

"You would," she says, but her look has softened.

"Sister—," I say, "*Janet,* why did you ask me to come? Why did you want me?"

She closes her eyes and sighs. There's such a long pause I think she has fallen asleep again.

"Do you know who I am, Sister?" I touch her shoulder.

"I'm not brain-dead."

"If you're going to treat me like this, I'll just go."

"Go back to the woods. Go hide."

"Okay." I don't move. I'm still holding her hand.

We sit in silence for some time. Sister Monica brings one tray of food for Janet and returns a few minutes later with a tray for me. The smell of cream of mushroom soup fills the room. We don't eat.

"It'll seem impossible for most of your life," she says finally.

"What will?"

"Not running to hide."

She slips in and out of consciousness all day. I leave her side only to use the toilet. After I send the cold, congealed mushroom soup away, uneaten, they send cold, congealed chocolate pudding. Janet won't eat or drink, so I eat both dishes and ask Sister Monica for some coffee. My insides feel raw from the sugar and coffee, but I think about my peanut butter–cereal balls and beer by Cougar Lake and decided I've prepared my body for this kind of fast.

When she talks, it's in snapshots of her life, some names and places I don't know, some I do, all on a slow loop, certain words and phrases stressed for reasons I can't decipher. When she talks about the Colony, it's mostly about Maggie. Maggie was the one who was there for the dying. At the end, she was the midwife who ushered the living out of the world. But there's more to it for Janet. I suspect there was only one bed in their cottage, and in the end they were separated; sent to different facilities.

"Is Maggie getting some rest?" she asks.

I wonder what I am supposed to say to a dying woman. Is this a time to play along with the delusion, or is that condescending? Is the lie worse? Will she realize that Maggie can't be here? I think about what it might feel like, to be surrounded by women, but not the one woman you believed would be by your side when you went.

"Yes," I say. "She went for a walk. And she's having some tea and some of that cake with the honey and dried berries."

She smiles.

"Good woman. It's good of you to stay, Kate," she says.

My heart catches in my throat; I haven't heard about Kate since the sentencing, and even then, it wasn't from her. She didn't write me. My mom called to give me the news.

"Of course, Sister. I'm glad I could be here with you."

"I thought you were gone for good."

"You did?"

I watch her eyes focus on me—she's struggling to make sense of something—and I wonder if I'll be caught in the lie.

"You shouldn't have run off like that. They'll be looking for you all over those islands."

"Why would they do that, Sister?" Kate's in Bellingham with her parents: house arrest; community service. Tuck is serving fifteen to life.

"Because you told me in your letter."

"I don't remember what I wrote."

She groans and closes her eyes.

"You wanted to die."

"That was horrible of me. I'm so sorry if I gave you a scare."

She looks more alert again, suddenly. Her eyes clear and I see Sister J. in them for a moment.

"Lucie," she says, louder. In her fatherly voice from the island, like she's about to deliver a sermon.

"Yes, Sister."

"I knew you'd come."

"I'm here." I sigh. This loop. This loop again.

"Kate is gone; she's long gone," she says. "She was going to bring me what I needed. She was going to tell them her name was Lucie, so they wouldn't know."

I wait for her to say more. She's staring me down. I see her grasping at thoughts, but unable to speak them.

"She's not with her parents?"

She shakes her head.

"Did someone tell you she was missing?"

A nod.

"How long ago?"

Nothing.

"You don't remember how long?"

She squeezes my hand. She opens her eyes, and I can see she's in pain. It's been painful, remembering. Maybe she remembered everything at once—the whole picture of where she is and why, and what is left.

I pull the tin of mushrooms from my pocket and open it.

"I have something for you, Sister."

She opens her eyes and tries to focus on what I'm holding in my hands. She lifts her head. She can't focus her glassy stare, but she knows what they are. She nods. Her head falls back to the pillow.

She's bereaved and she's in pain. She's as ready to leave this world as anyone I've ever seen. I hadn't thought about how I would give them to her. She can't chew them—she might choke if I just put one in her mouth. What might Maggie have done at the Colony with a patient who couldn't eat, couldn't swallow a pill? She reaches a mantis arm toward me, and I take her hand. I know what I need to do. I put them in my mouth and chew. I take a breath, close my eyes, and lean down to kiss her sunken mouth.

Sister Rosie brings me an extra blanket and some tea around 10 p.m. One sister at a time comes to sit at the end of the bed to pray, silently. Only the occasional rustle of cloth or mouth-breathing or jangle of the rosary breaks the silence. Janet stopped making any vocalizations some time ago, after the kiss, when the room lit up so bright I couldn't stand it. Enough of the psychedelics had entered my bloodstream from my saliva that I was having a mild trip of my own. I watched her body glowing and shaking under the sheet, then she was calm. She was so hot, a fever of burning off what was left of her life. Janet's eyes never open, but I speak softly in her ear. "You're on your way, Sister. Do you feel it? Is this what you wanted?"

At some point I rest my head beside Janet's and hold her hand, her arm laying cold against the inside of my arm on the sheet. I think of Maggie, asleep at the women's penitentiary, sending my thoughts to her like beams of light, so that she can please, *please*, be with Janet in the end. I watch her chest rise and fall by the millimeter, every ten seconds, then every twenty, then the quietest fireworks I've ever seen and my head is on fire.

Early in the morning, I wake to Sister Monica's hand on my shoulder. The priest has come for Janet's last rites. I stand aside while he anoints her forehead, her lips, and she lies still as a saint. He speaks to her, quietly, right in her ear, but she says nothing. I want to tell him she's already gone, that I saw what was left of her escape hours ago. Sister Rosie takes my hand and strokes it gently, awkwardly. When Father Peter has finished, the sisters file out of the room. Sister Rosie kisses my hand and says, "Bless you, child." I wonder if any of them will know what I've done. I'm still blinking away the shock. She guides me to my chair at Janet's side again. Her fingers have curled. I pick up her hand; it feels impermanent as a flower.

Eleven

THE ISLANDS

———

ORWELL ISLAND, WASHINGTON
OCTOBER 13, 2014

CAREY AND I didn't talk much on the crossing. I was holding fast to my cup of Oswego tea, riding the waves of seasickness like it was my only job. Without the energy to fight it, I decided to give myself to the feeling, to move with it, instead of fighting it. I watched Orwell and fixed my gaze on it, letting myself drift there on the sea welling up inside me.

On the dock, Carey asked if he could buy me a cup of coffee. We agreed to meet at the Nootka Rose, near the ferry terminal. In my car, the first thing I did was check my voicemail. There were two messages, both from Chris Lelehalt.

The first explained that my neighbor, Mr. Swenson, couldn't be reached and didn't appear to have been admitted to any nearby hospitals. His family had been contacted.

The second said that his family had been reached and was unaware of Mr. Swenson's location. They wondered if I might come in to make an official statement.

I thought back to what I had seen at Rookwood: the windows, the lamps, the suitcase, his glasses and medications. I tried to tell myself that there could be a logical explanation—but I couldn't find one. I couldn't remember if I had mentioned the red car under tarpaulins in the carriage house to Chris—

had they checked it? I wasn't sure I wanted to stay at the cottage by myself.

Carey was sitting at a table by the window at the Nootka Rose. I had spent many Saturday mornings eating pancakes with my dad at the same table. I always chose it for its view. When the waitress came, I ordered a full breakfast along with my coffee. Carey gave me an appraising look and did the same.

"My neighbor is missing," I said to him, and told him about the lamp in the window, the scene at Rookwood.

"That's troubling," he said.

"I'm not sure what to do. It's unsettling, staying out there alone."

I wanted to tell him the rest—about the Swensons' own-ership of the Colony, and how Jacob's disappearance would put their tenancy, and all their work, in jeopardy. The more I thought about it, the more it seemed likely that once the fam-ily knew what was going on out there—the remediation had increased the habitability and possibility for development—they would be evicted. But I still wasn't sure if Carey could be trusted—if he told the wrong person in the government bu-reaucracy, they could use the information to get them evicted, too.

Our food came, and I changed the subject. We talked about Marrow, the meal the night before—his only real experience of the Colony.

"It's interesting to me that they've given themselves to this environmental effort," Carey said, "with such a religious bent to it."

"You mean Sister's sermon?"

"Yeah, I mean, I've seen some earth-worshippers, hippies,

Wiccans out gathering herbs during the new moon—but I don't think I've ever seen a group like this. I mean—they're Christian, right? Sister J. is Catholic?"

"She was a Catholic sister, but she left the order. The Sisters of the Holy Family. They were the sisters who ran my high school. They're pretty progressive, but Sister's activism didn't go over well with the archbishop. I think she was about to be excommunicated."

"Well, it was a new one for me. What was your impression, after spending some time with them?"

I had been thinking about it, through the night and on the boat from Marrow to Orwell. Sorting through my feelings for Katie, her marriage, the devotion they all seemed to show Sister J. and her mission. And Marrow Island itself: a graveyard. It would always be a graveyard. And the Colony—Sister J.'s mission—it was a kind of salve to a wound that never healed. The resurrection Sister talked about didn't feel real to me—using mushrooms to remediate the soil was out there, but it was still biology, science—there was no promise of Heaven in that. But it did make me feel *something*. Hope, maybe. That the event that killed my father wouldn't be a footnote in the history of environmental science, but the beginning of a new field of research.

Carey was waiting for me to say something, watching me sort through these thoughts.

"I think they're brave," I said, finally. "I think that they're doing something no one else would dare to do, and it's this sense of . . . spiritual obligation that compels them to do it."

Carey's eyes narrowed. He knew I wasn't telling him the whole story. I waited for him to ask me what I knew, but he didn't. He was waiting for me to tell him, so I changed the subject.

"I'm thinking of living out here for a while," I told him.

"Oh?"

"I can write from here, and I can't really afford my apartment in Seattle anymore."

He asked more about the cottage, about Orwell Island. The more we talked, the more I liked him. There was something steady about him, an easy, thoughtful manner that told me he didn't react rashly to anything. I needed that kind of energy; I craved it. My dad had that energy. At his wake, his people praised him for being level-headed, trustworthy. He was the kind of guy who didn't run for help in an emergency, but examined the problem and stuck around to fix it himself. They said this is probably what got him killed. He probably died trying to put the fires out.

As soon as I made this connection—that Carey reminded me of what I remembered of my dad, what I missed about him—I felt my pulse quicken. I was conscious that I hadn't showered in two days, had only brushed my unwashed hair back into a ponytail. I replayed the things I was saying, asking myself if they were true, if they were interesting. Carey was looking for a more permanent place to stay for the duration of the assessment at Fort Union. If the park reopened, he would likely stay on as the park's ranger. The idea of staying at the cottage for a few weeks —even a few months—seemed like a real possibility, if he was going to be around. I tried to shut these thoughts down—the last thing I needed was a crush—but once I acknowledged the attraction, I couldn't ignore it. I hadn't been kissed in months, let alone touched with any romantic intention. Being around Katie again, remembering that first taste of desire—that charge of something new, of being on the brink of something—I wanted that again. I felt like I deserved it, as a reward for coming home again, finally, for being an adult and facing my past.

Before the meal was over, I had invited him to dinner at the cottage sometime.

The receptionist-dispatcher at the front desk of the sheriff's office told me I could "go get a beer" if I wanted, and she'd send Deputy Lelehalt over when he returned.

"It's eleven o'clock in the morning," I noted.

"Or coffee, whatever," she said. "He gets lunch at the tavern every day. He'll show up."

I had a bloody mary instead and made notes on the story that I wasn't writing—that I wouldn't write unless Katie told me I could—and made a list of questions: about squatters' rights, about verbal agreements, about property trusts, and about the Swenson Trust in particular. Assuming Jacob Swenson *had* gone off the deep end and someone else from his family was to take over, there had to be some sort of legal standing for the Colony. Laws of adverse possession might apply, considering the amount of time and capital the Colony had invested in Marrow —these were laws I was vaguely familiar with from reporting on the guerrilla gardeners: community gardens that sprung up on disused property had a greater chance of survival the longer they were in use by the community without the title holder's intervention. Combine that with the verbal agreement Jacob Swenson had come to—there had to be some kind of documentation, somewhere, in correspondence between Julia and Sister J., maybe? I might be able to make the case for the Colony in the right story.

The only aspect that gave me pause was the mushrooms— psilocybin was a Schedule I drug, and the fruits of the mycelium were illegal to cultivate and possess. But they grew wild all over the Northwest, and their presence might be glossed over or explained away, so long as they weren't harvesting them.

Chris Lelehalt joined me at the bar at noon and ordered a burger to go and an iced tea.

"Do you want me to come back to the station to give my statement?"

"Sure." He seemed to have something on his mind.

"Can you tell me anything? His family has no idea where he is? Did he check himself into a hospital or something?"

"Why do you ask that?"

"I've heard some things about his mental health — you know how people talk."

He nodded.

"No, he's not at any hospital nearby. Anacortes, Bellingham, Port Townsend. We even tried Everett and Mount Vernon, down to Seattle. And his car's been parked in the garage for at least a week, probably longer. He's a missing person."

"Do you have any leads at all?"

"Are you asking as a concerned neighbor or as a reporter?"

"A neighbor." I didn't hesitate but glanced down at my notes. I didn't think he had seen them. He smirked.

"I'm just kidding. We don't really have any leads, just a history of mental illness and alcohol addiction. Crashed his car into a ditch a few years back — it's all public record or common knowledge. Didn't have any enemies, and we don't have any witnesses to anything strange. Except you."

"I don't have much to tell," I said, waiting for him to ask me about my trip to Marrow. If Jacob's alcoholism was common knowledge, it seemed like his relationship with the Colony would be, as well. "I've never even met him, that I can remember. Maybe as a kid?"

"If you hadn't trespassed, we still wouldn't know he's missing."

"I didn't trespass."

He chuckled. "We'll leave that part out of the report. But you've got nerve, checking up on a neighbor you've never met, after you've been back in town for, what? Twenty-four hours."

"Something like that." He was angling for something.

"Well, somebody from his family will be out if he doesn't turn up soon. You might have a neighbor again before long."

"Do you think he'll show up?"

"I don't like to speculate."

"What are you doing to find him?"

"Couple of us spent the day walking the woods around the property and the shoreline around there. Aren't a lot of places to go on Orwell, so next step is the other islands. We're getting his picture out to law enforcement, the hotels, the ferry terminals, the Coast Guard, the media. After that . . . there's a lot of water out there."

He watched my expression casually, glancing at me, but never looking at me straight on, catching glimpses of me in the mirror behind the liquor bottles on the other side of the bar.

"You think you'll be headed back to Marrow anytime soon?"

I shook my head, looked him in the eye and held it, dared him to ask me something about the Colony. "I don't know. I have some things I need to work on at the cottage."

He looked down at his hands.

"Are you thinking of selling the place? Moving back?"

"I'm considering all the options."

The waitress brought him a paper plate covered in foil. He

finished off his drink and said, "Come on back to the station anytime to give your statement. I'll just be having lunch." I told him I'd be over when I finished my drink.

I wrote my account of trespassing at Rookwood in about fifteen minutes. When I was done, Chris read through it and asked if there was anything else I wanted to add. I said no.

"It can be anything—not just what you saw at the house. If you've heard anything, seen anything else that might pertain to the case."

My cheeks reddened slightly, and I forced myself to smile warmly at him. "Gotcha. I think that's all I've got."

"You can add to your statement later, if anything else occurs to you."

"Okay, thanks." I rose to leave.

"Oh, Lucie, one more thing." I turned around; he wore a goofy, sheepish grin that made him look ten years younger. "My mom asked after yours. When you talk to her, tell her Deb says 'hi.'"

"Of course, I will."

While my laundry was going at the Wash-O-Mat, I sat in the coffee shop with my laptop. I wanted to make sense of what I knew about Jacob Swenson and about the Colony. Katie had said that Tuck sometimes helped around Rookwood. Sister J. had known Julia. Maggie was a nurse—she may have tried to help Jacob. Then there was Katie, who had been in Rookwood often, when we were girls. I wasn't sure about other members of the Colony, but I listed as many of them as I could. Tuck was at the top. But I didn't know his full name. Basic search results for "Tuck + Marrow Colony," and "Tuck + Orwell Island" brought up no matches. I tried the AP News Archive. I worked my way through different facts I knew about him. He had gone to UC Berkeley. He had protested divestment in fossil fuels. He had worked for Greenpeace. I tried "Tucker." And that got me a piece from an article from thirteen years ago about activists arrested for blocking passage of an oil rig headed for the Gulf of Mexico. "Alex James Tucker, 22" was one of the activists arrested in the protest. There wasn't a picture, so I did more searches under that name. The first hit was an article about an arson at a logging camp in northern California. I scanned the article—the crime had caused millions in damages to logging equipment and a truck driver had nearly burned alive while he slept in his cab. The crime was attributed to the Earth Liberation Front. A raid on a house in Arcata had led to warrants for three young men. "Alex James Tucker, 24," was the only man not in custody. There was a mugshot from his previous arrest: a clean-shaven, young white guy in a polo shirt, more frat boy than salt of the earth; but the self-righteous pride in his blue eyes was the same. It was Tuck.

The warrant had been issued ten years before. Tuck had been hiding from the FBI for the last ten years.

I called the Colony's number and left a message.

"Katie, it's Luce. I need you to call me as soon as you get this. Please. It's important."

In my time reporting on radical environmentalists, I had heard stories of activists targeted as domestic terrorists, phones tapped by the FBI, houses full of sleeping families raided, and beloved family dogs shot. I had also heard stories of firebombs at car dealerships, sabotage on forest roads, people chaining their necks to logging trucks. I tended to give the protesters the benefit of the doubt. The government did seem quick to label the burning of SUVs in Springfield, Oregon, as terrorism, while anti-government nuts who shoot at park rangers and set tripwires on public lands are called "militiamen," like they were good old boys. But if Tuck had been hiding out on Marrow for this long, whether he was guilty or not—what might he do if Jacob found out he was wanted? What would happen to the Colony if Tuck was discovered?

That night I tried to think about Carey, soothing my mind with fantasies of a lover. It had been so long since I had a body to attach my longing to. I wanted to feel something other than distress for Katie, for the story I couldn't write, if it revealed what I knew about her husband.

If Jacob had become as paranoid as Katie said, he might have fled the house in panic, afraid of some imagined threat. He might be living in the woods, in one of the smaller outbuildings on the estate—the potting shed, the old kiln. There were lots of places to hide from two deputies stomping through the underbrush. He might be watching me, waiting for me to leave to come out of hiding. He could be sneaking back into the house for food, for water . . . It sounded far-fetched. And with so much at stake for the Colony, why hadn't they tried harder to get help for him? Had he really deteriorated so quickly? If he had found out about Tuck, an already-paranoid person might do something drastic, knowing there was a liar in his house.

The doors were locked, my phone by my side.

Katie would call. She would call me. And if she didn't call, I would drive to Coombs's house at dawn and ask him to take me back to Marrow.

Twelve

THE ISLANDS

———————

MARROW ISLAND, WASHINGTON
OCTOBER 14, 2014

THEY WERE CARRYING the body to the woods when I came over the hill. It was wrapped in a bolt of unbleached muslin, on a makeshift stretcher—two long poles of windfall spruce or cedar and a tarpaulin slung between. Six of the youngest and strongest carried it; among them I could see Elle and Tuck. Most of them didn't see me. Those who did looked confused, probably unsure whether Katie had been in touch or whether Sister J. had invited me back. They made quick eye contact or nodded, but didn't say anything.

I hung back, following at a distance. The entire Colony processed through the fields, through the orchard, beyond the fence, into a wooded area I hadn't investigated before. It was overcast, several layers of cold clouds soaking up with light. I watched one colonist after another disappear into the shadows of trees ahead of me, walking on after them, over a well-worn path, marked with cairns of river stones large and small. The stones glowed in the low light, against the brown and green of the forest floor. The path let out onto a narrow dirt road lined with rhododendrons and white birch, then a wide clearing that opened onto a bluff and the sea.

Everyone gathered, leaving space between one another,

some near and some far, from the place they had set the body down in the earth. As I approached, I could see a rough outline in the dirt from one edge of the clearing to the other, marking a rectangular field, and I realized that this had been the site of a house destroyed in the quake. This field was the foundation; I was standing at what was once the front door. The green expanse stretching off to the bluff, the yard; the dirt road, a dead end.

There were plots all over, hidden in the weeds, but marked by small wooden carvings and driftwood sculptures. I counted nine, in various stages of heap and sink, the soil settled over some of the plots completely. And everywhere, mushrooms. Small, black caps like umbrellas beaten in the wind, similar to the *Psilocybe* Tuck had shown me before. Some sprouted at the edges of the graves, others in clusters over the heart.

Sister stood at the head of the grave. I kept to the back but crept around to the other side so that I could see better. The body was still covered with the shroud. They lowered it gently into an oblong hole no more than three feet deep, on a bed of sawdust. Sister nodded, and Elle and Maggie pulled the shroud from the body. She was completely naked, the woman, gaunt and pale, skin dull like putty, eyes bulging under the lids, hands resting over her heart. Her white hair had been braided with flowers. She looked ancient, holy. We gazed at her silently for several minutes. Then, one or two at a time, people approached the grave, closed their eyes, and released bundles of flowers and shells and lichen over her. I felt my throat tighten. There were baskets of offerings. They tossed them over the body until she was covered almost completely. No one spoke, not even Sister. Only the tokens placed lovingly around her, the prayer was the act itself. Then each bowed a head to the dead woman. There was no song, no prayer. Then Elle and Tuck and the other bearers shoveled bark and soil into the grave, and after that laid branches and stones around the edges. The rest stood quietly, heads bowed or eyes closed, hands on hearts, until they had finished. Eventually, one by one, the colonists peeled off and began the walk back.

I tried to shrink into the trees, but Katie saw me. Tuck looked up and followed her gaze. He looked weary, the hollows of his eyes almost bruised; he had been crying. He kissed Katie on the temple and followed the others back. I felt a pang of remorse for imagining the things I had about him, or for knowing what I knew about him. I watched them go and approached the grave. Katie and I stood on opposite sides.

When the last person had disappeared into the trees, I spoke. "Will you talk to me here?"

"Yes," she said.

She stared at the grave. "You should have waited for me to call."

"I'm sorry. I didn't know."

I walked over to her, to see her face. I wanted her to see that I meant it—that I hadn't come to intrude.

"This is Sarah?" I asked.

"She died night before last."

"That was the night of the harvest supper," I said.

Katie nodded.

"You've done this before." I looked around at the other graves. "Others have died here?"

"You know people have died here, Luce," she scoffed. She turned away from Sarah's grave and wandered the plots.

"Of course I do." I said it softly, baffled by her tone, by the viciousness. "I meant at the Colony. This is—it's shocking, Katie, to come across a funeral procession like this. And a burial ground; this is like a pioneer cemetery — is this even legal? Is this part of Sister's mission?" I followed her across the plots, careful not to walk over any of the graves.

"People die everywhere, all the time," she said. "Death isn't part of the mission; it's part of life. We found a way to deal with it — a safe, humane, natural way. It may not be legal, but it's what they wanted — to return to the earth, to continue to be part of the island, not pumped full of chemicals and artificially preserved."

She stared at her feet. We were standing at what would have been the back of the house, in the west corner.

A bedroom, I thought. We're standing in the bedroom. This is where the window would have been, looking out at the sea.

I stood there and watched the clouds darken behind Waldron Island, until I noticed that Katie was still staring at our feet. I looked down. At first I saw nothing but milkweed and Queen Anne's lace, then I made out the indentation in the earth, the small black mushrooms pushing up at the edges, the tiny cairn, nearly swallowed by the grasses. But this one was so much smaller than the rest; it was the length of a shoebox. There was another to my left, only slightly longer. I searched the grass to the right, turned around to look behind us. This entire corner of the plot was marked with small graves. Some of them looked very old; only their cairns stood out.

"Oh my god, Katie."

She wept and said nothing.

"Are these graves?" I started to count them but stopped myself. "Katie, what the hell? Are these animals? Tell me they're animals."

Nothing. Silence. She held her breath and wouldn't look at me.

"If they're not animals . . . ?" I was shaking.

"They're babies."

I let this thought settle, the jaded journalist in me sorting through all the plausible reasons why they might have so many dead babies on Marrow.

"How many are there?"

"Six. This is Sucia. She was the last one. Her heart stopped beating at six months' gestation. Her mother carried her for three months after that and delivered her dead."

"Who's her mother?"

"Me. She was mine." She wasn't crying anymore, but there was a distance in her eyes, her body and her mind were on different islands.

"Jesus, Katie, why didn't you tell me? When did this happen?"

"In the spring, right before I wrote you."

I looked at her baggy overalls and sweater. The way she had grown into a woman's body since I'd seen her last.

"We were hopeful; conditions had improved so much. But all the early exposure must have built up. Ten years here, plus living on Orwell for the years after the quake—all the dispersants that washed ashore, you remember?" She looked at me again and I nodded. Her voice was low, firm. "The early exposure was the worst, before the remediation. Maggie was really careful about charting cycles. After a year or so, periods were irregular among almost all the women. Skipping months or bleeding every other week a little bit. Everyone was supposed to be practicing birth control, but accidents happened. Miscarriages are common everywhere, so it didn't alarm anyone for some time. Maggie has herbal recipes for abortions, too. Some chose to go that route. But when the babies started dying in the womb or coming too soon—there weren't that many, but enough—they knew. They knew." She squatted and plucked the mushrooms from the grave. Put them in a small basket she'd carried shells in, for Sarah's grave. She crawled around on her knees, plucking the mature mushrooms from all the graves.

I got down on my knees to help her. Most of the graves had the small, wavy-capped brown mushrooms, but others, the older ones, had only a few shaggy-topped white and brown fruits. I gathered as many as I could hold, then crawled over to Katie and added them to her basket.

"What are these for?" I asked.

"Medicine," she said, not looking up. "At the end of life, they help with pain."

She stopped, sat on her butt, and stared at Sarah's grave. I joined her.

"Sarah had cancer?"

"Yes."

"Does Sister have cancer?"

She nodded.

"This is fucked up, Katie."

"You have no right to judge," she said, shaking her head calmly. "No one knows when or how they'll die—no matter what choices they make. The Big One could wipe us out tomorrow, thousands of us at once. We're killing ourselves slowly with carbon emissions, melting glaciers. At least we want to do something with the time we've got."

"But you've been selling honey from your bees, milk from your goats, eggs from your chickens. Do the people buying these things know the risks they're taking?"

"We only started doing that recently. The water and soil samples for the last few years have shown levels of heavy metal contamination better than soil in sample gardens off the island.

Water from the wells has come up clean, again and again in the last two years. Cleaner than water you drink in Seattle. It's working. It worked."

"So you were crying because the experiment worked and you have *no* regrets?"

She picked up her basket and stood up.

"Just because I have no regrets doesn't mean I can't grieve what we've lost and what we're losing."

She was standing over me, crying again. I reached a hand out to hers, but she wouldn't hold it. She shook it off, wiped her nose with her sleeve.

"Katie, I don't know what to do with all this."

"What do you mean?"

"I mean, I came here." I stopped, my fingers digging into the dirt and grass. "I thought I could write about this place and find some way to be okay with it — with what happened here."

"And what, Lucie? What? Now you can't write your stirring memoir? Your redemption in the wilderness piece? Did we fuck that up for you?"

I saw in her eyes a Katie I had known before — one I didn't like to remember. There was pity and disgust. And fear. This was the Katie who would say anything to hurt me, to see how much she could say to me before I walked away. This was the Katie who had looked me in the eye when we were eighteen and told me that she had never loved me the way I loved her, that she had only been practicing with me.

"I know something about Tuck," I said.

She was silent for a moment.

"What do you mean?"

"I know that his name is Alex James Tucker."

She stared down at me, bleary-eyed.

"Okay," she said. "What are you trying to say?"

I found it hard to believe that in a place with so many secrets, she wasn't also in on this one.

"I'm saying I know who he is. And I think you knew I would find out, eventually."

She shook her head. "You don't know anything. He's not the man they say he is. He didn't hurt anyone. They were set up."

"I get it, Katie. The government has it in for radical environmentalists — you don't have to tell me."

"You won't say anything."

"There are too many secrets here, Katie. The Colony has been operating under the radar for a long time. If you know what happened to Jacob Swenson, you need to tell me. They're looking for him, and it won't be long before they come asking you questions."

"You're sitting there by my child's grave, accusing me of keeping secrets? Killing our landlord?"

I looked down at my hands. I was still holding one of the mushrooms, which had turned blue under the pressure of my fingers.

"Where is he? What happened to him?"

"We didn't do anything, Lucie. We have no reason to hurt him."

I stood up.

"I can't unknow any of this, Katie. I don't know how to help you or the Colony. I'm just worried about you — you can't stay here." I gestured to Sucia's grave.

She turned abruptly and started walking between the graves back to the path. I followed.

"Katie, please," I called after her.

She walked faster.

"I'm sorry." I was crying. I would've said anything to stop hurting her. "I won't say anything." I knew I was lying when I said it.

She stopped in her tracks but didn't face me. She let me catch up to her.

"I love you," I said.

She had stopped crying. She took my hand and started walking.

"I love you, too."

We were both lying.

Tuck was sitting on the steps of their cottage, waiting. When she saw him, Katie looked back at me, her face a calm veil. She dropped my hand and adjusted her basket. He waved as we came closer, stood up to hug Katie. He didn't look angry, just grim. He didn't seem like the violent type. I was willing to believe that he had been young and stupid, involved in a direct action campaign gone awry, and that he hadn't intended for anyone to get hurt.

Katie would tell him, of course.

"I'm so sorry for your loss," I told him, holding out my hand. Katie pulled away from him.

"We appreciate that," he said, and pulled me in for a hug. His affection — if that's what this was — was disorienting.

"Sister wanted me to ask you to have tea with her," he told me. "She's waiting for you in her cottage."

I wanted to be alone for a few minutes, to sort my thoughts. Part of my brain was trying to find a way out of knowing what I knew; the other wanted to try to get a cell signal and call Carey. But I didn't know what I'd tell him. That there had been a funeral? That they had a burial ground? It was unnerving, yes, but

I didn't actually know if it was illegal. They were skirting the
county coroner and avoiding the scrutiny that would no doubt
come their way if a medical professional autopsied their dead.
There were probably regulations on where cemeteries could
be, and how bodies had to be prepared for interment. When
I thought about it, their method made more sense to me than
embalming or cremation: let the mushrooms do their work and
turn the bodies into dirt.

I just wanted to hear the sane, clear voice of someone who
wasn't drinking the Marrow Colony tea. I checked my phone. It
was still charged, but I had no signal.

Sister's cottage was nearest the chapel. It was easily the oldest
structure still standing on the island. The front door was open so
I stepped inside. I could hear rattling in the kitchen and found Sister loading a tray with three cups and a teapot. She was stronger
than her frame suggested, but I offered to take it from her when
she turned around, and she passed it to me with a gracious smile.

"That's kind of you," she said. She followed me into the living room, where I set the tray on a coffee table between a loveseat and two armchairs. "Thank you so much for coming to see
us." The authority of her voice, the undulating rhythm of the
oratory, was gone. I sat on the loveseat.

"Us?"

"Maggie will be back from her walk soon."

I nodded. I couldn't remember if someone had told me they
lived together or not.

"I'm so sorry for the loss of your friend, Sister." I wasn't sure
what else to say. "She must have meant a lot to all of you."

She watched me very carefully. "Some people come into your
life at just the right moment, and without any awareness of it

themselves, they bring something you never knew you needed. Sarah was one of those people."

We sat in silence. Sister leaned forward to pour the tea just as Maggie walked through the door. She closed it behind her. She stomped off her boots and hung her field coat on a hook. She looked tired, but her cheeks were flushed from her walk in the island air. Her gray hair was pulled back into a messy bun, strands blown about around her face.

She reached out for my hand, took it in both of hers firmly, then sat in the other chair opposite me, next to Sister.

I repeated my condolences. Maggie smiled gratefully but seemed resolved to carry on with some sort of business.

"Your visit happened to coincide with our loss."

"I don't believe in coincidences," Sister said. "Lucie is here for a reason, like all of us."

"I don't know about that," I demurred.

"You lost your father on the island."

There was a familiar sinking in my chest, but I knew how not to react. I had many years of practice, hearing the pity in voices, the oblique references to my failings, my brokenness, as a result of my deep, untamed sadness. Everything I did, good or bad, for years after the quake was traced back to that loss, by everyone who knew.

"It was a long time ago." I didn't want them to use my father against me.

"And yet, here we all are," Sister said. "Brought together in grief."

I said nothing.

"How did Sarah die?" I asked, finally.

"Cancer," Maggie said. "But you guessed that." The ebullient woman I had met in the dairy was gone.

"Your tea is getting cold," Sister said, to either or both of us.

Maggie and I looked at her. Sister picked up her own cup and drank it down. I watch the steam rise from our cups on the table. I could smell mint, other herbs, and an underlying bitterness—some root, maybe? I picked up my cup and took a sip. It was lukewarm, not pleasurably hot anymore. The mint was there and something lemony, but there was a dirty undertone, something gritty and fermented, like rotting apple.

Maggie saw the look on my face.

"Reishi mushrooms," she said, flatly. "That's what you're tasting. We drink them, we eat them: they're in everything. The Chinese have used them for thousands of years medicinally."

"For cancer," I said. I was aware of the reishi sold in supplement form and the health claims.

"And fertility, and the circulatory system, and the liver . . ." Maggie said.

"But Sarah's cancer—the reishi didn't save her?"

Maggie looked disgusted. "It's not magic. Not everything works for everybody, for every illness. Sarah tried many different treatments. We did everything we could."

"So everything here is part of the project? Even your bodies?"

"We have an opportunity to use the oldest of the earth's medicines against the newest of the world's diseases."

"What happens when they don't work?"

"We manage the pain," Sister cut in. "Just like the doctors in hospitals do, after they've irradiated and poisoned all the cells in a body and the cancer returns."

"But you knew that you would make yourselves sick. There are babies in that graveyard, burial ground, whatever you call it. Women lost their children. You lost another generation. You put yourselves in the way of certain suffering and death." The cup was getting colder in my hands, the taste of the tea sour on the sides of my tongue.

"Lucie." Sister's voice was soft, pliant. She wasn't the orator now; this was a plea. "We have nothing but *this*. We have one life each and one death. What comes between birth and death is up to us. You put yourself in the way of death every time you get in a car, every time you drink alcohol or eat hamburger. The entire population of the industrialized world is putting itself in the way of certain death and suffering. The only choice for us is to live in service to each other and to the planet itself. That's how we put ourselves in the way of God's love."

"What am I supposed to do, Sister?" I searched her face, her expression. She searched mine. She was the kind of woman who would be ignored, written off, invisible to almost everyone outside this island: fertility gone, beauty gone, vanity—if she ever had any—gone. But her eyes shone; her heart and mind certain. She had no doubt, no fear. She would walk into the fire whether anyone followed her or not.

What did she see in me? Would I walk into the fire with her? Or would I turn and run?

"You can do whatever you want, obviously," Sister said. "You could stay here with us awhile longer. Spend more time with us, with the project. If you wanted to write about this place, it would be unfair to do so in haste. We've been here almost twenty years. We've invested our lives. Give us the time to show you."

Sister looked to Maggie, who stared out the window, across the boundary waters, miles away.

"Whatever you do," Sister said, "I would ask you to think of the harm it might do to our work here, all the work we've done to honor your father's resting place."

· · ·

The tide was out, the muddy flats stretched away from the shore around the island, seaweed and driftwood and shells. The sun was trying to burn through the clouds, but the wind was blowing in more, bringing in darker clouds from the northwest. I had pulled on a sweater, but the wind blew right through the wool weave. I had packed so quickly, in the darkness before dawn. My windbreaker was hanging in the closet at the cottage, next to my dad's field coat.

Everyone took the afternoon off from their work. Meals were makeshift — leftovers and bread and cheese and shellfish cooked over the fires they were making on the beach. They would stay as long as they could, on the shore, into the evening and night, Katie said, so they could send off paper lanterns and driftwood boats. If anyone boating saw us on the shore, we looked like late-season vacationers having a clambake.

I wandered the shoreline, looking for agates, moving my body to keep warm between sun breaks. There was a wet chill in the air; a portent of winter. Voices carried occasionally, a word here and there of conversation. Everything felt fractured. Where I had felt part of the gathering before, now I felt outside of it, outside of myself.

Katie came up behind me and took my arm. She didn't say anything but walked with me for a while. I had seen her talking to Tuck, to Maggie. They seemed to agree to something — to leave me to Katie. I didn't know how to talk to her. Something between us had gone astray — unapproachable but watchful, scavenging our scraps of conversation, feeding on our feelings. We sat on a log and watched the boats pass, the gulls pecking at the bull kelp and crab carapaces. I shivered and she put her arms around me, squeezed me tight. I tried to relax into her, but I felt a tug in my gut, like this was the end of us.

She released me and pulled out a flask.

"Thirsty?"

"What is it?" I asked. I realized I hadn't eaten much that day. I hadn't had anything but Maggie's reishi tea in hours.

"Birch liquor. It's like gin."

I took the flask and drank. It was sharp and herbaceous, astringent. "It's good."

"Have it," she said. "I have another one." She patted her pocket.

I took another sip and felt it burn its way into my stomach.

I needed to eat something, I told her. So we made our way back to the others and found mussels in broth and chunks of sourdough. We sat there quietly, dunking our bread into a cast-iron pot of broth. I had been sure the lack of conversation was about my presence—they didn't trust me now, they didn't want to say anything in front of me—but now I thought it was just another of their silent observances, like the work prayer.

I drank from the flask and gradually felt warmed, inside and out. Others passed around a bottle of dandelion wine, then a bottle of elderberry. When the alcohol had sunk in, there was more talk. When I caught the voices, I heard only words that soothed me. The sounds of words like *anemone* and *caldera* and *parish*—or maybe it was *perish?*

There was a languourousness to everyone's movements. Hymns begun in mid-verse then ended, minor chords suspended in the air around us then swept away by the outgoing waves. Jen looked at me, her eyes both dark and shiny, like stars. She took my hand in both of hers, looking at it, feeling the weight of it, then she placed it tenderly back in my lap. I looked to Katie, who was stretched out at my feet. Katie smiled warmly at me, but we didn't speak.

My stomach started to ache.

"I think I've had too much," I told Katie. I felt the sudden need to shit. I started quickly up the beach to the Colony. It seemed miles away. I felt lightheaded. I didn't notice Katie following me, but when I reached the closest toilet, behind the chapel, she was there behind me.

"I'll get you some water," she said, and I heard her feet trod off up the path.

I emptied my bowels but the cramping in my stomach continued. I tried to take deep breaths, but every inhale caused a stabbing pain.

I left the toilet and started walking. The fresh air and movement seemed to help. Katie caught me halfway up the hill to the bluff. She handed me a canteen, like the kind we carried as Girl Scouts. I stopped and looked at the pattern on the side for a moment—*chevron*, I thought—and Katie nudged me and told me to drink. The water was so cold going down my throat, but it didn't help the pain and nausea rising. I kept walking, but slower.

"Katie, I feel really strange."

"It's okay. Keep walking. It'll feel better in the woods. It always feels better in the woods."

She took my arm and led me up the path, away from the Colony. I knew I had been on this path before, but I couldn't place it.

"Where are we going?" I asked.

"I want to show you something," she said.

"I don't feel right, Katie." All the plants looked like they were lighting up at the tips, flickering with green flames. Long fronds of fern vibrated, giving off waves.

"Do the trees seem taller to you?" I stepped off the trail and walked up to a cedar; its bark was warm to the touch and responsive like human skin.

"Katie! Come here!" She came and I reached for her, pulled her to the tree. "Feel this."

And she did, stroking the bark like it was fur. She was wearing a sweater so I reached a hand under her shirt at her hip to feel her skin. She looked down at my hand curiously. With one hand on her body and the other on the tree, I felt a humming run through me. I pulled away.

Ravens called, loud and various, sometimes speaking in English.

"Katie, what's happening?"

"It's okay," she said. "It's part of the grieving process."

"What is?

"We all do it." Her voice came rolling toward me, soft, then loud, then louder, then crashing into my ear. "It reminds us how connected we all are. We give them to the dying, too, to ferry them along to the lights."

"Am I dying?" I asked, but I wasn't angry with her—I felt unreasonably calm. I knew that I should be mad, but I couldn't feel it. I felt the parts of my brain that reasoned, that wanted to make sense of everything, falling back, into the shadows. I noticed things, but I stopped forming coherent thoughts about what I saw or felt. I couldn't feel the pain in my stomach anymore, though I sensed that something was happening there. I could feel the movement of the organ, its machinations. And the nausea—it was still there, still rolling and rising up through me in the same seasick waves I was so used to, but I wasn't alarmed. It was a sensation that was happening in my body that made me want to move, so I pushed on through the trees.

I heard Katie behind me—heard her breathing in my ear—but when I looked back, she seemed so far away, down a long tunnel of green. I took her hand for a moment, but we slipped apart. We weren't on the path anymore. I was pushing through bushes that scratched and spiderwebs that could choke me—I was sure of this—if I didn't hold my breath.

I broke into a meadow full of tall grass, a barn at the far end. Two ravens sailed through the air. I ran into the meadow but felt like I was sailing, my arms out skimming the top of the grass like it was water. The sun came through the clouds, and it seemed much lower in the sky than it ought to be, lighting up silver cumulus with dirty yellow rims. The sea beyond, down the hill past the trees. I could see all the islands—every one of them—from this place. There were so many of them, teeming with life. I could feel everything the islands felt. Every drop of rain, every footfall, every car and bike wheel, every bird landing, every insect crawling.

I fell down in the grass and stared at the clouds. I heard Katie calling me. I heard the trees calling me. The ravens inscribed a circle in the sky above me. *Everything,* they said, back and forth to each other.

"Everything," I said. "Everything."

Katie lay down beside me in the grass.

"Do you hear them?" she asked.

"Yes," I said, because I was sure I had.

"This is the way they go," she was saying, or maybe "This is the way you'll go."

I looked at her freckled nose, her eyes closed. I closed my eyes and reached for her, that soft spot on her hip where her sweater fell away. I felt her warm skin and the beating of her blood, the movement of her bowels, the growth of tumors on her ovaries, clustering out like fungi, like witch's butter, in clumps of yellow and orange, feeding on her, eating her away from within, hastening her decay.

"They're the ones we picked from the babies' graves," I heard her say.

I sat up. Was I dreaming? I was sweating. It was so humid, this weather. I threw off my sweater. I struggled to get out of the sleeves, yanked free and dropped it in the grass where Katie had been laying. Where was Katie? I hadn't felt her leave. I hadn't heard her go.

I called her. The ravens called back.

I looked again at the spot where she had been lying, the grass pressed in the shape of her body. I looked off across the field toward the trees, but there was nothing. Only the trees, sparking and dancing. Then my knees buckled as if I'd been struck, as if I had been standing on the shore, struck by a sneaker wave. I could hear it, like an earthquake, rolling toward me. I threw up in the grass. The mussels, the bread, the wine, the honey cake —I tasted it all, coming back up. I heaved so hard it came out my sinuses. I coughed and spit and gasped between waves, one after another, until everything was out.

It was suddenly much darker but lit up by lightning. I wiped my mouth on my sweater. Then the thunder cracked above, and I saw the rain falling out over the water.

I called for Katie again. She was gone.

The rain started down in fat droplets, then harder. I ran for the barn at the far side of the field. I cranked open the old door and took a breath of the air. It was heady with the remnants of animal droppings and hay, the way that musk never leaves a barn. I felt all the energy drain out of me. I lay down near the doors, where there was some light, on a soft pile of dirt and bark, thinking, *This is where the bark lives,* and listening to rain shattering over the roof, dripping to the earthen floor.

I felt the storm pass above for hours, or minutes. A steady rain began to fall. Time moved in and out like a telescope. Sometimes I felt the presence of animals, breathing in the dark, their white globes of eyes fixed on me. Then I realized there were white globes at the back of the barn, in the shadows, but not eyes. *Not eyes,* I told myself. Or maybe I spoke. I crawled over the floor slowly, trying to get a better look at the glowing orbs, floating all over the ground. Closer and closer, but it was so dark. Cracks in the walls of the barn let in just enough steely light, just enough to set the orbs alight. They weren't floating, I could see, but coming out of the bark and dirt, bubbling out over a pile of earth and bark like the one I had been lying on. But this one had more contour. Parts of it had fallen, causing little avalanches of mycelia and soil, uncovering long pale bundles of sticks, like fingers. I caught sight of a swatch of plaid flannel. *I'm hallucinating,* I told myself. So I crawled closer, reached out my hand to the swatch of plaid, and tugged until the dirt gave way to reveal buttons, and a cluster of white mushrooms tumbled down and maggots and beetles went scattering over the hand and fleeing across the barn floor.

I clambered to my feet and ran. I left the barn, the rain coming down in a light sheet, soaking me through until I reached the woods. It was getting dark. I cowered under the skirt of a cedar and shivered. I didn't know where I was, but the island was only six square miles. As long as I kept the sea to my left, I would come to the Colony eventually. But I didn't want to find them. What had they done to me? What would they do if they found me? How could Katie do this to me? If I stayed under that tree all night, I would be safe. I could wait till morning. The trees all around had light trails like comets when I moved my head from side to side.

I lay down on the needles and felt something hard against my collarbone. I felt for my shirt pocket. It was my phone. I turned it on. It was seven-thirty. If I could find a signal, I could call Carey, but I would have to walk. I would have to leave the safety of the cedar. Eleven hours till daylight.

I sat in a timeless fog, trying to figure out what to do. Whenever I closed my eyes, I saw tumors growing out of them. I saw my eyelashes covered in them. I could feel them over my face, through my airways, creeping up my sinuses to the inner rim of my skull, down into my bronchi and the fat red slabs of my lungs.

Despite it all, there was still one separate channel of my brain that seemed outside the sensory chaos, where logical thoughts occasionally surfaced. I realized that I was going to get cold, and that I had thrown up my last meal, and that I had had maybe an ounce of water in the last several hours.

I also knew they were looking for me. I could hear voices in the trees, far off, maybe across the field. They would look for me in the barn. I didn't know if this was real, but it felt real. I could hear Katie calling me, and Sister. I could hear them both, first one, then the other. Singing. But maybe it wasn't them at all. Maybe it was the shrike, calling me out of my hiding place.

I heard a clear call—my name. It was closer. I crept out of my den and made my way from tree to tree. One at a time, away from the voices. Sometimes arms reached out for me, but they were only branches. Sometimes I picked a tree that was across a great expanse that I was sure was full of fox dens. It stopped raining, but I was wet and shivering, teeth chattering. At every tree I wanted to stop, to climb up into its branches and hide above, wait for them to pass. But I kept moving to keep warm.

The sound of the water echoed in my ears, was getting closer, and the voices had ceased. I waded through high grass at the edge of the trees and ran into a chain-link fence. Beyond, the sky, though dark, seemed to open up. I saw great expanses of cloud reflecting light from some source I couldn't see. I walked along the fence until I found a place where a tree had fallen into it, bending it down to the ground. It was an old tree, long stubs of thick, bark-stripped dead wood jutting out of it. I held on to one, then another, slowly negotiating my way over the tree and the fence. My feet touched the gravel field on the other side of the fence, and I ran toward a red glow in the distance. Rocks jabbed my soles, wedged themselves between my toes. The air whirred with insects I couldn't see.

The red glow became a fire, set back against a wall. A bonfire. Or bigger. A pyre. Something to burn witches on. But it was so far away. There were hulking shadows to my right and left, the ruins of tanks; water tanks, fuel tanks. Piles of concrete and rebar overgrown with weeds. The sound of the sea echoed off the wall and all around. It could be a trap, I thought. They knew I'd be attracted by the warmth of the fire. And it was warm. I could feel it. I became aware of asphalt under my feet, somehow hot, though wet. I walked toward it, wary of the shadows. The fire moved when I moved. It was always just a bit farther away. Though it flickered and charred the walls wherever it went. I saw shapes in it. Arms reaching out, legs beneath, dangling out like logs. My father's voice came floating out among the echoes of waves, singing "O My Stars," just like he did walking up from the shore, climbing the ladder to my room, the crackle under his voice like the needle on the vinyl record, but the crackle of a fire, of limbs, charring, the water left in them steaming out, blistering and popping, the flesh bursting. Farther and farther into the ruins, through the naked steel skeleton of the cooling pipes, the empty metal vats the size of small houses, right up to the base of the tallest of the smokestacks I followed it, till it shimmied away into the wet dark cavern of night and was snuffed out.

"Come back!" I sobbed. My voice circled round the cooling towers and smokestacks. *Come back. Come back. Come. Back.* I sunk down in the weeds and hugged my knees. I felt the cell phone in my pocket and pulled it out. I was on the southeast corner of the island, where I might pick up a cell signal from Waldron or Orwell. The phone lit up and my eyes blinked shut. I thought I was dreaming; there was one bar. I dialed Carey's number. The ringing was jarring. It continued to ring, sometimes cracking up. On the last ring there was a break, then voicemail.

The words I wanted to say and the words that came out of my mouth may not have been the same, I couldn't tell. There was a body in the barn; not the graveyard, where the babies are, the barn. They fed me poisonous mushrooms. They fed me dead baby mushrooms. They feed the dead to mushrooms. I was incoherent, not sobbing. I stared around me in the weeds. They were flecked with down and feathers, fish bones. I picked at them. Bald eagles slept a hundred feet over my head in their smokestack nest. I looked up, as if I might see them. When I looked down, I realized I had dropped my phone. The light on its screen went out, but I found it in the weeds. I put it back in my wet shirt pocket.

I wandered into the woods. I listened for the sound of the ocean and kept it to my right this time. My right. I found a sheltered place and clung to a tree that looked out over a bluff onto the water. I could just make out waves, I thought. Reflecting something. A deranged glowing orb in the sky. *The moon, idiot. Just sleep.* I wrapped my whole body around the tree. Hugging it with my legs, pressing my face to the bark. I held on to it and prayed that it would hold me till morning, though some part of me didn't care.

I felt myself falling and woke. My face was in the moss and salal. There was light in the sky, still gray. A light rain fell, but I was sheltered by low branches. I was three feet from a sheer drop to the rocky shore.

I scooted myself away from the bluff, used branches to pull myself up. My legs were weak and my head swam, but I felt warm. I was aware enough to know that I might be hypothermic. I went slowly, weaving and holding on to any bush or tree sturdy enough to support me, and in this way I found the road. I wasn't sure which way to walk, so I went right. When I found an old trail marker, I knew I had reached the outer edge of Fort Union. I followed the road to the end, the entrance to the park on one side, the path through the trees to the Colony on the other. What time was it? Would they be awake? The way was clear, through the trees, and in the light of day, the effects of the mushrooms wearing off. I wasn't afraid anymore of what they would do to me when I made it back. At the hill above the kitchen on the bluff, I scooted down on my butt, afraid I would fall headfirst down it. A few bodies were moving about in the drizzle, heads down, deep in their work prayers. I crept to the doors of the chapel and lay down, tried to turn on my dead phone, dropped it. After a while: the approach of a boat on the water below, the bellow of someone's voice breaking their vow of silence. I kept my eyes closed. I didn't say a word.

Thirteen

THE WOODS

———

MALHEUR NATIONAL FOREST, OREGON
JULY 12, 2016

CAREY'S WORKING LONG hours, helping organize the fire crews, coordinating with the Bureau of Land Management and the National Interagency Fire Center. Sometimes he's on call at the cabin; sometimes he just doesn't come home. They have cots in the back of the station and take turns catching a couple hours' sleep each when fires are burning. They're already working on two fires, one near homes to the northeast in the Umatilla, outside Baker City, threatening farms and houses. A smaller one in the Ochoco. These are all far enough away that his station is merely on alert; ready to pitch in if needed.

It's been the warmest, driest season on record, with the lowest snowpacks in the mountain ranges, with more of these drought years expected to follow. I listen to the talk back and forth at the station. A few smoke-detecting cameras have been set up in some forests, but not all—not out here. The early summer heat is already toasting the undergrowth, and the warm waters out over the Pacific have been creating unseasonable storms, coming inland—breaking out over the Cascades, dumping their moisture in the valley, but not their velocity, not their electricity. Lightning strikes cause fires some of the time—most of the time it's people, campfires and cigarettes and sparks from railways, fireworks. Then the storms bring winds that spread the fires, whip them up higher and toss them across containment lines, create their own weather systems, massive heat and smoke storms that can be seen from space.

They're manning the fire lookouts this year—the ones they normally rented out to backpackers. I convince Carey to let me man the lookout I've been going to all spring. His boss says, "Sure, that's great." But Carey says he'll keep looking for another volunteer.

He goes over how to use the CB radio again. It's a silver and wood laminate box, covered in knobs and little red and green lights, a frequency meter. I suspect the machine is older than both of us.

The first rule is "Just don't touch any of these knobs." He gestures to an area of the box with buttons and abbreviations like RB and ANL. "Just don't bother. There's a manual somewhere if you get desperate, but just remember: Channel nine for emergency calls, that's the station dispatcher. If no one answers, try nineteen—you might get a trucker on Highway 7 who can get a call through to some other station's dispatch. After that, just try all the stations. But be patient. Always come back to nine."

He sends a test call to dispatch at the station. It's Darlene, the office manager for the Forest Service. She sounds like she's been eating something, but maybe it's just the interference. "Weather disturbs transmissions all the time. Certain conditions can bounce a call off the ionosphere and send it hundreds of miles away," he says.

I give an impressed whistle. "Win for Mother Earth," I say.

Carey shakes his head.

"I'll come up on my days off —"

"If you get any days off," I say.

We heat some beans and kielbasa and eat on the deck and watch the sunset. I light citronella coils, and we sit at the edge, legs dangling. We don't talk; we take in the view and the air. When we're done, I take our plates inside and bring a camp blanket out, wrap us both in it while we drink cans of Oly.

"Do you miss the firefighting," I ask him, "when you're at the station pushing paper and dispatching?"

"No," he says. "I'm too old now; it wouldn't be the same."

"You're only thirty-eight. What would be different?"

He thinks about this for a while, then he tells me about his first year with the Snake River Hotshots, stationed in some quaint postage stamp in Idaho, waiting to head out. He went to the library—a perfect Carnegie model, all brick, high arched windows, silent as the grave—to get away from the constant noise of the camp and crew. On the last day before they went out on their first job, he sat in the still, dusty room in an old chair, just breathing in the calm. He pulled a random book from the shelf next to him, flipped it open to a page somewhere in the middle. It was a passage in a long poem about life and death, and it struck him so much that he found himself reading it over and over again, and eventually tearing the page from the book and folding it into his pocket. He put the book back on the shelf and stood up. The librarian was asleep behind her desk; there were no other patrons in the place. He walked out the door, exhilarated and horrified. He was an Eagle Scout. He did everything to the letter. He was filled with shame. But after that, on the line, he took the page out every night he could and read those words before falling asleep, filthy and exhausted, eyes sore and throat raw.

"What poem was it?" I ask.

He reaches in his pocket and pulls it out: a paper so worn and soft it could be a hanky. He carefully unfolds it and hands it to me. It's T. S. Eliot, from *Four Quartets*.

"A modernist," I say, impressed. I was expecting Longfellow; Manley Hopkins. "Do you know about this poem?"

"What about it?"

"This page—it's from a poem Eliot wrote about living in London before and after the Blitz. He was a Christian, Eliot; fire was complicated for him: it was death, but it was also the purification of the soul."

He's silent, and I think that I've ruined it for him. That I've somehow belittled him and intruded on his love for these lines.

"I'm sorry," I say, "it's apt, is all I meant to say. It seems really —telling, that you kept this page with you."

The bats are out, feasting, their wings beating the air silently against the pale pink of the sky. Where we're sitting, it's already so dark, I can barely see his face.

I reach my hand out to touch his chest, and he catches it and holds it. He kisses the inside of my wrist and my elbow. His lips linger over my skin. I haven't shaved in weeks, but he buries his face in my armpit and pushes aside my tank top, tastes the tender side of my breast. My skin is covered in sweat and dust and DEET, and when we kiss, I taste it all in his mouth with the warm sour of beer. We spread the blanket out on the pine planks of the deck. We're still wearing our hiking boots. He unhooks my bra, kisses my belly, unbuttons my shorts, and slips his hand between my legs. He's pushing my shirt up with his face. The stars light up the treetops. When I close my eyes, I can still see them. And the shapes of the trees, too, the outline of them, flaring up in the night sky.

Later he asks, "What are you doing out here, Lu?"

I'm not sure if he means the woods or the lookout, or both. But I'm caught by that nickname. He just started using it, at the Dollar Save on our way back from Baker City. We were standing at opposite ends of an aisle, each hunting for something, distracted by the discount store oddities. "Lu," he had called, softly; the store was eerily quiet. And I looked up. He was grinning, holding a can of Armour Potted Meat. I choked on a laugh and held up a package of Ekonomik Boy Cream Cake. It's a moment I go back to in my mind now, instead of thinking of an answer.

We're lying naked in the cot, his ear pressed into my breast. I can't lie to him.

"I don't want to be anywhere else," I say.

My first night alone at the lookout I am terrified, sleepless, listening to the sounds of a cougar prowling the deck. Maybe my period is coming. Thinking of the old wives' tales about menstruation and wild animals, how the smell of blood draws the carnivores. I imagine there's a niche market of erotica based on this superstition. A woman alone in the wilderness: so vulnerable, so delicious; she goes mad, consorting with the beasts.

I convince myself I'm imagining the stealthy footfalls, the deep padded, furred tread, the velvety disruption of the air around its ears, its nostrils. It's only the wind, blowing pine needles on the boards.

I sleep late, for once.

My coffee water is about to boil when I hear the sound of footsteps on gravel. It's not early in the morning, but it's not late. It seems early for a hiker. I know it can't be Carey. The footsteps come closer. Not an animal, not the scurry of small mammalian feet, and not the soft waltz of deer hooves, the languorous 3/4 beat of their steps. I recognize the sound of thick rubber soles on the rocky terrain because they were just like mine, the echo of my own lone footsteps up and down and around this mountain. I freeze. I cannot imagine the person attached to them. A lost hiker, someone in need, perhaps. But what if it's not? I feel the electric surge of adrenaline, and I turn off the burner, take the pan of boiling water by the handle for protection, and force myself to go to the door, to step out onto the deck, and peer over the side in the direction of the path.

Katie stands below, shielding her eyes to look back at me.

The pan of hot water splashes me, and I curse and run inside and put it down on the burner. Katie stands halfway up the steps when I come out. Her dark hair is shorter now, cut up around her ears, sticking out from a red bandanna. She's wearing backpacking gear, but she's cleaner than I am. I hug her and she smells like Katie, the way she smelled on Marrow, like vetiver and seaweed—but also musky from walking in the sun—oily hair, warm sandstone. Her nose and cheeks are burned.

"How did you get here?"

"I walked." Her voice is a husk. She clears her throat. "I'm out of water."

"Come inside."

I pour some water from the jug for her, take her pack and set it aside — it's lighter than it ought to be, for someone backpacking or traveling anywhere. She sits at the small table and drinks. I want to wait for her to be ready to talk again, but I can't.

"Sister J. passed away, two months ago."

She doesn't look at me but only nods. She's looking around the room, her eyes resting on the CB radio.

"I was with her," I say. "She was thinking about you."

She holds out the cup, and I get her more water. I notice now the circles under her eyes, how they're lined with red inside the rims.

"You're not supposed to be here."

She looks directly into my eyes. "I am dead," pulling off her bandanna, hair felted to her head. "I'm not here. If anyone comes looking for me, you haven't seen me."

She lies back on the cot, and I remove her shoes. She groans as I pull them over her blistered heels. I strip her holey socks — she has one more pair in her bag — and see the swollen knobs of her toes. I roll up the leg of her jeans — they were Tuck's jeans, I think — she has belted them; her legs are unshaven and pale, with blue and green bruises up and down the shins. I take the water I had boiled for coffee and pour it into my dish tub along with some cold water, set it on the floor beside the cot. She lets out a howl of agony and pleasure as I ease her first foot into the water; she's breathing like a woman in labor.

"If you can manage it, we can go down to the creek later and have a cold soak to bring down the swelling. Let's just clean you up, now."

"Okay." Her voice is small, an octave higher, like a child's.

I make oatmeal while her feet soak, and she lies, senseless, on the cot. I think she's sleeping, but when she hears the bowls of oatmeal hit the table, she sits up. I put extra brown sugar and evaporated milk in hers. She lifts her feet from the basin and hobbles to the table. The oatmeal is scalding but she eats quickly.

"Let's bandage your feet," I say. I take some Ace bandages and antibiotic ointment from the first-aid kit and attend to her sores and blisters. I don't know that her boots will fit again so soon and I tell her so.

"I'm fine," she says, lying back on the cot. "I just need to rest." Then I think she really will fall asleep, but I don't want her to rest.

"Okay," I say. I'm afraid if I take my eyes off her, she'll slip away.

"Tell me about Sister," she says, closing her eyes.

I think about this, sitting at her feet, watching her drift away.

"They sent a letter saying she asked for me," I say. "She wanted me to bring something, but she wouldn't say what it was. At first I thought she was just losing her mind. But that was my clue, the not naming: I knew it was something the sisters couldn't give her, and that she couldn't name in front of them."

Katie opens her eyes and watches me.

"Did you figure it out?"

"I did. Or I was pretty sure I did. I hiked every day, hunting for them." Katie opens her eyes wide at me, delighted.

"I lost my way, wandering off the trail, looking for the right fallen tree, the right pile of bark. I looked for bear scat and tracks and followed them to trees with the bark clawed off. I couldn't find them anywhere. I found other kinds, I found them and picked them and brought them back and dried them, but they were never the right ones. I thought about bringing them anyway. I thought, *She's dying anyway, what does it matter?*"

"But you found them?"

"I went to visit Carey at the ranger station one day, and getting out of the truck in the parking lot, I saw them. Wavy caps, in the landscaping around the building. They had mulched with wood chips in the fall. When I was sure no one was around, I picked them all, wrapped them in a bandanna, and kept them until I could get back here. I knew they were the right ones because they turned blue when I pinched them, like the ones we picked off the graves on Marrow. I remembered what you said to me, when we were high in that field. That the best ones grew on the babies' graves."

She smiles at this.

"I went to see her after that."

"How far gone was she?"

"I was almost too late, I think. She wasn't eating. I didn't know how to give them to her."

"How did you do it?"

I swallow, feel the burn on my tongue from the oatmeal. Katie's pupils are large and deep, her eyelids droopy, but she keeps her gaze on me. I look out the window at the cloudless sky.

I tell her how I waited until she was somewhat lucid, not really lucid, but almost awake. About how she reached for them or for me. About how I broke down the bitter, gritty caps with my teeth, mixed them with my saliva. About the strangest kiss I've ever given.

I look back to Katie. She is grinning.

"You're an angel of mercy, Luce," she says. "And a badass."

She closes her eyes.

"And she went peacefully?"

"I saw the life leave her like sparks from a roaring blaze."

• • •

There's nothing to do but watch her sleep in my cot, in my look-out. The breeze blowing through the window screens, the way they wave with it. The light on the leaves outside like the day of the earthquake, pure and unredeemable, the gift of the moment. She came back to me. And I wonder what this means, because I realize—it's written all over her—*I cannot keep her.* I find my phone and take a picture of her sleeping.

I cook bacon and eggs for dinner—using up more than I had rationed for myself, but knowing I could go down to the cabin for more if I needed. Every so often a transmission comes through on the radio—I keep it on to hear the weather. In the strange mechanical voice of emergencies, the robotic man declares that the National Weather Service has issued an alert for the area. Storms are expected tomorrow morning through early evening. The possibility of dry lightning. I'm waiting to hear from Carey, too. And anxious. I don't know if he'll believe me, if I tell him that Katie is here. Or if I should tell him. He never trusted her—he seemed relieved to hear she had taken off.

Katie wakes up to the smells of cooking. She's been living off trail mix. She's been shitting it for days, she says. Every squat in the woods is like giving birth to a little granola bar. A Christian family who picked her up gave her a tuna sandwich and some potato chips, she said. And a generic cola. It was her first drink of soda in several years, and she said her eyes teared up from the syrup, and they thought she was so grateful she was crying. They prayed for her: the mom, the dad—who was driving—and the two kids in the back of the minivan, who were seven and ten. She swallows the eggs in under a minute, then takes her time with the bacon.

"I never would have eaten bacon before," she says.

"But now that you're dead, you can eat what you want."

I open two cans of beer and hand her one. She smiles for the first time.

I let her borrow my extra shoes, and we walk down to the river. She's used to walking on her sore feet, but she's not used to resting. Her body protests being back in motion after the rest in the lookout. We walk slowly, and I take her arm or hand for the steeper parts. It's only a mile to the creek, but it's not always easy climbing.

This part of the river is wide and shallow; the sun heats it, but there's shade at the edges. I haven't showered in a few days, so I strip off everything but my bra and underwear and wade in. Katie keeps to the bank and soaks her legs, watching me.

"I can't remember my last period," she says.

I sit on a rock in the middle of the stream, water just covering my crotch. I look down to my thighs, half expecting to see blood in the water.

"I can't remember mine, either. Maybe we're both pregnant."

She looks at me and smiles.

"Dead women can't have babies, Lu."

"Oh, right." We're still pretending. But it's making me uncomfortable.

"You must have had at least one period since you left Bellingham, right?"

She gives me an indifferent grunt.

I count the days in my head, but I am counting my own. Thinking back to the Palouse, to Prairie City on my birthday, to the month before that. April. Washing bloodstains out of my panties in the morning, hanging them outside to dry in the sun.

"I can't be pregnant," I say. "I don't feel pregnant."

"How do you know?"

"I was, once. With Matt."

"You were?" she asks, like it doesn't surprise her at all, her face blank.

"We hadn't been together long. I was in love with him, but I couldn't tell him." I'm staring at her body, her bony frame that carried a dead baby for weeks.

"You couldn't tell him you were in love? Or that you were pregnant?"

"Either."

"What happened?"

I remember it, the quiet but certain knowledge I felt. That it wasn't right. It wasn't time.

"Motherhood seems like a dangerous experiment, in this world. How can you love someone and leave them with the mess you've made?"

She watches me, then looks up to the trees.

"You don't have to tell me," she says, finally.

There's a washcloth and a little chunk of soap tucked in the front of my bra. I wash my underarms in the cool water, my feet, between my legs. A trout nibbles at my toe, and I kick it away, lose my balance, slipping off my rock perch and landing in the stream, sharp rocks on my ass and hip. I come up coughing, soap lost to the current. Katie laughs. I stay there, dunk my face and head and rinse the soap from my body. When I look up, Katie is still smiling. She looks content, calm. I try to understand how this can be: she ran away; she found me. But for once, I don't want to question the joy I feel. She was my first love.

"Come in," I say.

She wades in farther down, where the rocks dip, creating a small waterfall. Her back is to me, and she's saying something, but her voice is lost downstream. I can't see her face, her expression.

"I can't hear you."

She says it again. I can hear parts of the stressed syllables. I think she says, "I'm trying to save you." But maybe it's "The fire will save you."

"I can't hear you when your back's to me."

She turns, just to look over her shoulder.

"I didn't say anything," she says.

"You said something, just now. I heard you."

She shakes her head no, wades deeper into the current, up to her hips, sweeping her arms against it to stay upright.

"It's like limbo," she says. I hear her this time, see her lips move.

That night we lie in the cot side by side, and I tell her about the cougar I hear sometimes, how I think I can smell him marking the area around the lookout—sometimes the heady odor of cat piss wafts through the trees.

"I talk to him a lot."

"What do you say?"

"I sing him songs. I tell him stories."

"Which stories?"

"About the islands, mostly. About what it was like before the quake and after. My dad going out in his boat, chasing me around with live crabs. 'Crab hands! Crab hands!' Remember? I tell it about the sound of the quake, the shapes it made, the geometry of it. Looking out the classroom window and seeing the earth rolling in, the trees tipping sideways. I tell it how I thought: *I am going to die.* Then I looked into your eyes and saw you were thinking the same thing."

"Aren't you supposed to be writing all of this down in a story?"

"Yes. But I'm not sure I want to write it down."

"Does it help, telling the lynx?"

"It's a cougar."

"The cougar, does he respond?"

"No. Wherever he is, he's probably just thinking about eating."

"That's bleak."

"I had a therapist in Seattle. I used to tell her these things, thinking it would help. But she responded by asking if I was having suicidal thoughts."

"Were you?"

"If I wanted to die, I'd be dead already."

"That makes two of us."

"Carey thinks I'm here writing it all down. My mom thinks I left the city to write. I go day by day, starting with the day I arrived on Orwell after twenty years. I write a page and it takes me all day, and then evening comes and I burn it up and bury the ashes."

"How many pages have you burned?" She is drifting off. My arm lays parallel with her arm, and she traces my index finger over and over with hers.

"I'm not counting."

"Where are you in the story?"

"Lost."

"Lost?"

"Yes."

It's dark but I can feel her tense. She's looking at me. The whites of her eyes glow.

"I went looking for you," she says.

"You disappeared and I found Jacob in the barn."

"That was an accident," she says, kissing my temple.

"That I found him or that he was in the barn?"

"Both. You were both accidents. He fell down the stairs; you had some bad mushrooms."

"That was not an accident. *You* didn't take them—the *Amanita*," I say, pleading. "No one else could have had that kind—only me. Why, Katie?" I just want to hear her say that she knew, that she gave them to me.

"You're fine, look at you. You're still here." She runs her hand down my waist and back.

"I'm not fine. I see the filaments everywhere."

"What filaments?" Her hand stops.

"Like threads on fire."

"Oh, those." She relaxes. Her voice is soft; her hand resumes.

"You see them, too?"

"No. But I've heard about them. Only some people get them after the mushrooms. You're lucky."

"What are they? Will they go away?" I'm drifting off. It's harder to speak. There are unnatural pauses. We used to talk ourselves to sleep like this; we used to confess our deepest thoughts and secrets, then pretend it was all a dream.

"Saint Lucy tore out her eyes and God restored her sight, but ever after her eyes were made of light."

"Why did you do this to me?"

"I wanted you to see."

"See what?"

"How your dad became part of the island, the millions of particles of him, his ashes. How they were in the air, in the trees, in the soil. Couldn't you feel him?"

"You didn't have to kill me to show me."

"I only meant to show you how close you could be to him."

"I never loved you," I say.

"I never loved you more," she says.

She winds her fingers into my hair and kisses me, mouth open just enough to taste her. I fall asleep to her slow exhale.

When I wake, dawn is streaking through the clouds and she's gone. Her bag is gone. Her shoes are gone. There's a note on the table, paper pulled from my journal. There's a pen next to it, but the page is blank. I hold it up to the light, looking for impressions, but all I see are the ghosts of my own words.

I run outside, looking for her footprints, stopping to listen. I hear nothing. I find nothing. There's no trace of her down the path to the fire lane and the cabin. I run a mile down the trail, two, knowing she can't be moving quickly, but she's not there. Has she heard me coming? Is she hiding in the trees? I call her name once. Then again. Nothing.

She took nothing with her from my stores. Maybe some water from my tank. No food. She had nothing for shelter, no warm clothing. She left nothing behind. Not even tracks. It was as if she hadn't been here at all.

I call down to the ranger station on the radio to see if anyone has come across a female hiker recently. I get Darlene, who says she doesn't think so. No lone female hikers. Not with the closures to the west and the northeast for the fires burning.

"Were you expecting somebody to check in with us?" Darlene asks.

"Maybe," I told her. "Can you have Carey check in with me when he can?"

"Sure thing."

I think about what Carey will do, if he knows she was out here — that she's out here still, somewhere. He would send out search and rescue. He would call the sheriff.

I set out myself, not the way she came — up the trail from the logging road and the highway, where she must have hiked past our cabin, or hitched past it, maybe with other hikers, with campers or fishermen. I set out the other way, up along the ridge and down the other side toward Cougar Lake. The trails there aren't marked well. They open up into dry forests, some still coming back after fires. Without a map or guide, it would be easy to wander off the trail and become disoriented. If it's your intention to get lost, the landscape will only help you.

I hike the trail for an hour, then two, calling Katie's name until I'm hoarse. Not a footprint, not a scuff. When I start the descent down to the lake, I hear thunder in the distance. It's early afternoon. The storms are coming down over the mountains to the west, just like the radio said. I make my way down to the lake, its shores muddy, the film of algae thicker, like a velour blanket. I can feel it — the change in the troposphere — the pressure descending, the hairs on my arms rising, that weight on the lungs, like when a plane lifts off the ground, the first ascent. At this altitude the body has its own barometry. The hum of insects amplified by the charge in the air. The birds keep up their calls, the pitch increasing, ready for the rain that will not come, that will evaporate before it reaches the ground, sucked right back into the wreckage of storm clouds. It'll take me another forty minutes to circle the lake, but I try, calling her name less now. The panic I felt earlier was gone; replaced by a sinking.

I look for her red bandanna, listen for the sound of another human, the way our movements are different in the woods than any other creature's; I close my eyes and feel with my skin—I am sure I will feel her, if she's close, if she knows I am close.

I climb the ridge back and come up out of the trees to the sight of lightning flashing across the opposite ridge. The sun is completely hidden, trees thrashing. And there they are again, the filaments, wriggling up to the tops of a pine thirty feet away. There's a spark and a flash, and I close my eyes. I'm breathing hard from the climb. I sit on a log, but it gives way under me, and I slide on my rear back to the trail, the log hitting my back. I keep my eyes closed. I breathe slowly and dump the last of my water over my face. I'm a mile from the lookout. If I jog I can make it in fifteen minutes. When I open my eyes again, the filaments are gone. The clouds are lumbering in and it's darker, so I get up and run, walk, run, until I'm back at the lookout. From the deck I watch the storm rolling through, feeling sick to my stomach. When the lightning flashes, the filaments follow. Red, gold, white. It goes on like this. The thunder shatters the air, and I count. One . . . two . . . three . . . four. Lightning streaks, my retinas fill with tiny flames. It's getting closer and closer, the thunder breaking right on top of my mountain, and I go inside. There's a hammering in my head. I lay down for just a minute, on the cot.

I smell the pillow, but even her scent is gone.

I've been asleep for three hours. It's unnaturally dark outside, clouds still hanging over the foothills, but the worst of the storm seems to have passed. Carey's voice comes through on the radio.

I jump out of the cot and pick up. "Hey, I'm here."

"Darlene said to check in with you about a female hiker?"

I hesitate.

"Lucie, are you there? Over."

"I'm here." I'm shaking; I don't know what to tell him.

"I just wanted to check on conditions."

Pause.

"Lots of lightning but no strikes that we know of, yet. What's it look like up there?"

"Lit up like the Fourth of July, for a while. Quiet now."

"Any strikes?"

"I don't think so. I'll keep watch."

"Did you have a hiker?"

"I did," I lie. I'm about to keep lying. "But I only saw her from a distance. Red bandanna. Tan pack. Headed down the mountain, toward the river. Not a backpacker. Day hiker. She didn't have any gear."

"Nobody like that has checked in with us, but day hikers usually don't. There are campers out at Strawberry Wilderness, maybe they were checking out the trails. Strange not to go up to the lookout, though."

"Yeah, I thought so, too," I say. "Let me know if somebody checks in? She could've been caught in the storm."

Twenty-four hours pass. At night I lie awake, forcing myself to imagine different scenarios in which she saves herself.

She makes her way out of the woods, meets another car full of Christians or hippies, hitches a ride to town—any town. She borrows a phone. She calls Jen and Elle. Or her parents. She turns herself in at the nearest sheriff's office. Someone comes for her. Someone takes her home.

But I can't help seeing the other possible scenes. Her foot stepping off the trail, her path into the unfamiliar wilderness. She hunts the site of an old fire—years old—scanning the felled trees, the rotting logs. She would find what I have seen there before: the *Psilocybe*, the wood-eaters. Like fireweed, they come back to the scenes of disasters; they thrive where others were destroyed; they make a place for another generation. She only needs a handful of the mushrooms. These would ease the discomfort. But she would need something else—something acutely toxic. She could have plucked many kinds from the woods of the Cascades, even in a drought year. She could have collected more than enough *Amanita smithiana*, the ones they fed me; she would know how much to ingest. Once I imagine it, it's like a bad dream that can't be undreamt: it infiltrates all the other scenes. There she is, choosing the place, taking off her pack, settling against a pine trunk, looking out at the bend in the river, drinking the last of her water while dog ticks climb up the leg of her shorts, mosquitoes drink until they're heavy. It would happen to her like it happened to me: the immediate sickness, the hallucinations, abatement, then weakness, deterioration. She would feel how I felt, and she would understand. It would be her way of confessing to me. But of course, even if we found her, no one would be able to carry her out in time.

The fire breaks out five miles to the northwest. An hour away by foot, if I'm running, but I know fires can move faster than that, especially with the wind urging them. They've already started digging containment lines, redirecting some of the crews from the Ochoco fire, which is 90 percent contained. The men are exhausted.

"It's the other side of the river, so you should be fine for now," Carey says, "but you should come back down to the cabin tomorrow."

"If I leave now, I can get back to the cabin before dark." Or I could stay, I think, in case she comes back tonight. But instead, before signing off I say, "Carey: make sure everyone knows about the hiker. Just in case."

I throw my books and clothes into my pack, leaving the food, the toilet paper and the hand sanitizer and all the other things I've brought.

As I close and lock the door, overhead one raven, then another, then another. They're loud, calling out to each other. There are other birds on the move, too, a strange migration: Steller's jays, in pairs, songbirds so fast I can't tell them apart, a solitary magpie. They scatter, alight on high branches, call from tree to tree. Particles of ash drift by on the breeze.

I remember reading about the unusual movements of wild animals before earthquakes — this was long after our quake, in a geology class in college. Days, even weeks, before there are shifts in the earth's plates, animals flee. Getting as far away from the center of the disaster as possible. The evidence is anecdotal, of course, but often cited to demonstrate the abject ignorance of the earth and its movements that humans live with, the utter divorce from the relationship with the environment that nurtured us through millions of years of evolution. The animals know what's coming before we do; they heed the instinct to flee. But we humans, even when we know what's coming, we do nothing. We watch the animals disappear.

I stop at the bottom of the path before I head off into the trees. I turn back to the lookout, for a last glance.

• • •

At the cabin I see the evidence of the early fire season, of nights Carey has spent at the field office in Prairie City: cold coffee in the pot, moldy oatmeal on the stove, dirty dishes, a stale smell —windows have been closed—a pile of unopened mail on the table. There's a blanket and pillow on the couch. He sleeps there when he's on call; it's a horrible place to sleep, so it's easier to wake up.

The light on the answering machine is blinking. There are three messages, and I can guess that at least one of them will be from my mother. Her voice comes out, as if from a can attached to a string, stretched along the five hundred miles between us.

"Lucie, it's Mom. Please call me when you get this. I love you." She sounds anxious. The cord of tension travels through my ear and into the back of my head, down my neck and spine. The message is from yesterday; they're all from her. Each one is shorter, taut with anger, with worry.

I open a window and lie down on the unmade bed, press my face into the sheets to smell him. They're cold. The scent of him makes him real to me, and I sink into the bed. But I smell someone else there, too. It takes a moment of shock for me to realize it's not some other woman I'm smelling, but my own scent, from before the days at the lookout, bathing in the river. There's a fermented odor to me now, an activity in the cells that wasn't there before. I inhale the remnants of us on the sheets, and there's a clarity to it, a certainty, if just for a moment. It's the sanest I've felt in weeks. I need to bathe.

Cellar spiders have woven webs in the bathtub; he's been showering at work. And I realize how alone I was all those nights at the lookout—how much farther he was from me than I realized. I wonder how Katie found me at all—how she would have known that I was up there, and not here, at the cabin. I grab the broom and collect the spiders, shake them off outside, let the water run in the tub until it's only lukewarm and get in anyway. It feels like a hot tub compared to bathing in the river.

Night falls before Carey comes home. I heat some soup and cut the mold off a log of Tillamook cheddar, salvage what I can to eat with crackers. The radio is on, tuned to the only station that comes in out here, which favors old country and country-gospel. I fall asleep on the couch, waiting for the sound of his truck.

It's almost ten when he comes in, dropping his overnight bag and gear by the door. I sit up sleepy-eyed, but I am anxious to see him.

"Don't get up," he says. He comes over and picks me up, carries me to the bedroom, lays me on the bed, and sits next to me.

"You smell like a campfire," I say.

"Biggest campfire you'll ever see," he says, kissing my knees open. I'm wearing underwear and one of his T-shirts and nothing else. He puts his face in my crotch and inhales.

"The hell?" I say, laughing.

"I've spent the last twelve hours running interference between a raging fire and the BLM, state and federal forestry, and the fire chiefs of three counties."

"That's quite the weenie roast."

"You smell amazing."

"I took a bath."

He crawls up next to me and kisses me, closes his eyes and falls back on the pillows. I unbutton his shirt, loosen his belt. He grunts as I undress him down to his undershirt and briefs.

"Oh, hey," he says as I'm pulling his shirt off.

"Yes?"

"Before I forget: that hiker you saw."

I drop his shirt to the floor.

"Yeah?" My heart pounds in my chest.

"I think I found her when I was evacuating the campground."

"You did?"

"Brown hair, red bandanna. Mid-twenties. I didn't talk to her, but somebody else in the group said they had all been out hiking near Cougar Lake."

"You saw her up close?"

"So that mystery's solved," he says.

"Maybe . . ."

He turns around and kisses me.

"Are you still worried?"

I look into his eyes and wonder if it's too late. Even if I tell him, what could he do? She's gone two days now.

I nod.

"Did she look like Katie?"

"What?" He pulls back.

"She looked like Katie."

He looks confused, then there's pity in his eyes, his voice.

"No, not really. Not up close, Luce." He wraps his arms around me. "Is that why you've been acting so weird? You thought you saw Katie?"

"I really did see her."

"I'm sure you did—in your mind. You wanted to see her, so you did. From a distance, with the dark hair, her height . . . this woman could've looked like Katie."

We lay down and he holds me for a while.

I say, "Do you want a beer?"

And he says, "Sure." Eyes closed.

When I get to the kitchen, I take deep breaths, open a bottle, and take a swig. Back in the bedroom, he's asleep on his side, facing the room. He falls asleep like that—instantly—like a giant knocked out by a clever village boy. I stand there drinking the beer in the rim of lamplight, an owl marking the hour out in the trees somewhere.

In the night the fire slows down, the containment lines on the west side are holding. We decide I should go to Prairie City, though. Carey wants me to take his truck, but I refuse.

"Your car is falling apart, Lu."

"It's falling apart, but it runs. I drove it to Spokane, didn't I?"

"And you haven't driven it five miles since. It's fifty miles to Prairie City. These roads are dangerous, especially during a fire. I just want to know that you're safe."

"You need your truck more than I do. I'll stay on the paved roads. I'll be careful."

He pulls on his jacket and kisses me, heads out the door. I don't hear his truck starting up, so I open the front door again. He's fussing around with something in my car. He sees me in the doorway and sticks his head out.

"CB radio," he shouts.

I walk out to the car. He's duct-taping the radio to the top of the dashboard.

"I worry about you, too, you know," I say, staring him down.

"I'm a pencil-pusher now, not a fire jumper." He steps out of the car and looks back at me, hard.

"I am not going to die."

I bring his hand to my face, resting my cheek in his palm. I am sure my father believed the same thing every time he left for work. I should tell him I've missed two periods, but it seems so dramatic.

"Call me when you can, so I can hear your voice."

Carey warned me that the roadside motel in Prairie City was booked with Missoula hotshots, so I end up reserving the same room we stayed in for my birthday, at the inn. I think about calling my mom back but decide I'll do it from the hotel.

I find my suitcase in the closet and throw it open on the bed. Stand over it, bewildered, not remembering what I filled it with when I came out here. I look around the room. My dirty laundry is in the canvas bag and ready to go. I have two drawers of the dresser, so I pull them out and dump them over the suitcase. A hairbrush in the bathroom. A small, cluttered bag of makeup and toiletries. A few books. I take everything, right? I pack it all, just in case? In case I never come back. In case there's not a cabin to come back to.

I turn on the radio to settle my nerves. The country-gospel station doesn't seem to have a DJ or advertising of any kind, no interruptions in the broadcast for weather or news, no emergency broadcast alerts. As far as I know, it's broadcast from outer space. I wash the breakfast dishes and the coffeepot, watching out the window, thinking of Katie. I look down at the soapy water, my hands doing circles around the inside of a coffee cup. When I glance back up to the window, for a second I let myself believe she will be there, limping up to the cabin. I dry my hands and force myself to walk away from the window.

I should have told Carey everything. I will tell him all of it. When the fires are out.

I wander the cabin, opening cupboard doors and drawers, marveling that I have nothing else. Nothing. I left everything behind. Everything I ever loved is in Seattle, collecting dust in my apartment. I sink into the couch. What if it all burned down? My soft gray sofa covered in pillows, my shelves of vinyl records, books, the closet full of decent clothes (the ones I knew I wouldn't need out here), my French press and my favorite coffee cup, pictures of friends, of my parents when we were all still together, on the islands, the jar of agates collected from the windowsills, the latch-hook rug by my bed that Grandma Lucia made, Grandpa Whit's old coat, the photograph of the two of them, standing next to the cottage, the other things I asked my mother to collect from the cottage before I sold it back to the Swensons.

Margaux and Charles, they were Jacob's sister and brother. I met them in Seattle during the trial. They weren't the monsters Katie had suggested, but they were pragmatic businesspeople. Rookwood and the cottage would go on the National Historic Register, in honor of their aunt and grandmother; Marrow Colony they dismantled and sold, along with the ruins of the refinery. They allowed those colonists who seemed not to have been involved in Jacob's death to collect what they could before they were evicted from the property.

What did they take away with them?

The suitcase yawns from the bed, so I pack a few of Carey's nicer shirts—ones he never wears—and a pair of jeans I'd only seen him wear twice, his only books, *Moby-Dick* and *Lonesome Dove*, a duo I've taken to calling *Lonesome Dick*. Then I pick up random objects from each room and pack it till it's full. I pull on sneakers and a sweatshirt and load the case and the laundry bag into the trunk of my car. There are a few things left inside when I hear the CB radio in the car. I sit in the front seat and listen. It's Carey, talking to someone else, another ranger. He left it on the dispatch channel for me, so I hear it all. They're moving the fire line, winds shifting, driving the fire downhill. Carey isn't in the field; he's at the station, handling dispatch. Relieved he's safe, I listen to the chatter, then they both sign off, and all there is to hear is the river and the breeze in the pines, shaking down dry needles. Flakes of ash blow by. Inside the cabin, the lights flicker and blink out.

First, I think I'm seeing things again. But my visions don't flicker—they ignite. The kitchen window remains dark. I step from the car and approach the cabin. The front door is wide open. I stand at the threshold. There's no more radio twang, just fitful cabin sounds, old wood shifting and settling, the drip of the faucet. I stare into the dim rooms, wondering if I am alone. Did she walk up from the river, sneak in the back door? Is she hiding in the shadows? I uselessly flip the switches near me on the wall. The circuit breaker is behind a landscape on the far living-room wall. The fire has caused a power outage, I tell myself. But I go room to room, saying quietly, under my breath, "Where are you? Where are you?"

I call Carey from the hotel room. I tell him I've brought his favorite belt, clean underwear. The innkeeper is letting me use their washer and dryer. Carey's heading to the Sunshine Guard Station to hose it down. There are several old lookouts and cabins in the path of the fire. They'll try to save as many as they can. He reminds me to call my mom and tells me not to wait up for him.

I start a load of laundry and take the service stairs back to our room on the third floor, the way the innkeeper showed me. When I explained the situation over the phone, she put us in the honeymoon suite at the discounted "fire season rate." I remember the last time we were here, jumping on the bed, doing a striptease, deflecting Carey's concern. I can't muster the shame I think I should feel, for not saying what I should have in that moment. But I dig through my backpack for the GPS watch. It blips a greeting. I put it in my back pocket and walk to the post office.

Prairie City looks like a ghost town most days, even in the summer, but today it's bustling. There are cars everywhere with official logos on the doors and license plates. In the three-minute walk to the post office, I see all of the uniforms of the major agencies affected by the fires: U.S. Forest Service, Oregon State Forestry, Parks and Recreation, Fish and Wildlife, and the Bureau of Land Management. They're mostly men; the few women among them seem tense and miserable. They're probably being treated like secretaries. I gather our mail, stuffed into the small PO box; we haven't picked it up in a while. I go through it next to the trashcan, tossing out junk mail—how it follows you wherever you go, even all the way out here, I'll never understand. In the end there's an *Audubon* magazine, a few bills, a card for Carey from someone with his last name, one of his four younger sisters probably, and a small manila envelope for me, with a Spokane postmark and the shaky handwriting of one of the sisters Rose. I won't open it here. I put the envelopes inside the magazine and tuck it under my arm.

On the way back to the hotel, I stop into the gas station/country market. It's the only grocery in town, with a room full of DVD rentals in the back and soft porn behind the counter. I pick up a basket and wander the aisles, staring at things I'm sure I've never needed: cookies shaped like elves, canned yams, off-brand toothpaste. Everything has a neon sticker with a price on it; it's a throwback I find oddly comforting. Somehow I come to an arrangement with myself, so that I will pick one thing from each section of each aisle. I fill the basket with packages of things that appeal to me; sometimes I choose the thing that seems least like me, just to feel the thing in my hand, to see it among the things that I'm buying. I feel a surge of power every time I make a decision. I choose onion crackers and strawberry-flavored instant oatmeal, fudge-striped cookies and powdered donuts and honey-roasted mixed nuts, a yellow legal pad and Irish Spring soap, a six-pack of Rainier and a quart of chocolate milk. When the basket is full, I unload it at the counter, trying to decide if I should choose something from behind the counter, too. The owner, a taciturn, crusty old booger in a flannel shirt, doesn't even give me the once-over. Not even when I ask him for a Western Family pregnancy test. He pulls it down from the pegboard behind him without looking and types in the price.

"Can I have one more?" I ask him. "Please."

I dump my mail on top of the groceries and carry the paper bag back to the hotel in my arms.

You're supposed to test your morning urine, but I take the first test as soon as I get back to the room. I leave it on the edge of the bathtub and sit on the bed. *I don't feel pregnant*, I think, opening a beer and the cookies. I unpack the groceries and put everything in the mini-fridge, even the things that don't really need to be refrigerated. The soap I inhale as I flip through the five channels on the television, waiting it out, thinking about calling my mom and what I will say. I promised her I would always keep in touch; I promised her I wouldn't give her another scare. I assume that she has heard about the fires, that she has been worried.

By the time Mom made it to the hospital in Anacortes, Katie was in police custody. Not charged, just being questioned. But I wouldn't see her again for months. Carey had gone, too, though he would come back almost every day until they let me out. I was alone in a room with three beds, bars and curtains between them. They put me by the window, though there wasn't a view of anything but gray sky.

"What the fuck happened out there, Lucie?" It was her I'm-not-yelling voice; a soft shriek.

"Mom, you said 'fuck.'" I was loopy with morphine.

"It's a 'fuck' kind of situation, Lucinda. I don't ever, *ever* want to get a phone call like that about you again." She was trying hard not to cry.

I learned how to swear from my mom, a longshoreman's daughter. She may have remarried into a higher social class, but she let it slip sometimes. Even her pearl earrings could look pissed off. She gave me a good chewing out while she gripped my free hand in both of hers. Greg was at a job site in Lake Chelan, and she had driven herself up to the hospital, earning two speeding citations and a lecture from a trooper young enough to be her grandson. I dopily marveled at her ability to mask her fear with anger. I knew if she was swearing this much, she was terrified.

It hadn't occurred to me to call her. That first night in the hospital, I thought the worst had passed. Within sixteen hours, my guts were on fire. Piercing pains ran along my spine and under my ribs. I had an unrelenting urge to piss molten lava. When Carey came back to check on me, he found me having emergency dialysis. The doctors were mystified—lab results were slow, and no one knew to look for mycotoxins—so Carey told them what he had gathered from my rambling voicemail. Of course neither of us knew what kind, or how much, I had ingested. He asked the nurse to call my mother, so they dug through my bag and found my phone. They had to interrupt dialysis to ask me her name. I had her listed as "Marie," not "Mom."

The next day, I woke to a nurse prepping me for surgery. They removed a portion of my right kidney. A lab in Seattle examined the dissected tissue and discovered the culprit: amatoxin, which concentrates in the liver and kidneys twenty-four to forty-eight hours after ingestion of *Amanita smithiana*. Also present: traces of psilocin, from the wavy caps, which were likely in the broth with the mussels, likely why everyone was so strange at the wake. The *Amanita*, though, was for me alone. No one else on Marrow had fallen sick. It must have been in the birch liquor Katie had handed me, given me. I couldn't prove it—the flask was lost. Later dried *Amanita* were found in the apothecary, along with samples of hundreds of other hallucinogenic and toxic species.

Mom paced the halls fretfully while I gave a statement to the state police—I insisted on doing that alone.

"When did you notice you were hallucinating?"

"In the woods, the trees were talking to me. I remember thinking that was strange."

"Was this some sort of . . . ritual or something? Was everyone hallucinating?"

"No. That's—no. Katie was hallucinating too, I think—I'm not sure. But I think that was just the wavy caps. We picked them off the graves earlier."

"You picked hallucinogenic mushrooms earlier in the day?"

"I can't be sure, but I think so, yes."

"Off of graves? Which graves would those be?"

"I'm not making this up."

"I don't believe you are, ma'am. I just need to clarify."

It went on like that until I pushed the button for the nurse and told her I was experiencing a seven on the pain scale. Mom told the detective to take a hike and called a lawyer. She stayed at a hotel nearby until the hospital released me, a week later. Greg came eventually, showing more fatherly concern than he ever had. And I was genuinely grateful when he brought me tabloid magazines and Peanut Buster Parfaits from the Dairy Queen up the street. Carey brought my car back from Orwell, along with the things I left at the cottage. My mother's eyes lit up when he walked in the door. I shooed her from the room so that he could tell me what was happening, but I'm sure she only went because she thought we were making out.

They had found Jacob Swenson's remains the second day, and a search of Rookwood turned up traces of his blood on the stairs and floorboards. The theory was murder, possibly manslaughter. Tuck was the primary suspect, because of his past, and because he was known as Jacob's occasional handyman. But how many accessories were there? Why had they left the body in the barn? No one from the Colony would say, so they were all implicated.

Carey said, "I know, I get it. But it looks bad, Lucie. Really, really bad for all of them. They didn't even bury him in their own cemetery."

"It was probably part of the experiment, like the whale — maybe they were trying something new," I said. "He wanted to be a part of the project. But the only ones who knew about it were Tuck and Katie, Sister and Maggie."

"How do you know that?"

"I don't," I snapped. "I'm trying to understand. They couldn't

bury him in the usual way, or everyone in the Colony would
have known."

"You were wandering around hallucinating and you found
him. Someone else would have found him."

"Between the mycelium and insects, I don't think he would've
lasted very long."

I don't know why I wanted to spare my mother the details. She
saw it all on the news in her hotel room anyway.

"That cult could have buried you alive on their mushroom
farm!" she said.

"Stop it, Mom. It's not a cult."

"Jesus Christ. You have Stockholm syndrome, Lucie. It may
be some kind of eco-cult, but it's still a fucking cult."

If I had just told her everything from the beginning, would it
have made more sense to her, how easily the fight for something
fundamentally good can go astray in human hands? It's still a
fight; fights get bloody. She accused me more than once of still
being under the influence of the psilocybin. She tried to talk the
internist doing rounds into ordering a psych evaluation.

"That's good, Mom, just ship me off to therapy again," I hollered at her.

Months later, in a deposition, Elle would tell what she heard
one night: Maggie and Tuck having words. Sister J. had asked
Tuck to check on Jacob. Jacob had been drinking a lot, going on
and off his meds. They had all been worried. He found Jacob
at the bottom of the stairs, bloody but breathing, barely conscious. He panicked. If Jacob's family took over the Trust, the
Colony would face eviction and worse, when someone found

the graves, the psychedelics they'd been growing. Tuck wanted
to get Jacob back to the Colony to clean him up. He had loaded
him into the Colony's boat, taken him back to Marrow, to Maggie. But on the way, Jacob started convulsing. He died in the
night. They knew his injuries looked suspicious. What could
they do, but protect the others from culpability by hiding his
remains, disposing of them away from the rest of the Colony's
dead? But by then, everyone had made up their minds. Tuck,
Maggie, and Sister all pleaded no contest in exchange for an end
to the investigation. No contest. They didn't have any fight left
in them. Tuck was extradited to California to face the arson and
attempted murder charges. Katie, Elle, and Jen pled down and
received house arrest and community service.

When the next commercial comes on, I take my beer into the
bathroom and pick up the test. Only one pale pink line; not two.
I bury the stick under toilet paper in the trashcan. I drink the
rest of the beer and pull the phone onto the bed. My urine may
be unreliable, with my kidneys the way they are now, so I'll try
again in the morning.

I pick up the receiver and dial Mom's landline, staring out the
window at the main street, burly men piling out of a van at the
town's only diner. She picks up on the third ring.

"Hi, Mom."

I hear her take a deep breath and let it out slowly.

"Lucie, I've been calling every day." Her voice is strained but
soft, spent, like she has been crying.

"I know, Mom. I'm sorry." I'm tense already, hearing her
voice. "I've been up at a fire lookout. Carey's been staying at
the station a lot. The fires are really bad right now. But I'm in

Prairie City now; we've evacuated the cabin. You don't need to worry."

I hear her measured breathing.

"So you haven't heard?"

"What? Heard what?"

"Oh, Luce. I'm so sorry."

I know what she's going to say before she says it. Her voice gets younger, all of a sudden. It's her voice from years ago, when she was telling me that Daddy wasn't on the boats coming back from Marrow.

"They found Katie on Marrow. She killed herself, sweetheart."

I feel something pull my insides to the floor; then I draw back up as if on a spring and fly right up into the air over my body, on the hotel bed, holding the phone to my ear. My mother is saying something else now, and maybe I see the words in my mind's eye, as if in a thought bubble above me, but they don't mean anything yet, as if I'm not reading them.

Then I'm saying, "When?"

And I'm hearing her answer, "Yesterday." And I'm counting back in my mind, trying to find some measure of the distance between here and there, on foot, by car, by bus, by train, by ferry, by whatever means necessary. How?

"She was here," I'm saying, and my mother is protesting.

"How is that possible? When?"

"It's not that far away," I say. "It was . . . a few days ago. I can't remember when exactly. She could have taken a bus . . . How did she do it?"

"What?"

"*How* did she kill herself?"

"Oh, Lucie. It was with her father's handgun."

"What? That can't be right, Mom. Why?" But I know why. She didn't want to be found, to be revived. Like I was. I go numb. I hardly hear my mother's voice.

"Lucie, you can't be alone right now. Call Carey. Is there anyone else you can call?"

The mail is spread out on the bed. The manila envelope is slipping out of the magazine. My fingers are wooden; my limbs are numb. I lift my hand, watch myself pull the envelope from the magazine. Inside there is a note from Sister Rose Gracemere, along with another envelope, addressed to me, care of Sister J., in Katie's hand. The note explains that the letter came recently, dropped in the prayer box at the end of the driveway. I'm shaking and slice my finger across the paper as I open it, watching the blood appear in the crevice. I hear her voice.

Dear Lu,

I know this letter won't be what you want it to be, but I don't know how else to say goodbye. A letter seems so dramatic. And one that won't find you until it's too late—god! If there were a hell, I'd be going there for this letter alone. I've never given you what you wanted. I don't know why. It just always seemed that if I did, we'd have nothing left between us. I was always a part of you, and you were always a part of me. No matter how far apart we were. But now you're so far away that I don't know how else to reach you. I know the sisters will get this to you, if I can get it to them. They'll probably even throw in a prayer for us both, no questions asked.

I won't drag it out: there are so many tumors they won't be able to find them all. They want to take everything out of me—

all the lady parts—but the cancer is everywhere. It's so strange, that the body can look so normal when the insides are a cellular clusterfuck. But here's the beautiful thing: when they showed me the scans, all lit up on the screen in the dark room before the surgery, the tumors looked like Clavaria—like coral fungi. They are growing in me, breaking me down, sending me back to the earth. I could feel them, then, so hungry, so efficient. I just stared at them thinking: I know you, I know you.

You know them, too. You've seen what they can do.

Life and death, they're always together, hand in hand, like inseparable friends, like sisters. And the space between them is an endless cycle of growth and decay. This is nothing to mourn. The whole fucking thing is a celebration. Every moment of it.

I love you, Lucie. Always.

—K

The letter isn't dated. I look to the postmark: it's from over a week ago. I laugh. How is it possible? How did she make it to Spokane to leave the letter with the sisters? How did she make it back to Marrow? How did she travel over a thousand miles round trip, being eaten alive with cancer?

I remember the picture I took of her—Katie, sleeping in my cot at the fire lookout. I can see the picture if I close my eyes: it's the whole of the lookout—the windows stretching round, the view of the mountains to the west, the conifers knit into the sides, the robin's-egg sky and long streaks of cloud. And the plain cabin room, with the efficiency kitchen and the table with the two oatmeal bowls, crusting over in the dry high mountain heat. And in the lower left-hand corner, the shape of her body on the cot, under a sheet in shadow, hair falling into her face; the brightest point, her hand resting against the pillow in a patch of sunlight. The picture is on my phone. I search for my phone, through my backpack, my suitcase, my jacket pockets. When was the last time I saw it?—I can't remember. I remember shutting it off completely. The battery is old, it needs charging constantly. I only turn it on for the clock and the camera. I could prove that she had come to me, somehow. I could prove that I'm not crazy. I know what happened. I just need to find the phone. We talked and she ate my food, and drank my beer, and bathed in my river. I touched her, smelled her, and tasted her. She was as real as Carey; she was as real as my reflection in the mirror. I see myself, red-cheeked, panting, tearing everything apart looking for my phone.

"How could you fucking leave your phone behind?" I ask my reflection. Everything from the cabin is strewn across the king-size bed and floor.

I decide to take a shower. I need to calm down and think. The water flows over my hair and face, over my skin. I start to feel my limbs again. I run my hands over my belly and wonder whether there's something growing inside me, too. Maybe it all goes back to the earthquake, to the fire, the smoke in the air, the debris onshore, the oil in the water, the dispersants. Long before the Colony. That early exposure. We were there for months, waiting for Dad to come home, waiting to bury him. Katie and me, combing through junk on the beach, wading in the water. Maybe it's in my brain, in my eyes. Fungi cells, burning across my corneas.

Wrapped in a towel, I drink a glass of water on the edge of the bed. It's three o'clock. I try Carey but Darlene says he's out in the field and she'll have him call me when he gets back. I don't let myself think about it. I grab my keys and walk out the door. The lobby is busy—with refugees or journalists or fire-watchers, I can't tell. I slip out the door and to my car. It hasn't been long enough. The fire will still be miles from the cabin. I just need to get up Highway 7 and hope they don't have all of the Forest Service roads closed. If the first is blocked, I'll be out of luck, but maybe I could get Carey to radio, to tell them to let me through, just to get back to the cabin and back. If the second is blocked, I could go past it and around the back by the logging road along the river. I've never been that way to the cabin, but when we came back from Baker City, I remember Carey pointing it out—"That's the old logging road that circles round and meets up with Road 821." I'm sure that's what he said. I had drawn a map in my mind, like the maps you see sometimes at trailheads. I had done that. I have the wherewithal to draw maps in my head, so I'm fine. Fine.

In the car I keep the radio tuned to dispatch, listening for word coming through about the fire and where it is. I take the road out of town and up through the hills toward the mountains. In the rearview mirror, the deep green-gray clouds of a storm roll across the plain. The radio's quiet for some time, just the crackle like a needle skimming the blank end of a record. I'm an hour from the cabin.

There's nothing to listen to but my own thoughts, that storm getting closer behind me. Golden sunlight slashes through the trees ahead, but the air is hazy. There's a wild breeze whipping up dust and smoke. What am I headed for? What am I running away from? These are the only questions that matter, but I refuse to answer them. Other voices creep into my head.

My mother saying, "They found Katie on Marrow."

And Katie—or her ghost, or a figment of my hallucinations, my psychedelic sister-lover-other—her breath on my face, saying, "I never loved you more," before she kissed me. And Sister, before she died, calling me Katie (her protégé, her daughter, her younger self). I kissed her, too. I did what Katie would have done.

Then my father's, singing—but I can't actually remember his voice (how is it that I can't remember his voice, when did it slip away?), and it comes out like Carey's—that same song I sing to the bears and the wildcats.

Trees blur by, the light going out of the sky. The clouds overcome me. How fast am I going? Have I slowed down? The radio comes alive: there's chatter about the wind, a containment line jumped. Will there be rain? Or only wind and lightning? There's no panic; they are professionals; there is protocol.

I turn off the highway onto Forest Service Road 76 as the rain pelts the windshield and pounds the roof. Thunder breaks over the car. I keep driving, slowly. There's a low murmur from the radio, but I don't recognize the voices—it's not Carey. He's not looking for me, yet.

I'm halfway there, picturing my phone in its solar charger, on the window by the side door, the sunniest window, and the smallest one. The one with the little sun-catcher in the sill that sends a stained-glass flare across the floor at midday. I'm so close, crawling through the storm at twenty miles per hour. Then the rain ceases and the clouds charge on to the east, to Idaho. I'm approaching the next road, the one that heads straight to the cabin, and there are orange and red lights flashing. I don't want them to see me—whoever they are—because they'll tell me to turn back, so I step on the gas and hurtle on up the highway to find the spot Carey showed me, the Forest Service road that circled back along the river and met at the other side of the cabin, near the Cougar Lake trailhead.

I'm flying down the road, and the mist is rising off the pave-

ment as the sun comes out again. All the green wet leaves gleam.
I open the window to let in the air, to inhale the petrichor. And
I do. I take in a lungful before the wind shifts, and I smell the
smoke again. It smells so close, but I hear nothing. Nothing in
the woods nearby. Nothing on the radio. I keep on the road,
weaving up and down the heaves in the old asphalt, farther into
the woods. I watch the odometer, looking for the seventh mile
past the first turnoff — I think it was seven miles — but seven
miles pass and I cross a bridge over the east fork of the river. I
think I've missed it when I just see the brown painted Forest Service Road 821 sign, half hidden behind some bushes. I slam on
the brakes and pull onto the one-lane road.

Trees lean over the cracked and pit-marked asphalt that
winds through the pines, up and down, away from the river. I
am sure the road is heading east, but the cabin is east-southeast.
The windows are down, and I can't hear the river anymore. Mist
and smoke collide at bends in the road. I am doubting what I
remember — about the road, about the phone. When the road
takes a sharp turn to the southeast, I relax. I feel a stillness, feeling the breeze through the car, the occasional bursts of sunlight
through the darkened forest, listening for the river.

I speed up as the road straightens, and I crest a small hill. I let
off the gas to coast down the hill when I think I hear the river
to my right, a rushing through the trees, a sound I might hear
in my dreams. But a swift river, a strong river, with rapids and
waterfalls. The haze is thick as the hill bottoms out, and I see
the shape coming out of the woods only after I've hit it, slam-
ming into its thick brown body as I feel my own volley against
the steering wheel as the car comes to a shuddering stop, and
I hear the body slide off the hood and onto the pavement. It's
been only seconds and I can't see anything, but there's another

crash from the right and the car is pitched sideways in the road. There's a careening bellow coming from outside the car. Then hooves. I hear them before I open my eyes. When I do, a familiar prickle of light pierces my eye sockets. I blink and groan. There's lightning again, then it's gone and the after-lights dance in front of me, inside the car. There's blood on the windshield and on my face. I gasp for breath. There's an acrid smell. Elk are clambering out of the woods at a clip, up the ditch and across the road and into the woods on the other side. A few backtrack to avoid the fallen, the one I've hit, still alive, but broken, unable to lift its body. The one that ran into the passenger door stands, stunned, staring through the window at me before it drunkenly trots off into the trees after the others. Their woolly, angular bodies keep coming, harrowing through the tree trunks at a clip, pounding and scuffing at the ground like the trees themselves uprooted and fleeing. It's a cow-calf herd; the antlers on the young bulls are small velvety nubs. They are wet from fording the river, dripping and steaming. My blood thunders along with their movement, the whole herd of them. I'm shaking and laughing, tears filling my eyes and running down my face. There must be a hundred of them. They keep coming and coming, calling to each other. The car idles and coughs and dies. I watch them go, gripping and ungripping the steering wheel, keeping still. They trundle off into the trees, smoke in their wake.

Legs quaking, I step out of the car, brace myself against the side of it to keep steady, and breathe. The windshield is cracked. The hood has a deep metal rift running all the way down to the grill and bumper. Clumps of gray and brown fur and bloody hide cling to the broken metal. The engine sputters; steam escapes through the dents.

The elk on the road has stopped struggling to get up and follow the herd. There's a gash in her side, giant ribs protruding. One of her front legs is broken and bent beneath her. She's nodding her head and breathing heavily, like she's in labor. I breathe along with her, approaching slowly. Her large eye tracks me, and she makes a high mewling sound. There's an answer to the call, not far off in the trees. She has a calf. The calf always responds to its mother's call. I search the trees for it and finally see her small head. I can still hear the mewls and chirps of the cows, fading up the mountain.

"Go!" I say to it. "Go with your herd!" But she locks eyes with me and doesn't move.

Her mother calls to her, and I know she's telling her to follow the rest. I can hear her pleading.

I approach the beast from behind, speaking softly. I want her to know I'm coming.

"I'm so sorry," I say. "I'm so, so."

Her eye rolls around wildly. She's at least five hundred pounds, and taller than I, if she were standing. If she were to summon some last surge of power, bolt, drag herself from the road to protect her calf, she could kill me with one hind kick to the skull. She could cave my chest, plow open my ribs like I did hers. I kneel behind her head, and she stops calling to her calf, sensing me there. But she becomes very still. She's paralyzed, by terror, by instinct, in the presence of an animal more dangerous than she. She blinks every few seconds, lets out short huffs of breath. I reach out a hand to the back of her head, between her ears. She's so warm, her fur so dense.

"I didn't mean to do this," I tell her. "There's something wrong with me." I stroke her head, talking to her while her calf looks on. She's blinking less now, her chest rises and falls, but she's close. She's so close to the end. Her calf calls, but she can't respond—there's a brief moment of awareness in her eyes as she recognizes her child, alone, separated from the herd— but she cannot move, and she doesn't respond. Her eyes water, her gaze settles on something in the near distance, something above me in the air. I look but there's nothing there, not even a bird, just the orange glow of the clouds, the black smoke. I run my hand down the back of her neck where the brown-gray fur curves down her chest. Her waning pulse reaches my palm. My hands are slick with her blood. I lie down next to her, resting my head on her, my ear below hers, the wild smell of her so strong I can taste it, like iron and wood and shit, on my tongue, in the back of my throat. I'm breathing with her, still.

"Why did I have to run toward the fire?" I'm asking her.

I need to imagine my way past the pain in my head, physically redirect my mind from the searing behind my eye. Where do I go from here? Where to begin? At the end.

"Is this the end?" I ask, or maybe I'm thinking it. Yes, I'm sending the thoughts to her. She's an elk, telepathy is as good as English. I'm feeling the thoughts. I'm feeling them as energy and sending them into her.

"I don't have a map." I stroke her neck, feeling the power, the life still in her. She's fighting it. She wasn't supposed to go like this, bones smashed, breathing blood. Her baby watching her from the ditch.

My eyes are watering, and I realize it's from smoke, blown this way. I remember that the fire has jumped the river. The fire is on both sides of the river. The elk were headed up the mountain, away from the fire.

I can't remember the last words I said to Carey, but they weren't enough.

I follow the hours and days back, further and further, like

hiking deeper into the woods. Did I come to the Malheur to be with him, or to get away from everyone else? I could have gone back to the city; I could have gone anywhere. I didn't have to go to the woods at all. I didn't have to call him after his deposition or let him sleep on my sofa that night. I didn't have to kiss him; he made no move on me. I kissed him because I had been thinking about kissing him—I remember—I had thought about it every day since Orwell, breakfast at the Nootka Rose. I thought about him as I lay alone in bed at night, unable to sleep.

I came here and I put myself in the way of loss, of death. I put myself in the way of love.

The trail looks different from this side, just like Carey said it would. From this angle, I see all the danger, all the risks. The choice to tell what I knew in the deposition, what I saw, even though I might have saved them all if I had lied even a little bit. The choice to go back to Marrow, after I found out about Tuck. Trying to save Katie. The choice to visit her, after all those years of silence. Sneaking into Rookwood. Going back to the cottage.

I close my eyes and try to see her thoughts, try to feel what she's feeling. The elk quivers; she reverberates. There's a last flicker of light in her eye, a reflection of me. She bellows at her calf, then she's still. I see her letting go. I'm weeping.

The radio comes alive in the car, and I hear my name. I startle. The elk is gone. I stand, her head falling away from me. Her calf mewls from a ditch, and I yell at her, wave my arms.

"Go! Go!"

There's a snapping of branches and rustle of leaves as the calf flees. Her mother's blood is all over my hands and arms, my hair, soaking through my clothes to my skin. I turn away from her body to vomit.

I hear my name again and look back to the car. I know that

it is dead, too, that it won't start again. Carey's voice comes through the radio.

Flames dance on either side of the road ahead, flitting from branch to branch. They're not raging; this is no roaring blaze. There's no urgency to the fire's hunger at this moment, just instinct. It licks at anything made of carbon, grazes on the bark and grasses, saplings and pinecones, like a herd of ruminants.

"I can barely hear you," I say.

I walk back to the car, knees shaking.

I pick up the handset and say, "I'm here. I'm here."

For a moment there's no reply, and I'm suspended between radio silence and the burning road. There's a balmy stillness over the wreckage I've made. Not even birdsong; the birds are long gone.

"It's dead," I say. "My car is dead. I'm three miles down"— trying to remember, breathing out more than in —"FSR 821. I need to get out of here."

There's a crackle on the line, and Carey says something but I can't hear it. I can stay with the radio and wait for help. Or I can go. I can get out on my own.

"The fire jumped the river," I tell him. "Over." I see Katie in the rearview mirror, behind the car, almost out of sight, bandanna like a gash at her neck. I drop the radio and turn. She's not there. The radio hums.

I step out of the car, stand between the road and the smoke-red sky.

Then I am running, ashes falling like rain.

ACKNOWLEDGMENTS

Though this story is fictional, I was inspired by real places and things. I would be remiss if I didn't thank Paul Stamets, author of *Mycelium Running* and many other books, for opening my mind to the possibilities of mycoremediation, and for fearlessly advocating for the earth through his work. I would also like to express my gratitude to the Sisters of the Holy Names of Jesus and Mary, for my high school education, for some of my first lessons in social justice, for inspiring me to act and create from my faith, and for the few days, twenty years ago, that I spent with the elderly sisters at their provincial house in Spokane, Washington (it clearly made a lasting impression).

I often think (and have been known to remark) that I find it miraculous that anyone understands the words that come out of my head. But people do, and not only that, they encourage me to keep the words coming by giving generously of their time, their food and drink, their art and music, their endorsements, their unconditional love, and, even, their cash. Here, I would like to sully their good names by mentioning some of these folks in print: agent, first reader, and ringmaster, Seth Fishman; editor, mycophile, and miracle worker, Jenna Johnson; best friend, financial guru, and mopper, Amy Koler (this one's for you, Ames); tea therapist, Mary Zartman; collaborator and space witch, Nora Wendl; chicken wranglers and ace gay uncles, Andrew Pizzolato and Tom Alton; pink wine fashion icon, Amanda Morgan; narrative oracle, Karen Munro; ever-true work date and rock star, Cari Luna; landlady and saint, Kate Mann; trail-running soul sister, Michele Filgate; beloved retreat and birthplace of first chapters, the Sou'Wester Lodge; book-devourer and adventurer, Karin Ljungquist; letter-writer and portraitist, Zachary Schomburg; angel-faced cat lady, Amy Martin; adopted moms and sweetpeas, Ann and Pru; wildland firefighter and urban woodsman, Mason Purdy; father of my child and guy who handed me *Mycelium Running* eight years ago, Nick Barbery; crafty lady, Susan Waters; Reiki master and mom, Dorothy Brannon; rock hound and dad, Baker Smith; pimento cheese-and-pickle sandwich maker, homesteader, mystery-lover, and grandma, Betty Lois Baker Smith; inspiration, alarm clock, and son, Amos Leroy; and, at last, the woman who wordlessly followed me up a sand dune on Long Beach to see what the turkey vultures were eating just because she loves me, Kelly Lucey.

This book was made possible, in part, by a grant from the Oregon Arts Commission. I would also like to acknowledge the professional development support of the Regional Arts and Culture Council.

READING GROUP GUIDE

Questions and Discussion Points

1. How do you define a dystopian novel? Do you consider *Marrow Island* dystopian? Why or why not?

2. The last line of the prologue reads, "I forgive them for trying to kill me" (p. xi). What did you make of this when you first read it? What do you make of it after having finished the book? Why do you think Lucie Bowen chooses to forgive them?

3. Lucie's life has been punctuated by environmental disasters. How have these disasters shaped who she has become and who she wants to be? What role does nature play in her life?

4. "'Mycelium takes everything we give it,' [Katie] says, 'and transforms death into life. It communicates directly with the soul of every living thing that touches it'" (p. 47). Discuss this quote. How does the Colony use mycelium's prop-

erties to its advantage? How do you think this quote fore-shadows what's to come in the novel—both literally and figuratively?

5. Lucie is an environmental journalist. How do you think this colors her observations and her interactions with people while on Marrow Island? What are some of her driving in-vestigative questions? And, if you were in her position, what would some of your driving questions be?

6. Jen says to Lucie, "'Sister J. inspires different feelings in dif-ferent people—for me, it's not G-O-D'" (p. 107). What does Jen mean by this? Who is Sister J. to the different members of the Colony? What does she provide them with, and how has she roused them?

7. The novel alternates between two time periods, 2014 and 2016. What did you make of this structure? Did it increase the suspense for you?

8. "I was always a part of you, and you were always a part of me," Katie writes in a letter to Lucie (p. 232). What does Katie mean by this? Discuss Lucie and Katie's relation-ship—how it changed over the course of the novel and, more broadly, how it evolved since they were kids.

9. As you learn over the course of the novel, the Colony gives up everything for the well-being of Marrow Island. What would you give to save the thing you love the most? How much would you be willing to sacrifice?

10. At the very end of the novel, Lucie thinks, "I came here and I put myself in the way of loss, of death. I put myself in the way of love" (p. 241). What do you think Lucie has learned? How do you interpret the ending? Do you find it hopeful?

Q&A WITH ALEXIS M. SMITH

Your first novel, *Glaciers*, was a finalist for the Ken Kesey Award and a selection for World Book Night 2013. How was writing *Marrow Island* different after those successes?

When I wrote the first draft of *Glaciers*, my only audience was my faculty advisers at Goddard College and a few trusted peers. When *Tin House* took it on, I still didn't imagine any kind of audience beyond, say, my coworkers at Powell's and my family members. As a bookseller, all I really thought about was how easily books disappear in the stacks, get remaindered, then quietly go out of print. I feel incredibly lucky—even though we're not supposed to say that, right? I worked really hard on the book, I spent years studying literature, that all counts for something—nevertheless, I feel that *Glaciers* happened in the right place at the right time, and readers found it, and now I have an audience. Turns out it's no easier writing a book when you know you have an audience out there who might buy it. But it's not any harder, either. It takes some pressure off (I feel more legit as a writer than I did the first time), but the story still comes in its own way and its own time.

How has working as a bookseller influenced your writing?
This is probably an obvious answer, but the proximity to so many great books was extremely influential. Most books are either out of print or backlist, so used bookstores are the place to come across writers whose really great books are slipping into oblivion: their authors are dead, their original audience, too; their publishers no longer exist or were absorbed long ago into one of the remaining big publishing companies. Jean Rhys, Max Frisch, Sylvia Townsend Warner, Marguerite Yourcenar, Richard Hughes—all underread writers I came across in used bookstores or secondhand shops. (I love the NYRB Classics for reprinting gems like *Lolly Willowes* and *A High Wind in Jamaica*.)

The sense of discovery is powerful—it's an energetic connection to the time and place when the book was written, to the person who wrote the words. Just as all books come into being in their own time and place, I think there's a time and a place in which each reader is hungry for a certain book (though they rarely know the book until it is in their hands), primed to devour it. I like taking the long view where my own books are concerned; I hope they'll be around long after I'm gone, still meeting hungry readers at some cosmically appointed time. I'm certain this philosophy informs my writing, but how, exactly, is a mystery to me.

You go into a lot of detail about the mushrooms and fungi around the island. How much research did you have to do for the book?
It's difficult to quantify research. Numbers of books and articles read? Hours spent (reading, in the field, percolating ideas)? I picked up every book on mushrooms I came across—field

guides, cookbooks, natural philosophy, kids' books . . . Two of my favorites were Paul Stamets's *Mycelium Running* and *Mushrooms, Molds, and Miracles* by Lucy Kavaler. I also wandered the Pacific Northwest, photographing the fungi and lichen I found, consulting field guides and online mushroom forums, making spore prints if I had collected any, to identify them. Another exciting part of the research was interviewing everyone I could — my friends and family members, strangers at parties, my friends' parents — about their experiences taking shrooms.

Was there a specific place that inspired *Marrow Island* when you were building the setting?
The islands of Puget Sound, in general, inspired Marrow and Orwell. I haven't been to a lot of them (there are hundreds in the San Juan Islands alone), but as a group they have such a sublime presence. Part landscape, part seascape, they evoke feelings of loneliness but also longing to escape, to break free from society, to exist outside of the conventional, and in some ways outside of time.

The relationship between Lucie and Kate feels so real to the reader. Is their relationship reminiscent of any of your own?
Not so much, no. The original inspiration for Lucie and Kate's relationship was the folktale "Snow-White and Rose-Red," about two sisters who live on the edge of a dark wood with their widow mother. They wrestle a talking he-bear by their hearth every night and encounter a vicious dwarf every time they leave their hovel. I'm not sure I can articulate how this story inspired me because it's based on the kind of associative logic of dreams. What I can say is that like a folktale, I wanted Lucie and Kate's relationship to be visceral, murky, and a little twisted.

Did *Marrow Island* come to you first as a plot or setting, or did the voice of Lucie Bowen spark the rest?

The first seeds of the story came to me in a vivid postpartum dream: an environmentally devastated island, occupied by nuns. It took a few years to find Lucie's voice, and when it finally came, it was through the prologue, which all came out in one breath while I was on a writing retreat on the coast of Oregon.

What inspired you to write Sister J. as a nun? How important is the theme of religion to the novel?

I don't think religion is that important to the novel, but personal spiritual accountability is. I went to an all girls' Catholic high school run by the Sisters of the Holy Names. It was an impressionable time in my life, and the sisters were interesting people with whom I spent a good deal of my time for four years. I was inspired by them, even while I questioned their involvement with the deeply patriarchal institution of the Church. A couple of years after graduation, I ended up marching with some sisters during the WTO protests in downtown Seattle and learned more about the social justice activism the sisters took on when they weren't teaching. It was a complicated scenario—joining a patriarchal institution (the Church) to fight a patriarchal institution (global capitalism)—that has been sitting with me ever since, and I think it comes through in the book (albeit via different channels): How do we account for our own culpability? What if we can't even locate it because it's sewed into our entire way of life?

I should say: Sister J. wasn't modeled on any sister that I've known, though the Provincial House that appears in the book was loosely inspired by a real place in Spokane, Washington.

Did you write both the past and the present parts of Lucie's journey at the same time?

I did. The structure (going back and forth between the islands and the woods) developed organically as I wrote.

The ending of *Marrow Island* is heart-wrenching. Was it something you had planned, or did it develop along with Lucie's character?

I like to know what I'm writing toward, but I didn't know the ending until I was a few chapters into the first draft. I had a general concept, but the final scene didn't present itself to me for quite a while. Then, I was driving on a rural highway in southern Oregon just after a spring thunderstorm and had a flash of the scene itself. I pulled over to the side of the road to take notes, and from then on, I was writing toward that scene.

What do you hope readers take away from your book?

Oh, goodness. I hope they take away a positive impression of my work and want to read everything I write. Other than that, I don't want to project anything onto the reader's experience. I'm at peace with the fact that interpretation is out of my hands.